D1259153

BETH HAUTALA

VIKING

VIKING
An imprint of Penguin Random House LLC, New York

First published in the United States of America by Viking,
an imprint of Penguin Random House LLC, 2022

Visit us online at penguinrandomhouse.com.

Library of Congress Cataloging-in-Publication Data is available.

Book manufactured in Canada

ISBN 9780593463680

10 9 8 7 6 5 4 3 2 1

FRI

Edited by Liza Kaplan
Design by Ellice M. Lee

Text set in Palatino

For my readers:

THANK YOU FOR CHANGING THE WORLD,
JUST BY BEING IN IT.

1

AT THE POST OFFICE

Persephone Pearl Clark sat on her porch step one morning in June, the spring sun warm against her back, watching the tendrils of a small vine slowly twist around her finger. A heart-shaped leaf uncurled, colors and textures shifting, catching the light as it opened right before her eyes. She studied it, wishing she knew how it worked. She had never met a plant that wouldn't sprout or leaf, bud or bloom for her. The gardens that sprawled across the yard and around her small brick house were proof.

"You stay here," she whispered to the vine, smiling as she unwound it from her finger. It clung to her, like it didn't want her to go. She had no idea what kind it was. She could make things grow, but that didn't mean she always knew *what* was growing.

Persephone patted her pocket, feeling for the envelopes her mother had handed her that morning. Mom had pains-takingly written three checks, carefully tearing them from the checkbook and slipping them inside the envelopes. Payments for medical bills. Bills that never quit arriving in their mailbox.

Too bad money was one thing Persephone couldn't make grow on trees.

The little bell over the post office door jingled as Persephone pushed it open. Mrs. Rosalyn Howard poked her overly large, bespectacled nose from behind the front counter. She was fanning herself with an empty manila envelope. Her freshly permed hair curled damply against her forehead. It was shaping up to be a hot summer.

"Hello, *Persephone!*" Mrs. Howard exclaimed. "How's your family *today?*" The woman emphasized certain words as if she were afraid Persephone would miss the important ones. Then she clucked her tongue and waved her envelope-fan, creating a miniature breeze behind the counter. "Your poor *mother,*" she said to the post office ceiling. "That *poor* beautiful boy!"

Persephone cleared her throat and slid the bills across the counter.

"We're all fine." She offered a smile.

"*Any* changes?" Mrs. Howard pried. Persephone shook her head and continued smiling. But she clamped her teeth together. She wasn't about to say a single word to Mrs. Howard about seizures or treatments or bills. Everyone in town already knew more about her brother than she liked, mostly because Mrs. Howard was very good at *sharing things.* The woman's fan rustled the edges of Persephone's envelopes on the counter. She clucked her tongue again and then set her fan down, smoothing her hand across the counter like she was sweeping invisible troubles away. "Well. Enough of *that*," she said. "What can I help you with this morning?" She adjusted her glasses and examined the envelopes Persephone had laid on the counter. Two other customers had come in behind Persephone and they leaned in, listening.

Small towns have big ears, her father always said.

"Just stamps," Persephone said stiffly. Her smile was gone. "Whatever you have is fine." Mrs. Howard usually offered her several options, and Persephone usually loved looking through each newly released collection of stamps. But not today. Today she just wanted to slap a plain old stamp on the corner of each of those hateful bills and be done with them.

Mrs. Howard arched an eyebrow, noting Persephone's scowl.

"Why, Persephone," she asked, "whatever has you all *prickly* this morning?"

"That's none of your business, Rosalyn," Mr. Bartholomew Grove interrupted, glancing up from where he sat at his computer behind the counter. The postmaster was almost invisible behind the stacks of mail. Mr. Grove's gravelly voice somehow complemented his large handlebar mustache, and he gave Persephone a wink. She felt her smile returning. Mrs. Howard huffed and picked up her envelope-fan again, pressing her lips together so that no other nosy questions could escape.

"One book of stamps," she said politely, sliding them across the counter to Persephone before glancing at the two other customers waiting in line.

"Thank you," Persephone said. She smiled again and tried to sound as unprickly as possible. Then she stepped away from the counter and Mrs. Howard's breeze, and hurried over to her family's post office box.

Each morning the mail was filed into the boxes that lined the post office wall. Mrs. Howard or Mr. Grove filled them with letters from friends, packages, paychecks, fliers, newspapers, and of course, bills. Getting the mail every day was Persephone's job, and it used to be miraculous. So much possibility! So much hope! You just never knew what might be waiting. But that had all changed Last Year's June.

Persephone turned the little gold mail key in the lock and peered inside. She stared at the slim white envelopes and sighed miserably. It would have been so much better if the box were empty. Because there was nothing miraculous or hopeful about medical bills. Two of them waited for her today, and one was stamped with the word overdue in bright red letters across the front for everyone to see. She snatched the mail out of the box and shoved it under her arm. Mrs. Howard gave her a small sympathetic look from across the room as Persephone left the post office.

She stood outside in the warm sunshine, staring at the planter that sat beside the post office door, blinking back tears. It was filled with red geraniums, sweet alyssum, and a peculiar little vine. It reached for her—one small heart-shaped leaf and then another—as she stood there with the weight of the world tucked under her arm. Persephone ignored the outstretched leaves. Maybe that did make her prickly. But right now, it felt too hard to be anything else.

2

WATER TOWER CAT

Persephone trudged down the streets of Coulter, Wisconsin— population 523—with those two white envelopes heavy in her hand. She walked past familiar houses, counting curbside mailboxes as she headed home. Overhead, the canopy of fresh leaves was vibrant and alive, whispering in the warm air about hope and life and growing. And more than anything in the world, Persephone wished there was something she could *do*. Some miraculous way to deliver money, instead of this mail, to her mother.

Houses sat along the street on overgrown lots like sleepy monuments to a busier time. Persephone waved to her neighbor Mr. Hornberg, who was raking his lawn. Next door, old Mr. and Mrs. Tellington sat on their porch talking about everyone they knew. She waved to them too, and they waved back as she walked by. Dad said that being a neighbor wasn't about how close someone lived, but about how you treated them—how you thought about them—what you did to help them out. Which, if Persephone thought about it, made everyone neighbors in Coulter.

She walked a few more blocks and the trees thinned out, giving way to an open field and the chain-link security fence that wrapped all the way around the four legs of Coulter's water tower. It rose high into the air, overshadowing the tallest trees. It felt like the clouds barely skimmed the top of it. Craning her neck and raising a hand against the glare of the sun, Persephone studied the peeling black letters of her town's name painted across the side of the water tank.

The chain-link fence was meant to keep potential climbers out of range. But only human climbers, apparently, because as Persephone peered closely, she noticed a small gray cat had made its way through the fence and had scaled the ladder running up one of the tower's legs. It was perched on the circular walkway that ran all the way around the water tank, 130 feet in the air. A cat on a catwalk. It shouldn't have been possible. But there it was. Real and high and stuck.

"What are you doing up there?" Persephone shouted up at the cat.

It opened its mouth and seemed to meow, but it was up so high, she could barely hear it. Something inside her chest cracked a little. That poor cat was all alone and there was no one to help. No one except her.

Persephone used to have a cat—Mittens, an orange tabby with white stocking feet. He got hit by a car one Saturday morning a couple years ago, and Persephone had cried for days afterward. She was certain that if she had kept a better eye on him, or called him into the house that morning, she could have saved him. And now she couldn't stand the thought of anything like that happening again. Especially when she could do something.

She studied the fence with an appraising eye. A small vine with heart-shaped leaves had crept across one corner of it, rambling over the top rail. She glanced at the ladder, and then stared up at the catwalk. The gray cat peered down at her.

This was a very bad idea. How many times had her dad told her to stay off ladders unless he was with her? A million. Maybe a billion. People broke arms and legs and heads from falling off ladders all the time. Dad had told her. And he worked on roofs, cleaning and repairing chimneys all day long, up and down ladders almost every day, so he would know. But she'd been up and down ladders with him many times too. She could do this.

Persephone set the mail on the ground, anchoring it with a small stone so the spring wind wouldn't blow it away. Wedging the toe of her sneaker into one of the links in the fence, she scrambled up. She ignored the NO TRESPASSING sign and sat on the top of the fence for a moment before swinging over and dropping to the ground with a soft *oof.* Tiny grasshoppers windmilled away as she landed in the dry grass. The water tower felt even taller when she was standing next to it with her hand on the bottom rung of the ladder. The metal was warm from sitting in the sun.

High above, Persephone thought she heard a faint meow.

She began climbing.

"One—Two—Three . . ." She counted as she went, and the ground slowly fell away. After a moment, the trees lining the street didn't seem quite so tall. "Fifteen—Sixteen—Seventeen . . ." When she hit the twenty-second rung, she was the same height as the trees, and she wasn't even halfway up.

"*Meow*," said the gray cat, leaning over the edge of the catwalk. Persephone stared up at it; she could hear it crying plaintively now. She was going to be in so much trouble if she got caught. She squared her shoulders. At one point she glanced down and a bolt of fear raced through her, heavy and cold. She'd never been scared being on rooftops when she was on a jobsite with Dad, because he was good at making sure everything was safe. But the water tower was much higher than any rooftop in Coulter. She already knew it wasn't safe. And Dad wasn't with her. Persephone gripped the ladder rung with both hands and closed her eyes, trying to think normal thoughts about things that were not high. Like the ground. And floors. The bottom of hills. Basements.

"*Meow*," cried the gray cat again. It was the bravest cat Persephone had ever met.

"You're not afraid, are you?" Her voice shook but she forced herself up another rung, and then another.

The gray cat pressed its face against Persephone's forehead as she finally rose eye level with the walkway. It purred furiously, gazing into Persephone's eyes. It made her feel a little more brave. She clenched her teeth, trying not to let them chatter.

Leaning back against the warm steel of the water tank, Persephone peered through the bars in the guardrail out across town. She could see the post office—red brick, small and sturdy. The school sat just a few blocks over with the football field stretching out behind it like a green cape. Main Street was filled with small shabby shop fronts, sagging against one another in rows, like tired friends trying to keep one another upright. There was the bakery where her family went for donuts after chores on Saturdays. And the street Persephone lived on stretched directly below. She followed it, and found her house—small and square, with a peaked roof and brick chimney, a tidy yard, and the flower gardens she couldn't help but cultivate.

"Hey! What are you doing up there?" A voice interrupted her thoughts. Right under the water tower, just on the other side of the security fence, stood a boy. She was too high up to tell who exactly it was. Which was a relief, because that meant he couldn't tell who she was either.

"I'm just getting this cat," Persephone yelled down, picking up the gray cat and holding it close to her chest. The creature purred, butting its head under her chin.

"Are you stuck?" the boy yelled. *Was she?* Persephone glanced at the ladder and felt a little sick at the thought of having to climb down.

"No!" Persephone yelled quickly. "I don't think so!"

"Do you want me to call the fire department?" the boy yelled.

"No!"

He couldn't call the fire department. Her dad

volunteered for the fire department, and if he knew she'd climbed the water tower, she would be in so much trouble. Their family had enough to worry about without Persephone adding to the list.

"It's okay!" she added. She tried to sound braver than she felt.

This was bad.

This was very bad.

She rubbed the gray cat behind its ears, thinking quickly.

"I need you to be calm," she whispered to the cat. "No scratching, okay?" She tucked it under her shirt, soft against her skin, and then shoved the hem of her shirt tight into her jeans so the cat wouldn't slip out. It poked its head out from the top of her collar and nibbled Persephone's chin.

"I'm coming down! It's fine!" she yelled to the boy far below. She closed her eyes, took a deep breath, and with the cat purring and bracing itself against her chest, Persephone backed her way toward the ladder on hands and knees. The steel beneath her hands was hot and she wondered how long this cat had been up here—no food or water. Had its paws been burned as the metal baked in the hot sun? She would have to check when she reached the ground. *If she reached the ground.* She swallowed hard. The wind rushed around her up there at the top of Coulter, and her hair flew wild—a whirlwind of pale straw around her head. One foot on the top rung and one arm around the cat, she shivered in the wind.

"You can do this," she told herself. "You can do this,

Persephone Pearl Clark!" And step by step, rung by rung, she slowly made her way down, careful not to lose her grip on the cat, or the ladder, or her nerve.

"Oh! Persephone! It's *you*! Are you okay?" The boy had climbed over the fence and crouched down in the grass beside her as Persephone finally reached the ground. His eyes were wide. "You scared me to death!" he said. "What were you even doing up there?"

Persephone's legs felt like they were made of something other than skin and bones. Pudding maybe. Or water. But she was careful of the cat, holding it tight. The creature just kept right on purring.

She squinted at the boy, trying to remember his name. *M* something . . . Malachi? Yes, that was it—Malachi Rathmason. He was a year ahead of her in school. Brown skin, dark eyes, bright smile. Good at basketball, a little quiet, but he'd always been kind. Especially after Last Year's June. But now he was a witness to her trespassing. What if he told someone?

"I'm fine," Persephone said. Her voice sounded stiff. Far away and unfamiliar. She stood up on wobbly legs, brushing off Malachi's offer to help. "This cat was stuck up there." She untucked her shirt and pulled out the cat, cradling it in her arms and checking its paws for burns. Fortunately, it seemed all right.

"You could have fallen!" Malachi said. His voice was edged with something—irritation. Worry. Like he was her older brother and was supposed to protect her, or something.

"But I didn't fall," Persephone said firmly. And he was *not* her brother.

"All that for a cat?" Malachi asked.

Persephone gritted her teeth. "Yes."

"If you say so. Don't see it's worth your life, though."

"Don't see why you care so much," Persephone snapped, prickly again. But then she felt bad. "This cat's glad to be alive," she added with a hesitant smile. "Don't you think? I mean, who knows how long it was up there before I came along!"

"I guess." Malachi reached out and stroked the cat's head. It purred in the safety of Persephone's arms.

"Um, could you—could you not tell anyone about this?" Persephone peered up at him.

Malachi considered her request for a minute. "Okay," he said. "Do you usually do stuff like this?"

"Stuff like what?" she asked.

"Dangerous, foolish, brave stuff?" he said.

Persephone lifted her chin. "It wasn't foolish to this cat."

Malachi gave a small smile. "No," he agreed. "I guess not." And then he pulled the mail she'd left on the other side of the fence from his back pocket. "I think these are yours?"

Persephone stared at the envelopes. She wanted to shake her head. She wished the wind had blown them away. But instead she swallowed and nodded, stuffing the bills into her own pocket.

The gray cat didn't care about any of it—trespassing or secrets or bills—it just blinked at them both, and kept right on purring.

3

SUNSHINE AND SHADE

Persephone walked home with the cat cradled in her arms, her imagination filled with possibilities.

Maybe it's a valuable pet, and it's lost, and there's a huge reward for its return! Perhaps it isn't a cat at all, but something else—something more, *which would explain how it came to be at the top of the water tower. Or maybe it's just a normal stray cat, and I can keep it as my very own.*

But the closer Persephone got to home, the more the little gray cat squirmed in her arms.

"You want to walk?" Persephone knelt, setting it down. "Better?" The cat sat in front of her, curling its tail around its paws. It stared at Persephone with large green eyes, and then, before she could stop it, the creature slipped through the tall grass beside the road and disappeared into the underbrush.

"Wait—!" Persephone jumped to her feet, ready to run after it, but it was too late. Like a wisp of shadow and smoke, the cat was gone.

Persephone's mother was outside watering a lily when Persephone trudged up the driveway.

"Honey—what's the matter?" Her mother's brow furrowed.

Persephone hesitated. Today, the whole truth would worry her mother, and her mother had enough worry. Was it lying if you didn't tell someone *everything*?

"I found this cat on my way home from the post office and I really wanted to keep it." Persephone shrugged. "But it ran off before I could stop it." *That was mostly true.*

"Oh no, I'm sorry." Her mother wrapped her arm around Persephone's shoulders and squeezed. "I'm not really sure we could have kept it anyway," she said. Persephone nodded. She knew that, but it didn't change the fact that for a little bit, she'd been hopeful. She wanted something to look forward to—something small and warm and soft to cuddle and care for. Something that needed her the way she needed it.

"Was there any mail?" her mother asked.

Persephone hated those bills in her back pocket.

"Just the usual." She handed them over. And though her mother tried to hide it, Persephone saw the shadow that crossed her face. Her mom's shoulders drooped, matching the lily she was watering.

"I think that lily needs more sun," Persephone said quickly. "It's too shady here by the porch. That big oak tree blocks all the light." She pointed to the tree in the front yard and her mother nodded half-heartedly. Persephone grabbed a shovel and hoisted it over her shoulder like an explorer ready to unearth buried treasure.

"All right," her mother said, taking a breath and straightening her shoulders. She gestured dramatically at the drooping plant, banishing the bills from thought for the moment. "Where do you suggest we replant this languishing lily?"

Persephone led the way, and together she and her mother dug up the lily, careful of far-reaching roots and tubers, and carried the plant to a new spot in a sunnier part of the yard.

"It looks happier already," Persephone said, brushing dirt from her hands and studying her mother's face. She smiled a little, much to Persephone's relief, before turning back to the house.

"I think you should stand here and talk to this plant for a minute or two," she said. "I'm gonna go check on your brother."

Andrea, their home care nurse, had taken the afternoon off, and Levi could never be left alone for long. The threat of more seizures hovered over them all, and the bills Persephone brought home every day kept squashing the hope of getting Levi additional, advanced treatment that could help. Even with medical insurance, there were some things that just weren't covered, and they couldn't afford to pay for everything they needed.

"What do you want me to say?" Persephone called after her mother. "To the flower?" She wrapped her arms around herself helplessly.

"That's entirely up to you," her mother said. "Just make

that lily grow." She winked and Persephone nodded, dropping her arms. She could do that. Things grew when Persephone asked them to. They always had—even when she was little.

The day after Persephone was born, her parents discovered the cherry tree outside their hospital room window had burst into bloom, even though all the other cherry trees planted in the courtyard didn't even have buds yet.

"Your father thought it was because the sun hit that corner of the hospital courtyard just right," her mother always told her. "But we decided to name you Persephone, after the Greek goddess of spring, because the world bloomed and changed for her."

As Persephone grew, her ability to make things grow grew with her. The garden always did better if she was out playing in the dirt while her mother planted or weeded. In spring, the trees in her family's yard always leafed out before any of the others along the street. Dad told her once that he'd rather she didn't mow the lawn because it grew back twice as fast. And her neighbors even dropped off sick house plants for Persephone to look after sometimes.

No one understood *how* it worked any more than Persephone did, and not many people realized that Persephone's ability might be more than just a green thumb, because it was enough that she could make their plants grow. But Persephone knew there was something different about her. And while it was wonderful to be able to make things grow, she longed to be able to make other kinds of changes happen too.

4

TEN LAPS

The next morning, Persephone stood on the dock staring out at the surface of Galion Lake and wondering about that small gray cat. *Was it all right? Had it found its way home, if it even had one? Would she ever see it again?* She took a deep breath and shook out her hands, clearing her head. The lake was often so still this early, like liquid glass. Steam rose from its surface— the water warmer than the air this early in the morning. It made her feel strange, as though her ruffled thoughts didn't belong here. She glanced at the lifeguard chair, sitting just up the beach. The bright red paint was peeling and fading.

Her mom sat down on the dock, her back to the empty chair. The cup of coffee she clutched between her hands steamed almost as much as the water. It had been an unusually warm spring and Galion Lake had warmed just enough for Persephone to begin swimming laps again.

She adjusted the straps on her swimsuit and stared down into the shadows beneath the dock. What lurked there? A massive bass? A northern? Or nothing more than waving weeds? Persephone and her brothers used to dare each other to be the first one to swim under the dock. Levi always went first because he was the oldest and bravest.

"I chased off all the big ones!" he'd say with a grin, his voice echoing between the surface of the water and the underside of the dock. And then he'd splash her. And Owen, who was only six and not an experienced swimmer, would scream and scramble for shore as Levi and Persephone started a water fight.

But now Persephone was the one chasing shadows from beneath the dock. She straightened her shoulders. Levi had started working with her on distance swimming before his accident, and she wasn't about to quit now just because he wasn't here to help anymore.

"We need to make sure you're a strong swimmer!" he'd told her in his lifeguard voice. "Everyone who lives as close to a lake as we do should be able to swim at least a mile." And now that mile mattered to Persephone even more.

"How's the water?" her mother asked.

"Ch-ch-chilly." Persephone's teeth chattered as she eased into the cold lake. "But o-o-okay." She would warm up once she started swimming.

"How far today?" Mom sipped her coffee as Persephone looked out over the water toward the string of buoys. Galion Lake was huge, and as soon as the ice came off the lake each spring, a section was roped off so people could swim and play without worrying about boat traffic. The swimming area measured twenty-five meters from one side to the other. Same length as a swimming pool. Thirty-three laps—there and back again—made a mile. And that was exactly how far Persephone was planning to go before the summer was over.

"Ten laps today," Persephone said. Her mother nodded and took another sip of coffee. Persephone's goggles were fogging over, so she pulled them down, cleaning the lenses with her thumbs. A deep breath, then she slid beneath the surface. The world suddenly grew vast and quiet, her body weightless. She surfaced for air. And then she began to swim, first one stroke, and then another.

Reach—Pull—Breathe. Reach—Pull—Breathe.

Persephone crawled across the water, touched the far rope, and then turned back. She went slow and steady, focusing on her breathing and the movement of her body. If she didn't, her mind wandered, and then she forgot to breathe, and before she knew it, her rhythm was off, and she was gasping for air. Focus was key.

Eight laps later, she clung to the side of the dock and tried to catch her breath. Her arms were wobbly.

"How are you doing, honey?" Her mother leaned over the dock and covered Persephone's cold wet hands with her own warm dry ones.

"Good." Persephone grinned, breathless.

"Are you about ready to go?"

"Almost! Two more laps." Persephone took a deep breath, letting it out nice and slow, and then went under again. Resurfacing a few yards away, she counted strokes and breaths, reaching for handfuls of water, pulling them under her body again and again. Just like Levi had shown her. Just like they'd practiced, until she touched the rope and turned back toward the dock.

Between breaths and through the watery filter of the lake, she caught glimpses of her mother on the dock, coffee cup in hand, her feet dangling in the water as she watched. Persephone wondered if she was thinking about Levi too. About that empty lifeguard chair. No one ever thinks about saving the lifeguard.

Persephone gulped air.

Reach—Pull—Breathe.

Stroke after stroke.

Her lungs burned. But she didn't stop.

5

LEVI'S SECRET

Persephone left lake-water footprints on the sidewalk that ran through town as she and her mother made their way home, the morning sun warm on their backs. They didn't talk about the lifeguard chair, or Levi, or how these were the first laps Persephone had swum since Last Year's June. They were just quiet. But Persephone's mother gave her a wobbly smile as they walked up the porch steps. And she knew her mother was remembering too.

"Good job, sweetheart," she whispered, pulling Persephone's towel more tightly around her shoulders. But Persephone didn't feel like she'd done a good job, she'd just gone swimming, and Levi was still stuck. In this house. In his bed. Inside himself.

"I need to get some work done before lunch," Mom said. "Owen is going next door to play with Sam, so you'll be on your own for a bit, okay?"

Persephone nodded. Her mother was a medical

transcriptionist, which meant she spent a lot of time in her little office at the back of the house, emailing people at hospitals and turning notes, records, medication orders, and reports into orderly typed forms. Because of her work, she probably knew about the health of almost everyone in Coulter, and had done something to make sure they were all properly cared for.

Toweling off and pulling on a pair of shorts and a T-shirt, Persephone walked down the hall and lingered in Levi's open doorway for a minute. Andrea had given him a bath while they were gone, and his hair was still damp. He smelled like his favorite sandalwood soap—the one he used to use himself, before Last Year's June. Persephone liked that his nurse used it now, even though Levi couldn't tell her it was still his favorite.

In Persephone's imagination, her older brother turned and grinned at her, stretching and yawning as if she'd just interrupted a nap. But the image quickly faded, and she was left with Levi exactly as he was.

Her brother half sat half lay in a special bed that rose and lowered at the push of a button. His head listed to one side, a feeding tube running through his nose. He didn't talk—the doctors said his brain couldn't form words or thoughts in that way anymore. Nothing could make him go back to being his old self.

Persephone walked over to Levi's bed and rested a hand on his arm, hating the strange feeling of absence. As if he was there, but missing.

"Hey, Levi," she said. "I swam ten laps today." Her voice felt too loud in the quiet. She squeezed his arm gently. A reassurance. They were both still here. Levi said nothing. He didn't turn his head or grin. He didn't blink or sigh or twitch. He was just still; the only sign of movement was his chest rising and falling with even, measured breaths. Persephone felt out of place. Too awake. Too vivid against the backdrop of the machines that monitored her quiet brother's vitals. She stared out the window where the sun was warm and the world continued growing, bright and alive, while her brother lay almost motionless.

Levi used to laugh and tell jokes and pick her up and swing her around the living room. He would carry Owen on his shoulders and let him wear his hat, usually backward, because it was too big and the brim hung over Owen's eyes. Of course, like any brother, Levi bugged Persephone too—teased her and fought with her over stuff—dumb stuff, like who got the most marshmallows in their Lucky Charms, and who had to clean the bathroom on Saturdays. But she would give anything to have him back. She'd loved watching him swim. He was good. Really good. Freestyle, butterfly, backstroke, and that perfect backflip that only he could do. He'd been lifeguard for Coulter three summers in a row. And no matter who sat in that tall chair with its peeling red paint at the edge of Galion Lake every summer from now on, she felt like it would always belong to Levi.

Persephone climbed up on the foot of her brother's bed. "Do you remember where we left off? How many laps I'd worked up to?" She studied Levi—this version of him. The doctors told them it was important that they keep talking and interacting with him. At first, it had been hard to even look at him—tubes running in and out of his body. But even when the seizures had started, their family hadn't given up. And it had gotten easier with practice. Now Persephone liked to pretend Levi talked back. Sometimes, she could almost hear his voice in her memory, though lately, the exact sound of it had started to go a little fuzzy.

"I think you were up to ten or so," he would say, his forehead wrinkling as he tried to remember. *"We should check your log."*

Persephone frowned, glancing around the room. *That's right. Her log.* Levi had made a chart to help them both keep track of her swimming progress. It was probably still on his computer. She got up and pulled his laptop from the desk drawer where it always sat. None of them had messed with his things, other than to clean or dust around them. Persephone felt almost guilty as she climbed back up on his bed with the computer, like she was trespassing.

"It should be right on the desktop," she imagined her brother saying as his laptop flickered to life. She found it quickly—a single document: "Persephone's Swimming Log." It sat right beside a folder called "Small Town Revival Application." *What was that about?* Persephone let the mouse hover over that interesting folder for a moment, curious.

Small Town Revival was the television show she and Levi had watched together every Thursday evening—before Last Year's June. She still watched it with him now, even though things were different. It was a makeover competition show, only, instead of transforming a house, or a wardrobe, or a relationship, the show awarded prize money to the small town that made the most promising or impressive transformation over the course of the season's twelve episodes. It was fun to see the cool and inspiring things other places were doing as they improved their towns and communities. Levi had always loved the way the show worked to restore historic architecture and old buildings. Before the accident, he'd applied to colleges for architecture and design programs and had decided on an art school in Chicago.

Sometimes, Persephone and Levi even talked about what project they would choose to tackle—what they would restore or fix up or improve if *Small Town Revival* ever came to Coulter.

"One of the old buildings downtown would make the most sense," Levi had said.

"But maybe the whole town would look better if we did a bunch of smaller projects instead of just one building," Persephone had argued.

"Like what?" Her brother was skeptical.

"I don't know. Maybe if there were planters or something? Like on every street corner!"

"That'd be a lot of planters." Levi had laughed but nodded. "It's a good idea, Pip. The trouble is, it's not just about the idea. The towns that make it on this show make it because the person representing the town has a story to tell or something that makes them interesting."

"What do you mean?" Persephone had asked.

"The show makes money off viewers and advertisers,

so whatever or whoever they feature each season has to be a little sensational—to keep people watching. That's why you have to be at least eighteen to even submit a town for the show. These makeover shows sort of exploit people's lives and towns for the sake of viewership."

"Yeah, but isn't that always the cost of being famous?" Persephone had asked. "I think I could live with that for one hundred thousand dollars." Levi nodded thoughtfully.

"Yeah, Pip," he'd said. "Maybe I could too."

Persephone hit print on her swimming log, and then she sat for a minute, staring at that mysterious *Small Town Revival* folder.

In her mind's eye, she saw her brother grin conspiratorially.

And so Persephone clicked on it.

It opened, revealing a variety of documents and forms, several historical photographs of Coulter, an application, and a submission letter.

She could hardly believe it. Her heart pounded and her hands felt a little shaky as she clicked on each file, opening them one after the other and reading.

Small Town Revival was a well-known show. It was a big deal. And there was a lot of money involved—one hundred thousand dollars was awarded to the person who completed the winning project. And there was funding given for other improvements as well—like new collections for libraries, new streetlights, and building renovations. Sometimes, there was money given to individuals and families for things like education, home repairs, and emergencies. Viewers even had the opportunity to contribute. In one episode, a family lost their house when a river breached its banks and flooded everything. A fund was set up through the show, and people from all over could donate. Levi and Persephone had even contributed. It wasn't a lot, but as she watched the town come together to rebuild that family's house, Persephone had cried right along with the host of *Small Town Revival*. It felt good to be part of something like that, and she was so proud as she watched the family move into their new house—the whole town standing in their yard, welcoming them home.

Maybe Levi had been planning to submit Coulter to *Small Town Revival* in hopes of getting money to pay for college? Persephone stared at her brother lying in his bed. From the look of the documents, he must have spent hours and hours gathering information and filling out forms. He'd even talked to people in town, collecting their thoughts and ideas about what made Coulter so unique. Levi had been planning to submit their town to *Small Town Revival*, and he'd never said a word to her! Had he meant to share it after he submitted the application? Or did he want to keep it a secret until—*if*—their town was selected? And what project had he dreamed of completing? Now she would never know.

Persephone swallowed hard, trying to work around the ache building in her chest as she clicked on a document Levi had named "Application Letter," and began to read.

ATTN:
Francis Graham, Production Executive
Epiphany Television Inc.

Dear Sir,

Please find enclosed, the required forms and
documents (as detailed on your website) to
submit Coulter, Wisconsin, to your show, *Small
Town Revival*.

I appreciate your time and attention, and
sincerely hope you'll consider this historic and
friendly place when making selections for the
next season of your show.

A hundred years ago, Coulter was a mining
town, and thousands of pounds of iron ore were
pulled out of the ground in order to make the
steel that helped play a role in the victory against
Nazi Germany in WWII. Some of my neighbors
remember their fathers and grandfathers working
in those mines with great pride. But now that
the mines have closed, Coulter has become a
graveyard of memories and unrealized potential.
I would love to see it become a monument to
new dreams and new victories as we explore
opportunities for tourism and pursue the
preservation of history.

My little sister and I have loved watching *Small Town Revival* for several years now, and it has had quite an influence on my decision to pursue architecture and design as a career. I've always loved the restoration of historic places. I'll be heading to school in the fall—School of the Art Institute of Chicago—and I think it would be so rewarding to see my academic dreams align with the dreams I have for Coulter, my hometown. As the host of *Small Town Revival* says, "A little change can start a big revival." Thanks for considering Coulter; it's a place with a history worth reviving.

Sincerely,
Levi Clark

Persephone sat back, Levi's computer in her lap.

Her brother had wanted things to change too—maybe things she would never understand. The fact that she was sitting here right now with his computer on her lap, looking through an application to *Small Town Revival* was proof that there was stuff she didn't know about her brother. There were probably a lot of things she would never know. His reasons might have been different than hers, but maybe Levi had felt stuck, just like she did now. Maybe he had wanted more. More for himself. More for their family. More for their town. They had talked about things they would fix, if they could. For Levi, it was always restoring buildings and architecture—saving valuable old things. For her, it was always plants and flowers—growing new things. And she still wanted more for Coulter—especially now. Maybe this was how she could help her family, her brother, *and her town*. Maybe this was the answer to those medical bills, and a way to pay for those treatments her parents talked about—their voices hopeful, almost reverent, as they spoke in the darkness of their room across the hall every night. Levi couldn't change things for himself anymore. But she could.

Everything was ready. Levi had seen to that.

Now all Persephone had to do was mail a letter.

But first, she had to get it signed.

6

A NOT-FORGOTTEN GARDEN

Persephone was afraid that if she stopped to actually think about what she was doing, she'd lose her nerve. So she quickly forged her brother's signature at the bottom of his letter. She gathered all the forms and documents that she had printed, and slipped them into a large manila envelope. Then Persephone ran all the way to the post office.

She was hot and sweaty by the time she got there, and she stood outside, catching her breath and clutching that envelope against her chest. She was afraid to go inside—afraid of Mrs. Howard's questions and curiosity, afraid of the answers she didn't have, and worried about the lies she'd have to tell. Levi had been seventeen when he was getting the application ready. Maybe he'd been waiting to send it in until after his birthday. Only applicants eighteen years and older where eligible. And he never could have known how much everything would change by then. But Persephone was not eighteen, and forgery was against the law, probably even more than trespassing! And if anyone found out what she was doing just to submit the application to *Small Town Revival*, she would be in so much trouble. So she dropped the envelope into the mail slot outside the building before anyone noticed her standing there. She heard it land among the other letters in the bottom of the mail bin. She imagined it sighing softly, as if it were relieved to be on its way. There was no going back now.

A slow smile grew inside of her until she couldn't keep it from spreading across her face. It felt like hope.

"*Meow.*"

Persephone jumped, whirled around, and met a pair of unblinking green eyes. They belonged to a small gray cat who had appeared at her feet. The same cat she'd rescued from the water tower.

"*Meow,*" it said again.

It sat prim and unconcerned on the curb, the only witness to what she'd just done. It wrapped its long tail delicately around gray feet, the tip twitching just a little. The cat looked exactly as it had before it vanished into the underbrush two days ago.

"Hello again," Persephone said nervously. "Hey, you can't tell anyone about that letter, okay? I need to keep it a secret. For now."

The cat blinked.

"Where did you come from?" Persephone asked, glancing around. She reached down and gently rubbed the cat behind its ears. The creature leaned into her fingers, purring. And then it turned and began walking down the sidewalk, pausing once to look over its shoulder at Persephone.

"Are you coming?" it seemed to say.

Persephone had never been friends with a cat quite like this one before. Mittens had been skittish, self-absorbed, and prone to dashing for the door anytime they left it open. Would this cat run off again at the first chance it got? She couldn't be sure, but the invitation to follow didn't seem like the kind of thing you received every day, and Persephone didn't want to waste the opportunity. So she followed, the cat leading the way, until she found herself standing one block off Main Street, in front of Mrs. McCullacutty's big old white house.

Everyone said Mrs. McCullacutty was odd. She almost never came into town for anything besides groceries and the occasional bouquet of cut flowers from the little corner florist's shop. But when she did, she was always strangely dressed and aloof—old-fashioned, nodding gracefully at people as if she were a queen or something. She had lived in Coulter for as long as anyone could remember. People whispered things about her. That she had once been a famous actress . . . that she could do things no one else could— magical and sinister things—that she was much older than she looked . . . that she lured people into her house, and when you came back out (if you came out at all), you couldn't remember what had happened, but you were never the same. Things like that.

Persephone didn't believe the stories.

At least, not most of them.

"Do you live here?" Persephone glanced at the cat. "Is that why you wouldn't come home with me the other day?"

"*Meow,*" said the cat. It stood, purring as Persephone scratched under its chin. It let Persephone pick it up, pressing a soft warm head into her neck. Persephone examined the chaotic yard and tumbledown garden that stretched around the side of the house. A massive lilac bush encroached on the entire west side, standing guard over a cacophony of tangled vines, overgrown grass, and a collection of leaves, windfallen branches, and scrub brush. Buried beneath it all were the forgotten bones of flower beds, filled with choking perennials reaching for a sky they could barely see. Persephone could *feel* it all, like an ache somewhere inside of her, where the growing came from.

"That garden needs to *breathe,*" she said, stroking the cat all the way down its body to the tip of its tail. "It's stuck. Just like me."

"What are you doing with my cat?" said a loud voice from somewhere in front of the big old white house. Persephone dropped the cat, who landed on its feet, as cats always do. She stared at the house, trying to decide where, exactly, the voice had come from.

"Are you trying to steal my cat?" The voice was louder and more high-pitched this time.

"No!" Persephone shook her head. "I'm not trying to steal your cat at all!"

A pair of arms reached though the overgrown lilac bush, pushing aside the branches, and Mrs. McCullacutty herself peered through the bush. Or rather, through a window that was nearly hidden behind the bush.

"What are you doing?" Her voice was a little frantic now.

"I—I'm looking at your yard," Persephone stammered.

"Why are you doing that?" Mrs. McCullacutty asked.

It was a fair question. The new leaves in the trees rustled overhead, and a cicada buzzed from some secret spot. The cat purred from where she sat at Persephone's feet, and the chaotic, forgotten garden whispered restlessly.

"Um—because you have a nice yard and a beautiful garden . . ." Persephone hesitated. "But, um . . . it's overgrown. And maybe I can help."

"What?" Mrs. McCullacutty leaned so far out her window that she was almost entirely engulfed in the lilac bush.

"I'd like to help your yard—your garden," Persephone said, gesturing around and stumbling over her words before she'd had a chance to think them through. *What was she even saying?* "I'm good at making things grow!" she offered, as if that would help Mrs. McCullacutty understand. "Maybe I could clean it up a little. So it can breathe, and grow, and come alive again . . ."

At this, Mrs. McCullacutty leaned out so far she nearly fell into the lilac bush, but recovered just in time.

"Absolutely not!" The old woman was firm. And loud. Almost as loud as the garden itself. Persephone took a step back in case this woman could do magical and sinister things from a distance. "I'll not have some presumptuous, cat-stealing girl hacking up my yard! Now go away! And take your nonsense with you!" She shook the lilac bush. The little gray cat lashed its tail, almost annoyed with the old woman.

"Can you just think about it?" Persephone was caught somewhere between fear and curiosity. This garden's noise felt unusually loud. And she could almost smell forgotten peonies beneath the heady fragrance of the blooming lilac bush.

"No! Now get off my street!" The lilac bush shook some more, and the gray cat looked at Persephone and twitched its whiskers apologetically.

"Okay! I'm sorry!" Persephone said as the old woman disappeared from the lilac. She heard the window slam shut, and a moment later, Mrs. McCullacutty emerged at the door, dressed in a bright green silk housedress and pink slippers.

Persephone backed up.

"Go! Get out of here!" The old woman had an umbrella in one hand like she meant to jab it at Persephone. But she didn't jab. She merely opened it and held it over her head. Even though it wasn't raining. "And leave my cat alone!" She was almost tearful this time. "Come here, Blue. Come, girl!" she chirped to the gray cat, who rose and ambled toward the house and her crabby master.

Persephone didn't wait to see the woman close her door. She just turned and hurried back down the street in the opposite direction.

She could almost hear the yard and the forgotten garden begin to weep softly as she left.

"Don't worry," she whispered, glancing over her shoulder. "I know you're in there. You're not alone."

7

ONCE-BEST-FRIEND

"Dad?" Persephone asked later that evening.

"Hmm?"

"Do you think people get crabbier the older they get?"

Her father raised an eyebrow. "Are you suggesting I'm getting crabby, Persephone?"

"No." She laughed, rolling her eyes. "Not you. Other old people."

"Oh! Excuse me!"

"Dad! You know what I mean."

He chuckled and leaned back against the porch step where they were sitting. "I think people get set in their ways. It can be hard to think differently or see the world differently—no matter how old you are. Where's this coming from, Persephone? Was someone crabby at you?"

"Old Mrs. McCullacutty yelled at me today," Persephone said with a shrug.

"Oh?" Her dad sat up.

"I was petting her cat."

"That seems a little extreme . . ." he said carefully, already knowing there was more to the story.

"I also asked if I could help clean up her yard—fix her garden. Stuff like that."

"I see." Dad frowned. He didn't see. "Why do you want to clean up her yard and fix her garden? Are you already bored now that school is out? I'm sure your mother and I can come up with some more chores around the house for you . . ."

"No!" Persephone shook her head. "I'm not bored. It's just . . ." She frowned. It was always hard to explain how it felt to make things grow—how it felt *important* and urgent.

"You just want to make something happen—something change?" her dad suggested, and Persephone let out a relieved sigh.

"Yes. Yes, I do," she said.

"So do I," Dad said. "It can be hard to sit around and watch things stay the same." Persephone nodded. "It was nice of you to offer to help." Dad picked himself up off the step and brushed his pants. It was time to head inside and start dinner. "But sometimes, as much as you want things to change for someone, they might not be ready. Maybe that's why Mrs. McCullacutty yelled at you—maybe it had nothing to do with her cat or her yard. Maybe it was just the possibility of a change she wasn't ready for."

Persephone thought about that. It made sense.

"We can't force change, sweetheart," Dad said, opening the door. "We have to invite it in."

Persephone swam twelve laps the next morning.

Reach—Pull—Breathe. Reach—Pull—Breathe.

The water wasn't any warmer than the last time, and it wasn't any easier, but she did it anyway. One stroke at a time. One whole mile.

Her mother sat on the dock, feet in the water, watching and helping Persephone keep track of her laps. But by the time she'd reached her eleventh lap, her mother wasn't alone on the dock anymore, and Persephone knew exactly who sat next to her—legs folded beneath her, long brown hair swaying in the breeze.

Mya Lowry. Persephone's once-best-friend.

Her heart skipped a double-time beat and her stomach felt like lead, pulling her under. She didn't want to see Mya. She didn't want to talk to her. What was she even doing there, sitting on the dock beside her mom like nothing had ever happened?

Reach—Pull—Breathe. Reach—Pull—Breathe.

Persephone went underwater a few strokes from the dock, did a flip turn against the sturdy lip of the dock's edge, and headed back the way she'd come without surfacing. Her lungs screamed for air, but somehow it felt more important to not talk to Mya. To not cut her laps short. To not stop swimming. She had one lap left. She had to finish.

Reach—Pull—Breathe. Reach—Pull—Breathe.

Persephone touched the rope on the far side of the

swimming area and then reluctantly turned back. Her goggles were foggy and the world, both under the water and above it, felt messy. All the edges smeary.

Persephone surfaced as she touched the dock and took a deep breath, and then another. Her arms shook and her heart pounded. Water ran off her hair in tiny rivers and she was cold—from the water and the cool morning air, and from finding Mya on the dock.

I bet they were talking about me, Persephone thought. She didn't take her googles off and she didn't get out of the water. She just bobbed next to the dock, staring up at her once-best-friend.

It had been months since she'd seen Mya or her brother, Joseph. Or rather, since she'd seen them on purpose. She'd seen them at school of course. And their families had seen a lot of one another as they worked through some of what had happened Last Year's June with a special family trauma therapist. But Persephone had done her best to avoid as much of that as possible. Seeing them, and spending time with them, and talking about stuff wouldn't fix anything.

"Hi, Persephone," Mya said. Her blue eyes were wide as she waited for Persephone's response.

Persephone ignored her. She just stood up and walked into the shallows toward shore. After the weightlessness of the lake, gravity felt impossibly heavy. The earth spins at one thousand miles per hour, and it anchored Persephone with such force she struggled to lift one foot after the other as she walked away, leaving wet footprints—and her mother and Mya—behind.

When she got home, Persephone went straight to the bathroom and filled the tub with hot water, giving the bottle of watermelon bubble bath a generous squeeze into the faucet's rush. Bubbles rose and she eased into the tub, suit and all, and only then did she pull off her goggles. The world was suddenly sharp and hard-edged. She scrubbed her face with both hands, rubbing away the tight feeling the goggles had left against her skin, and then wrapped her arms around her knees as the bathroom filled with steam.

Mya had been Persephone's best friend since kindergarten. Mya's older brother, Joseph, had been Levi's. The two older boys were always off fishing, or exploring, or hanging out and playing video games, and Mya and Persephone were together doing everything else.

They rode bikes and pretended to be pirates and knights, space travelers and sword-wielding princesses. They ate Popsicles under the heat of the August sun, racing to keep their frozen treats from melting. The boys built a tree fort in the backyard oak. That tree reached long branches across the stretch of overgrown brush that ran right up into the towering pines, standing shadowed and serious behind the house. And sometimes the girls played there too, walking on quiet feet over fallen pine needles, leaning back and searching the tops of those trees for glimpses of sky. They would wrap joined hands around the mighty trunks, stretching to reach. Two girls. Grips firm. Making a perfect loop.

Mya knew everything there was to know about Persephone. All her secrets. All her fears. Everything in between. She was like her sister, really. A sister she'd never had and always wanted.

And then the accident happened.

And Levi was never the same. Because you can't hit your head on the edge of a boat and get swallowed up by a lake, and be who you were before. Even if they manage to bring you back.

Nothing would ever be the same again.

And it was all Joseph's fault.

Mya said it wasn't. She said it was an accident. She said her brother had tried to save Levi. But Persephone knew the truth.

And now after everything, Persephone couldn't go back to bikes and popsicles and space travel, tree forts and towering pines. She couldn't tell Mya things anymore. Their grip had slipped. The loop was broken. Because Persephone couldn't trust Mya. Not now, knowing that her brother was capable of hurting Levi the way he had. Just looking at Mya reminded her of Joseph and of her own brother, who was lying in his bedroom. Breathing, yes. But empty and gone.

There was a knock on the bathroom door.

"It's me. Can I come in?"

Persephone slid farther into the bubbles. She didn't really want to talk to her mother, but she knew that wouldn't stop her mom from wanting to talk to her. "Yes," she said after a moment.

"I brought your towel." Her mother came in and shut

the bathroom door behind her. She sat on the closed lid of the toilet. The towel Persephone had left in a heap on the dock sat neatly folded on her mother's lap.

"Thanks," Persephone mumbled into the bubbles.

"Want to talk about it?" her mother asked.

"There's nothing to talk about," Persephone snapped, and her mother raised an eyebrow.

"Mya just wanted to talk to you. She misses you, Persephone."

"I have nothing to say to her." The watermelon bubble bath suddenly smelled too sweet. The water was too warm. She felt a little sick.

"Maybe not." Her mom shrugged. "But Mya has some things to say to you, and the least you could do is listen."

"I don't want to hear what she has to say!" Persephone's voice came out louder than she meant, and she took a deep breath. "Nothing Mya says or does can fix anything."

"You're right," her mother agreed. "It can't fix anything. But it could change something."

"Not for Levi!" Persephone said.

"Not for Levi." Her mother nodded. "But maybe for you."

"Not for me either!" Persephone yelled. Her voice caught on the tears that were rising, pricking behind her eyes. She blinked them away angrily. "I don't want to talk about this anymore," she whispered. Her mom was quiet, her face sad. She stood up, laying Persephone's neatly folded towel on the toilet seat.

"All right," she said. "But I'll be here when you're

ready." She opened the bathroom door, releasing the humid watermelon-scented air into the hallway. "Persephone," she said over her shoulder, "nothing is ever going to change if you won't."

And then she closed the door behind her.

8

A VERY UNUSUAL CAT

Two more hospital bills were waiting for Persephone the following morning when she went to collect the mail. And nothing from Mr. Francis Graham, Production Executive, Epiphany Television Inc. Not that she really expected anything. She had only mailed the application a couple of days ago. But it was hard not to peer into the mailbox and wish something besides bills would miraculously appear.

Mrs. Howard was suddenly very busy with something on the other side of the counter as Persephone stuffed those fresh bills into her back pocket. She blinked away tears of frustration and wished she hadn't told her mom she would come home right after getting the mail. She needed some time alone, and an excuse *not* to hurry back. It felt like she kept handing her parents more reasons to be discouraged and sad every day. Just once she wanted to hand them something *more.*

Things used to be so different. Lighter. Easier. There

had always been bills to pay, but Dad had come home at the end of the day smiling through the grit of chimney soot and dirt. Mom had always hollered at her and Owen to "keep it down a little" from her office when she was transcribing medical notes and trying to rush reports, but she had never looked like she did now—a little lost and always tired. Even Owen was quieter. He cried more easily than he used to. He wanted to hang out and be with her more than he had before, almost like he was afraid she might disappear or something.

When Persephone stepped out of the post office, Blue, Mrs. McCullacutty's small gray cat (and the most marvelous excuse not to go home right away), was waiting for Persephone for the second time that week.

"Oh! Hello, Blue!" she said. "What are you up to today? Climbing any water towers? Hanging out with any crabby old ladies?" The cat gave Persephone a slightly offended look, and Persephone crouched down, sitting on her heels as she ran her hand down Blue's back. "Sorry, you're right," she said. "That was rude. I'm sure Mrs. McCullacutty is a very nice owner."

"*Meow.*" Blue blinked up at Persephone. And then, as she had done before, the little gray cat started down the sidewalk, glancing back as she waited for the girl to follow. As often as Persephone had thought about Mrs. McCullacutty's overgrown yard and the forgotten garden, she wasn't quite ready to face the old woman again. Not yet.

She shook her head.

"Mrs. McCullacutty told me to leave. I don't think I should go back so soon without a proper invitation." Blue sat down and licked her paw as if it were taking all her patience to deal with humans today. And then she got up and wound herself around Persephone's ankles before starting off down the sidewalk again.

"Please consider this a proper invitation," she seemed to say.

"Okay." Persephone sighed. "But if you lead me straight back to that big old white house and Mrs. McCullacutty is mad, I'm telling her it's all your fault." Blue simply twitched the tip of her tail.

Blue led her down Main Street and past the hardware store. She wove in and out of bike racks, around trash cans and fire hydrants, tiptoed delicately over tree grates in the sidewalk, and ignored a dog tugging at the end of its leash. She was decided about wherever she was headed, and Persephone followed closely, getting more curious the farther they went. Around the corner beside the hardware store she traipsed, into a blocked alley full of flattened cardboard boxes, used car wheels, two broken flowerpots, an overturned wheelbarrow, and a boy holding a can of spray paint.

"Oh! I— *Wait*, what are you doing?" Persephone went from surprised to indignant in the space of a breath as she noted the paint sprayed across the crumbling brick wall. She put her hands on her hips, and Blue sat down expectantly beside her.

Malachi Rathmason heaved a sigh and stared at Persephone for a moment before stashing his can of paint into the backpack at his feet.

"No water towers today?" he asked, kneeling and zipping up his pack. Persephone crossed her arms. He was the only person who knew about that. Well, him and Blue. And Blue wouldn't tell. She hoped.

"That's vandalism, you know," she said, ignoring his question and nodding toward the brick wall. "I could turn you in."

"It's not vandalism if you have permission," Malachi said easily. "And no, you won't. Because I could turn you in too. Climbing the water tower was trespassing. The signs were clear."

"At least I didn't destroy anything!" Persephone insisted.

"Neither did I," said Malachi, a little irritated. He tilted his head, studying his work. "Come see." Blue rose on silent feet and trotted toward Malachi. She sat next to him and they stared at the wall like they were at some gallery exhibit.

"Do you really have permission to do this?" Persephone asked.

Malachi sighed, refusing to answer.

She reluctantly joined the boy and the cat.

Using green spray paint, Malachi had transformed a broken and rusted drainpipe that ran up the side of the alley wall into the stem of a giant sunflower. The face of the flower was actually a broken window. He'd turned something broken and ugly into something wonderful. Something *more*. It was clever. *And really good,* Persephone thought. But she folded her arms again and Malachi rolled his eyes.

"Whatever," he said. "I don't care if you don't like it."

But she did like it. She just didn't like being wrong.

"*Meow,*" said Blue, ignoring them both. She'd made her way to where the overturned wheelbarrow lay in the alley. The handles were worn and cracked, the barrel rusted. Even the tire was flat. She rubbed the line of her jaw against one of the wooden handles and then sat, staring expectantly at both Malachi and Persephone.

"Nice wheelbarrow," said the boy.

"*Meow,*" said Blue. She blinked bright green eyes at him and then wound herself around Persephone's ankles.

"What is it, Blue, hmm?" Persephone reached down and scratched under her chin. This time Blue leaped, graceful as a dancer, and alighted on the edge of the wheelbarrow's rusty brown side. She stared first at Persephone, and then at Malachi, purring all the while.

"I think that cat wants you to get her a wheelbarrow," said Malachi.

"*Meow,*" Blue confirmed. Persephone bent to study the heart-shaped leaves of a small vine that twisted itself around one of the wheelbarrow's handles. She carefully untwisted the vine and lifted the handles, testing the wheelbarrow's weight. If she had learned anything since meeting Mrs. McCullacutty's small gray cat, it was that she was not a typical cat. Persephone righted the wheelbarrow with effort. One of its legs was bent, and the wheel wobbled on its axle. "Right," Persephone said, squaring her shoulders. "So, where do you want me to take this?" But Blue was already leading the way.

"I've got to see this," Malachi said, slinging his backpack over his shoulder.

The wheelbarrow was heavier than it looked. And more wobbly. Blue led Persephone with her wheelbarrow and Malachi with his backpack full of paint cans toward the post office, never bothering to make sure they followed. She just trusted they would.

"Where. Are. We. Going?" Persephone panted, setting the wheelbarrow down after several blocks. The sun was hot overhead. She could feel a trickle of sweat sliding down her back. Blue paused for a moment and leaped onto one handle, butting her head under Persephone's chin encouragingly. Then she leaped back down and waited.

"Almost there!" she seemed to say. Malachi chuckled and then shrugged when Persephone shot him a look. It's not like he'd offered to help or anything. But then, she hadn't asked either.

"I'm coming, I'm coming." Persephone sighed, picking the wheelbarrow back up and steering it awkwardly down the sidewalk.

By the time the small gray cat led them three blocks past the post office, Persephone realized exactly where they were going, and her stomach sank. One block later, they all stood in front of Mrs. McCullacutty's house, and in front of Mrs. McCullacutty herself.

The woman sat on one of the three steps that led up the walkway, fanning herself with a delicate fan made of ivory and blue-and-green peacock feathers.

"There you are," she said, rising and folding the fan before slipping it into her pocket. "And one extra, I see." She nodded to Malachi.

"Here we are?" Persephone asked, breathless, and sweaty, and a little confused. Mrs. McCullacutty had been waiting for them?

"Did you, or did you not, follow Blue and bring along the wheelbarrow as I asked?" She looked at Persephone like *she* was the peculiar one.

"You asked Blue to get a wheelbarrow?"

"Well, I asked Blue to get you, and the wheelbarrow is a necessary accessory. Unless you are uncharacteristically strong?" She eyed Persephone, looking for signs of hidden strength. "Blue insisted you were clever," Mrs. McCullacutty said. She stared at the cat and the cat stared back, eyes half-lidded, whiskers twitching. "Time will tell." She smiled. "It always does. Come along." She gestured for Persephone to follow, but Persephone frowned. Was this the part where Mrs. McCullacutty lured her inside and she forgot everything? What if some of those stories Persephone had heard about her were true?

Blue just sat there, purring. Maybe Mrs. McCullacutty wasn't actually sinister, but just a little eccentric? Persephone started to follow, but the woman held up a hand and pointed to the wheelbarrow.

"The wheelbarrow, dear," she said.

Persephone stared at her, and then at the wheelbarrow, and then at the stairs, and the walkway, and the front step, and finally at Malachi, who shrugged.

"You want me to bring the wheelbarrow? Into the house?" Mrs. McCullacutty glanced at Blue and raised an eyebrow, questioning both the cat's judgment and Persephone's cleverness. But the old woman just nodded and proceeded up the steps and down the walkway. She was wearing a pair of yellow rain boots and a lacy lavender dress.

Persephone hauled on the wheelbarrow and wrestled it up the three cement stairs dividing Mrs. McCullacutty's raised yard from the street—*Ka-thump! Ka-thump! Ka-thump!* It hit the back of each step as she tugged on it, the flat tire wobbling and protesting. She stopped at the porch, waiting for Mrs. McCullacutty to tell her what to do next, but the old woman simply gestured dramatically without looking back at Persephone.

"I think I'll just wait out here," Malachi said a little nervously.

"Oh. Yes, that's thoughtful of you, Malachi Rathmason." Mrs. McCullacutty nodded, even though Persephone had never told her the boy's name. "The house didn't know you were coming today, and it prefers to be prepared for visiting artists."

Persephone glanced back at him, and Malachi gave her a look that clearly advised her against going any farther. But she had gone too far to change her mind now. She wrestled the wheelbarrow up two more steps and onto the porch—*Ka-thump! Ka-thump!* Then into Mrs. McCullacutty's house she went.

9

INSIDE THE HOUSE

The inside of Mrs. McCullacutty's house was a little like the outside, and like Mrs. McCullacutty herself—*unusual*.

Three carved wooden carousel horses stood in a line inside the front door, nose to tail, galloping toward the interior of the house. A massive mirror stood on the floor leaning against the wall opposite them. It was intricately carved with small heart-shaped vines and flowers and over-laid in gold. It rose all the way to the ceiling, which was high enough to allow for a collection of many-armed chandeliers, all hung at varying heights.

All over the entryway walls, above the horses and around the mirror, hung portraits of people dressed in blue. There was a painting of Elvis against a black velvet back-drop wearing a blue-collared shirt and a handsome smirk. He hung beside a fancy oil painting of some long-dead king or dignitary, also dressed in blue. And opposite him, was a picture of a Black Madonna, also in blue, her hands outstretched beseechingly. These three were only a fraction of the faces that studied Persephone, standing there in the doorway with her wheelbarrow. She gripped the handles a little tighter.

"My late husband, Everett, was a collector," said the voice of Mrs. McCullacutty from farther inside the house. "He traveled the world, you know. He *curated*—that means he carefully selected—precious artifacts for museums and art galleries and private collectors."

Persephone studied her reflection in the giant mirror: a not-too-tall girl with sweat and dirt streaked across her face; gray eyes, and hair so blond it was nearly white escaping from a low ponytail, DREAMER written in white letters across the front of her gray T-shirt, jeans, sneakers, and a rusty wheelbarrow. Behind her reflection, dozens of faces of people dressed in blue stared back at her, and three carousel horses galloped where they stood.

Persephone blinked.

"*Meow.*" Blue sat in front of her, green eyes wide and dark in the dim light of the foyer. Persephone examined the small gray cat, framed on the floor between the wheelbarrow handles and her arms. There was something strange and surreal about it all. This was definitely the sort of place that girls in movies wandered into and never came out of. The wheelbarrow felt like the most real thing in here. She held on to it, tight.

Persephone tried to measure Blue's realness. She *seemed* entirely feline. But you could never be sure with cats. Glancing at their reflections in the mirror, Persephone tried to catch a glimpse of something other than gray fur and green eyes. Something *more*. Everything here felt like more than what it was. Even Mrs. McCullacutty herself.

Persephone cleared her throat. She'd told Mom she'd come home right after she finished at the post office, and while she'd wanted an excuse to delay the delivery of today's bills, this might be too much of an excuse. Her mom was going to be worried.

"I have to go!" Persephone called down the hall. Mrs. McCullacutty's voice had moved farther into the house and Persephone didn't know where she'd gone. "Can I leave this wheelbarrow here for you?"

"No, you cannot," Mrs. McCullacutty said, reappearing. "Goodness! Had I known you were in such a rush, I would have told Blue to arrange for a different day." She looked pointedly at Blue and the cat stared back, twitching her tail. "Come," Mrs. McCullacutty said to Persephone. "It will only take a moment."

So, despite Persephone's pounding heart, and the fact that Mom would be worried, she stayed. The whispering of the forgotten garden and the yard felt loud. She had no idea if there was anything she could even do, or if Mrs. McCullacutty was ready for change, but she was asking Persephone for help, and it felt important to try. Staying here, in this house, and following Mrs. McCullacutty down that hall, felt like the first step. After all, there was a lot she couldn't do. But maybe this was one small thing she could. Something dangerous, foolish, and brave. That's what Malachi had said. Maybe he was right.

Persephone adjusted her grip on the wheelbarrow. Blue leaped up to perch on the front, like the figurehead on the prow of a ship, and together they trundled farther into the house.

Persephone had always thought of Mrs. McCullacutty's house as just a big old mansion. And it was. But like Mrs. McCullacutty, Persephone now suspected it was also more than that. She swiveled her head this way and that, trying to get a better look at everything as they walked down the long hallway. In one room stood a magnificent piano. Dozens of ticking cuckoo clocks hung high on the wall, and a real stuffed lion prowled in one corner. It looked like it was hunting a real stuffed ostrich, which ran from it, frozen in time, in the opposite corner.

In another room, bookcase after bookcase lined the walls, but instead of books, butterflies and moths and other insects pinned in glass cases were on display.

An elaborate aquarium stood on a small decorative table, full of living seahorses, anchoring themselves around red and pink coral.

An antique dollhouse as tall as Persephone stood in another corner, full of miniature wooden people, and miniature wooden furniture, and miniature wooden pets, and miniature wooden food.

In a shadowed nook next to a bookshelf halfway down the hall, a giant horn rose spiraling all the way to the ceiling. It looked exactly like Persephone imagined the horn of a unicorn might—if a unicorn were as large as a whale.

And everywhere, everywhere, art—leaning against the wall at various heights, hung on spare wall space, and stacked on furniture. Faces, animals, flowers, landscapes, architecture. Watercolors and oils, acrylic and pastels, pencil and ink. She was almost dizzy from looking around and trying to take in what she saw.

Just before the hallway turned a corner, a beautiful bay window rose up on Persephone's right, and on a window seat in solitary splendor sat a massive potted flower.

This was nothing like the spindly, single-stemmed things you find in grocery store flower centers—small pots wrapped in brightly colored cellophane. This one stood in a many-paned glass terrarium, multi-stemmed, roots rambling wildly as they clambered over the edges of its pot. Moss grew in the roots, tucking them in here and there, allowing them to escape and breathe and wander. But where broad, bright green leaves should have been, there were yellow dying ones instead. And where exotic flowers should have dripped off tall stems, there was nothing. Persephone only knew what it was because its name was etched on a small brass plate: PHALAENOPSIS—MOTH ORCHID.

She hadn't stopped for anything else in the house. Not the lion and ostrich, not the seahorses or dollhouse, not the unicorn horn, or butterflies, or the art, but Persephone stopped for this. She couldn't have walked on by if she'd wanted to. It pulled at her, just as the forgotten garden outside had.

"What's the matter with your orchid?" Persephone asked.

"I don't know," said Mrs. McCullacutty. "I suppose it has nearly run out of hope."

Persephone reached out, wanting to touch the plant, wanting to bring it back to life, to make it grow. But Blue made a funny noise—not a purr and not a growl, but something like both—and Persephone pulled her hand away as the cat switched her tail, just once.

"*Do not touch*," the small gray cat said with her snapping green eyes. So Persephone didn't.

"It was a gift from a friend, a long time ago," said Mrs. McCullacutty, her voice soft. "But it's dying now. And perhaps it's my fault." She said it like you might say "I think it's going to rain today," matter-of-fact and resigned. But there was such sadness behind her words. Persephone could almost hear the *thip-thip-thip* of crying rain hitting the wet pavement.

They left the orchid by the window, alone. But as they walked away, the wheelbarrow's wheel squeaking down the hall against the polished wood floor, Persephone suddenly had to fight the bizarre urge to cry. Which was silly, because it wasn't even her flower. But it felt sad and lost.

Mrs. McCullacutty didn't say another word until they rounded the corner, and then she stopped so abruptly that Persephone nearly dumped Blue off the front of the wheelbarrow as she wrestled it to a halt just inches from the back of Mrs. McCullacutty's yellow rain boots.

"Well then, here we are," she said, standing outside the door of a small, worn study room. This room must be for living, Persephone realized, unlike the rest of the rooms, which were for viewing art.

A threadbare chair sat in one corner by the windows, and a lamp on a green wicker table sat beside it. A bright floral rug was thrown over the floor and wool roses wove in and out of the fading threads. Potted red geraniums sat on the wide windowsill. And standing tall and elegant among the geraniums was the only unusual thing in the room. A two-foot-tall bronze statue of a woman. She was clothed in a dress of gauzy bronze fabric. Bronze vines twined in her hair, and bronze narcissus flowers bloomed at her feet.

"The Maiden," said Mrs. McCullacutty, gesturing to the statue as though Persephone would understand some implied significance. "She's yours," Mrs. McCullacutty said, her voice level and decided.

"Mine?" Persephone asked.

Mrs. McCullacutty turned and clasped her hands in front of her.

"Blue refused to offer details, but she made it quite clear that you were rather instrumental in saving her life the other day. And for that, I feel I owe you an apology, and a thank-you."

"And a statue?"

Mrs. McCullacutty's lips twitched into what Persephone could only assume was a smile. The first Persephone had seen. It transformed Mrs. McCullacutty's face.

"And a statue." Mrs. McCullacutty nodded. "I was rude to you, yelling out my window like that, and I'm not in the habit of being rude. Though I am a little odd on occasion."

She smiled in earnest. Persephone tried not to look at her yellow rain boots. "You caught me in an unpleasant moment," she continued. "And I'm afraid I behaved rather badly. You see—" She paused. "I was terribly concerned for Blue's well-being. She was gone for several days before you happened along and came to her rescue. But I didn't realize you and Blue's rescuer were one and the same. The only thing I knew that day last week when you first stood in front of my house was that Blue had just returned to me. And when I saw her in your arms, I was afraid she might be on the verge of leaving again, and I couldn't bear it. Forgive me, dear."

"Oh. Well, that's all right." Persephone felt a little unsteady. "I—I forgive you." She wasn't sure that was the right thing to say, exactly, but it was the only thing she could think of.

"Marvelous!" said Mrs. McCullacutty. She clapped her hands. "So, *The Maiden* is yours. She has sat here in my geraniums long enough. Besides, it's rather fitting, after all."

"Why is it fitting?" Persephone really didn't understand why Mrs. McCullacutty was gifting this statue to her. It wasn't the sort of thing people did. Sometimes her mother brought a little gift to a neighbor who had been kind—a loaf of banana bread, maybe. Or a thank-you note. But people didn't just give bronze statues to each other as a way of showing gratitude.

"Why, the two of you share the same name!" Mrs. McCullacutty exclaimed, as if Persephone should have known that all along. "In the stories, 'the Maiden' is just another name for Persephone," said Mrs. McCullacutty.

Persephone felt the strangest thrill run straight down her spine all the way to her toes.

She'd never told Mrs. McCullacutty her name. She was sure of it. And yet, here they were. Sure, they lived in a small town, and it wouldn't have been difficult to find out her name. But something told Persephone there was more to it than that. Did Mrs. McCullacutty know who she was before she invited her inside?

Persephone glanced at Blue, who had made herself comfortable on the arm of the chair. The cat just looked at the girl, purring, green eyes bright. And it almost seemed like she was smirking.

10

SHOWING UP

"Are you sure you're okay?" Malachi frowned.

He'd been waiting on the steps for Persephone while Mrs. McCullacutty ushered her and the wheelbarrow inside, then back out with *The Maiden* in tow. The boy had jumped to his feet as Mrs. McCullacutty came out. She looked at him, a little surprised to find him still waiting.

"Have you been here the whole time?" she had asked. Malachi nodded.

"Well, I apologize for our delay," she'd said. "It's clear the house enjoys your company. But you can never tell. I once lost a local politician to the porch steps, you know." Mrs. McCullacutty winked. "The house is an excellent judge of character."

Persephone had raised her eyebrows and glanced at Malachi.

Regardless of what the house did or did not think of visitors, Malachi had gotten off the steps and waited from a safer distance on the front walk as Persephone made her way down. *Ka-thump! Ka-thump! Ka-thump!*

Mrs. McCullacutty had wrapped the statue in a bright yellow shawl, which she had almost certainly crocheted herself.

"For insulation," she'd said. "So she doesn't rattle around quite as much." The statute rattled anyway.

And now Persephone was trundling back through town toward home with the rattling statue wrapped in a bright yellow shawl, as Malachi walked beside her trying to determine if she was truly the same person she'd been when she first stepped into that old house. Then, to make matters worse, Mya Lowry joined them on Second Avenue. She hopped up on the curb, eyeing Malachi curiously. And Persephone realized just how much was happening that she would have shared with Mya, if not for Last Year's June.

A year ago, Mya would have laughed at Persephone, hands on her hips, eyes shining.

"What on earth, Persephone! Here, let me help!" And then she would have taken the wheelbarrow handles for a little while, introduced herself to Malachi, and listened to every part of their story, asking all the right questions. And Persephone would have told her everything. Because that's what best friends do.

But today, she just kept quiet as Mya fell into step beside them.

"Hi, Persephone," she said, just like she'd said yesterday morning on the dock.

Persephone said nothing.

"You can't keep ignoring me forever."

Persephone gritted her teeth.

"I'm just going to keep showing up, you know." There was iron in Mya's voice. "No matter what, until you look at me, and talk to me, and explain."

"You want me to *explain*?" Persephone whirled on Mya.

"Uh, I think I'll catch you both later." Malachi nodded at Persephone before hopping off the curb and heading for somewhere less confrontational.

She frowned, frustrated at Malachi for leaving, and at Mya, for not. Persephone dropped the wheelbarrow, and its wobbly legs hit the sidewalk with a grating screech that made her teeth ache. She stood there, clenching and unclenching her fists. "What exactly do you want me to *explain*?" She glared at Mya. "Because of your brother, mine is brain-dead!"

Mya flinched like Persephone had slapped her, and part of her—a small, shadowy part—felt good about that.

Mya lifted her chin. "Joseph explained everything to the police. And the paramedics. He explained it to my parents and your parents, and everyone! This was no one's fault." Mya's voice was getting louder. She loved Joseph. Persephone had loved him too. And Levi had loved him. He'd trusted him. They all had.

"Well, that's great!" Persephone's voice shook. "I bet, when I get home, if I *explain* everything to Levi, he'll just miraculously be himself again!"

Mya bit her lip, blinking hard.

"I'm sorry, Persephone." Her voice had gone small.

" 'Sorry' doesn't fix anything," Persephone snapped.

"I know," Mya whispered. "I'm not trying to fix it. I don't think there's any way I could. I'm just sorry you're sad. And I want to be your friend." She said the words like she'd been practicing them.

"I'm not sad. I'm mad!" But suddenly, Persephone wasn't sure that was completely true. "And I can't be friends with you," Persephone lied. "Not anymore. So, you can quit showing up like this."

"Can't be friends, or *won't?*"

"Both," Persephone said.

Mya flinched again, but this time Persephone felt sick from the anger that sat heavy and shadowy in the pit of her stomach. Mya's chin shook, the way it did when she was trying not to cry. But she took a deep breath and met Persephone's gaze.

And the look on her face was so fierce that Persephone had to look away.

Then Persephone picked up the wheelbarrow, somehow twice as heavy as before, and walked off without another word, leaving her once-best-friend alone on the sidewalk.

11

WHAT IF

If Persephone closed her eyes, she could sometimes pull herself back—back before everything changed.

Summer vacation had started. She'd just turned twelve, and Levi's senior year was over. They'd all attended his graduation—forty-six folding metal chairs set out on the Coulter High School football field, the sun warming the seats. At the end of the ceremony, he'd thrown his cap in the air, cheering along with everyone else. Levi would leave for college in the fall, and Persephone already missed him. What would life be like without him around all the time? Levi was planning to major in architecture and design—he wanted to design and restore and build things. Bridges and schools. Maybe whole cities. Her brother was amazing. And now the world would see it too.

In Persephone's memory, the warmth of Last Year's June breeze poured through the open window, the smell of growing things carrying straight into Levi's bedroom. Her brother perched on the arm of an overstuffed chair, his computer on his lap. He wore a frown and a green T-shirt with IRON COUNTY 4-H CAMP written in chunky white letters across the front. Persephone had wandered in looking for him, and now she leaned on his shoulder, peering at the blank screen and blinking cursor.

"Hey, Pip," he said. He always called her Pip.

"Hey. Whatcha working on?" Levi had leaned his head back and scrubbed one hand over his face and through his hair.

"Essay," he said. "For a scholarship. I have to answer this question in a way that's 'appealing and engaging and captures the reader's thoughts and imagination.'" He did air quotes with his free hand. "It's just, I don't want to tell them only what they want to hear," he said. "Which means I have to sound like I know exactly what I'm going to do with the rest of my life, so they're sure their money won't be wasted on me." He smiled sideways at Persephone. "Got any brilliant ideas?"

If she could, Persephone would have given him every dollar he needed for the next four years. Not even one would be wasted on Levi. She glanced at the bulletin board on his bedroom wall. It was filled with beautiful and intricate drawings of structures that Levi had imagined. They were glorious.

"What's the question you have to answer?" Persephone had asked.

"*How will you change the world?*" Levi groaned. "It's so pretentious!"

"Yeah," Persephone agreed, laughing. Levi had sighed heavily and stretched.

"You know, whatever. I need a break." He'd snapped his computer closed and slid his phone out of his pocket. "Joe and I were supposed to hang out this afternoon." His eyebrows knit together in a frown. "Maybe he'll want to meet up now instead—if he's not still upset," he mumbled.

Persephone frowned too, remembering what she had seen and overheard the night before. But neither she nor Levi said another word about it.

"Hey, answer that question for me while I'm gone, okay, Pip?" He ruffled her hair, and then he left.

Those were the last words he said to her.

She thought about that morning a lot.

What if she'd asked to go along? He might have said yes. She could have stopped it all. She could have saved him.

What if his text had never gone through? Cell reception was sketchy at the back of the house sometimes.

What if Joseph had never responded, because he *was* still upset?

But mostly, she wondered how things would have been different if she'd had a good answer to that question right when he'd first asked it. *"How will you change the world?"* She knew Levi would've stayed and started writing that essay, and not have gone out on the boat with Joseph.

In the days after the accident, Persephone made herself sick trying to make all those what-if's hold more weight than they ever could. In the end, none of those possibilities were real. And now, the only real hope she had was wrapped up in that application to *Small Town Revival*. She couldn't stop thinking about it. She knew it wouldn't change what had happened, but maybe it could be a way to answer the question Levi left for her. Maybe it could be enough to help him finish what he started.

"I'm back!" Persephone called as soon as she got home from Mrs. McCullacutty's. She was breathless from hauling the wheelbarrow and the statue of *The Maiden* all the way across town. "Mom?" No one responded for a minute or two, and then Andrea poked her head out of Levi's bedroom. Levi's nurse hadn't become a member of their family, exactly, but Persephone was always glad to see her. She cared for Levi in ways the rest of them could not.

"Your mom took your little brother to the park, Persephone," Andrea said. "She said she'd be back in a bit."

"Oh. Okay, thanks." Persephone smiled, relieved she could just drop the mail she'd collected that morning into the file basket on Mom's desk. It was easier than giving her those bills directly, and then watching her shoulders slump under their weight. She just wished she knew where her response from Mr. Francis Graham, Epiphany TV, was.

Persephone stood in the living room for a minute, looking around. She could hear the clock ticking from its spot on the fireplace mantel. The house was too quiet. Too empty. She went back outside and stood on the porch steps, staring at the bronze statue in the wheelbarrow. She'd parked it on the walkway in front of the house, but now she didn't know what to do with it. With any of it, actually—the statue, the dilapidated wheelbarrow, Mya who wouldn't quit showing up, the bills that wouldn't quit coming. She felt stuck. Stuck. Stuck. Stuck. *Stuck.*

Persephone clenched her fists and marched down the porch steps, angrily wrestling the wheelbarrow off the walkway.

Mom's car rolled up a minute later, and Owen was out and skipping up the driveway before the engine was even off. He had fresh holes in his pants from whatever he'd been doing at the park.

"Do you want to see my blood?" he asked, already rolling up his pant leg, which revealed a small cut across the top of his knee. "It happened like this"—he almost demonstrated how he had fallen and scraped his knee, but remembered that his knee actually hurt, and caught himself before he hit the ground a second time—"I hope I get a scar!"

"We came home for Band-Aids," Mom said, walking up the driveway. She dropped her purse on the porch as Owen ran inside, and then eyed the wheelbarrow. "So," she began. "It looks like you had a busy morning. I take it you didn't get that from the post office." She raised an eyebrow. "Care to tell me about the Greek goddess in the wheelbarrow?"

"Sorry I was gone so long," Persephone began, ducking her head apologetically, and then nodded at the statue. "That's *The Maiden.*"

"Is it, now?"

"Her name is Persephone." She felt that odd little

shiver run up her spine again, just as it had when Mrs. McCullacutty told her the statue's name. Her mother stared, frowning a little.

"That's very interesting. And where did *The Maiden* come from?"

"From inside Mrs. McCullacutty's house. She gave it to me."

"You went *inside* Mrs. McCullacutty's house?" Her mother stood up a little straighter. Her tone told Persephone this had probably been a very bad idea.

"She wasn't a kidnapper or anything," Persephone said, and her mother's face twisted into a wry look.

"No, she's not a kidnapper, honey. But we don't really know her. And she is a little—"

"Unusual," Persephone offered. Her mother nodded.

"Did anyone know where you were?"

Persephone remembered the alarmed look on Malachi's face as she stepped over the threshold and into Mrs. McCullacutty's house. But if she told Mom about Malachi, she'd probably have to explain why the two of them were hanging out all of a sudden, and that involved the water tower, a small gray cat, graffiti on a brick wall, and it was all more than Persephone could explain without adding half a dozen more lies to the mix. So, she shook her head. *A lie.* But only one.

"No. I was alone," she said. "But it was fine!" Her mother sighed, suddenly looking small and weary. Persephone quickly filled her in on the details she could share safely: the giant mirror and the lion and the ostrich in the piano room, the seahorses, the dollhouse, and the dying orchid.

"There's really a stuffed lion in her piano room?" Mom's face was a mix of wonder and confusion.

"And an ostrich," Persephone said.

"And the cat—Blue . . ." But Mom just let her question trail off. Persephone was glad she left it unasked, because she wasn't sure she could answer any questions about Blue anyway. "Hmm." Her mother steepled her fingers, pressing them to her lips, and then carefully leaned over the wheelbarrow like she was unwilling to get too close.

"Can I keep it?" Persephone was starting to feel a little protective of the statue. She didn't exactly *like* it, but it made her curious. It reminded her of that Greek myth about Pygmalion and Galatea—the artist who had created an impossibly beautiful statue. Galatea—the statue-turned-woman—eventually came to life, and she loved Pygmalion back. Persephone's class had studied Greek history and culture last year, and there weren't very many Greek myths with happy endings, so she liked Pygmalion and Galatea's tale. Maybe this statue could have a happy ending too.

Persephone's mother was quiet as she stared at the bronze woman in the wheelbarrow and then nodded.

"I suppose we should. Seems rude to refuse a gift. Even if it is an odd one. Where should we put it?"

"Can I keep it here, in the garden?" Persephone wanted to keep the statue, but she didn't want it in her room staring at her while she slept. She almost laughed at herself, but the statue had come from Mrs. McCullacutty's house, and

Persephone was pretty sure nothing that came out of Mrs. McCullacutty's house was ordinary.

"The garden sounds like an excellent place." Her mom nodded. "She is the goddess of life and spring and growing things, after all."

"She is," Persephone agreed. "Do you think it's weird? That Mrs. McCullacutty had a statue of Persephone in her sitting room?"

"I think that entire situation was weird," her mother said. "And I really don't want you going back."

"What—why?" Persephone felt a sudden urgency squeeze her heart. She had to go back.

"Persephone, I mean it—" Her mother hesitated. "There have been strange stories about that woman and her house for as long as I've lived here. It makes me uncomfortable having my daughter spend time with someone like that!"

"Someone like *what*? They are just stories, Mom! I have to go back!" Persephone dropped the wheelbarrow's handles. It came to a sudden stop in the grass.

"Nothing is ever *just* a story, Persephone—there's always a little bit of truth in things, even if it gets jumbled around." Her mother looked at her pointedly. "And why is it so important that you go back?" She folded her arms across her chest as she waited for a response. Mom was right. It was a reasonable question, but Persephone didn't have a reasonable answer.

"I just—have to!" Persephone grunted, pushing the wheelbarrow around to the back of the house. She and her mother lifted the statue out and stood her upright beside a patch of budding delphiniums, their blue spires reaching for the matching sky.

"How did you do this alone?" Mom asked, clenching her teeth as they heaved and strained to move *The Maiden*. "She must weigh a hundred pounds!" Persephone wasn't sure how she'd done it by herself. It had been heavy, but now it seemed like it should have been impossible.

"I have to go back to Mrs. McCullacutty's house," Persephone said again, once they'd finally managed to get *The Maiden* situated just right. She said it quieter this time. Calmer. "Mrs. McCullacutty is lonely. I think she needs a friend. And I like her cat. And she has a garden that really needs someone to help it. I can *feel* it . . ." Persephone trailed off and shrugged. Her mother sighed, a little exasperated.

"Let me think about it," she said. "I know helping things grow is important to you. But I don't want you over there again until your dad and I talk about it. It doesn't feel safe. And I *definitely* don't want you inside her house." She met Persephone's gaze. "Do you understand? I'm sure she's lovely, but we should get to know her better before you go over there anymore."

Persephone sighed.

Stuck.

12

TRADITIONS

On Thursday night, Persephone sat on the end of Levi's bed, bowl of popcorn in her lap, watching the panoramic shots of small towns flash across the screen in time with the familiar opening-credit jingle.

"This is my favorite part," she said into the quiet room. She imagined her brother grinning beside her as she tossed a piece of popcorn into her mouth.

"Why is this your favorite part—because everyone looks so obnoxiously happy?" She could almost hear Levi. *"Or because you think the host is cute?"*

"Ewww, gross! I don't think he's cute!" Persephone laughed, her brother's imagined grin growing wider as he teased her.

Thursday-night viewing of *Small Town Revival* had been their tradition before the accident, and she didn't see any reason to stop now, despite the tubes running this way and that, or the machines beeping quietly, monitoring her brother's life. If it were true that maybe, just maybe, Levi was still inside himself somewhere, then this tradition was medically important. They had to keep interacting, continuing familiar patterns and routines.

Persephone stared at Levi, studying him for signs of life. Of awareness. Her brother was stark in the flashing light of the television. The hollows in his face were deeper. His eyes vacant. It was hard to look at him. She hated thinking that the old Levi was gone. He was just lost. *Stuck.* Trapped. Because lost, stuck, trapped things could be recovered. Retrieved. Revived. Which is why treatment was crucial—like therapy for his body and his mind. There were treatments developed especially for cases like Levi's. She had heard her parents discussing them more than once.

Of course, there was no guarantee they would work, but Persephone had to try. Because Levi needed the treatments, and she needed Levi. So, one way or another, she would make sure he got them.

The host of *Small Town Revival* was halfway through his program and was emphasizing the need for each community member's involvement in order to make that particular town's project successful, when there was sudden movement on the bed behind Persephone. The bowl of popcorn fell off the bed and spilled all over the floor, and Persephone screamed for her parents as Levi's body began to convulse and seize.

Mom and Dad rushed into the room, calm and efficient but tense as they straightened tubes, checked machines, and secured Levi to his bed so he wouldn't fall out.

The host of *Small Town Revival* made lighthearted banter on the screen and Levi's monitors echoed the flashing lights of the TV. The show's host seemed to mock them with his perfect hair and easy grin.

"You can't expect change to happen overnight!" he said cheerfully to the camera.

"Shut that off!" Dad snapped. Persephone jumped, but she did as she was told. Somewhere out in the hall, little Owen began to cry—a small, frightened sound. Persephone bit her lip, remembering how Blue had cried at the top of Coulter's water tower. But this time there was no ladder for her to climb. No grand rescue. She fumbled with the remote and tried not to cry too, as Levi's body shook and shook and shook.

The television screen flicked off as Persephone's trembling fingers finally found the power button. The handsome TV host and his easy words about change went silent.

She pressed her back against the wall in Levi's room, watching and chewing her lip.

When she couldn't stand there a minute longer, Persephone turned and crept from the room. There was nothing she could do for Levi. But Owen was still crying somewhere in the house.

Sometimes, when her little brother got upset or scared, he would hide in small quiet places—under a blanket fort in his bed, behind the couch in the living room where the curtains hid him from view, or in the hall closet behind the winter coats. And that's where Persephone found him, blinking up at her from where he'd curled up with Levi's old blue puffer coat.

"Hey," Persephone whispered.

"Hey." Owen sniffed, wiping tears off his face with the back of his hand.

"Is there room for me in there?" Persephone asked, and her little brother nodded, scooching over until there was just enough space for Persephone to sit beside him, the heavy drape of winter coats brushing comfortingly against their shoulders.

"It's going to be okay," Persephone said, the darkness of the closet muffled and close.

"I know that's not true," her brother said. "I'm not a baby." Persephone turned, trying to see his face in the dark.

"I never said you were." She could just make out his small, pale face beside her. He was only seven, but tonight he seemed older than that.

"Sometimes you treat me like a baby though."

"I—I'm sorry." He was right. "I don't mean to."

"I know." Owen sighed. "And I know Levi's not going to wake up, Persephone. You don't have to pretend." Persephone frowned in the dark.

"You don't know that for sure," she said after a minute. "No one does." But her voice felt a little unsteady. Owen reached for her hand and squeezed.

"Will you play it?" Owen asked. "So I can remember?" Her little brother already knew she had swiped Mom's phone from the kitchen table. But then, Persephone always did, whenever Owen was sad and upset like this. She nodded and clicked through the saved messages—the light from the phone's screen suddenly much too bright in the dark. Her own heartbeat felt loud and too fast as she tapped on the video message Mom had saved, and then the speaker button.

Levi's voice poured into the darkness, his face animated and awake.

"Hey, Mom—just wanted to let you know I'll be late tonight. I have to guard at the beach until dark . . ." Everything about Levi was so familiar—the way he glanced away from the camera and then back again. The way he smiled, reassuring Mom that he was fine. The way he angled the phone's camera as he walked so Mom could see he was still at the lake. Persephone desperately wished she could wrap her arms around him. Owen brushed tears away, leaning his head against Persephone's shoulder as they stared at the screen. *"I'll probably grab pizza or something with Joseph, so don't worry about dinner. Okay. Love you. Bye."* Levi ended the call, the screen went black, and silence filled the closet again.

Persephone had found this message one afternoon when she was flipping through old pictures on Mom's phone. He'd sent it just a few days before the accident.

"Play it again?" Owen wiped his eyes on the sleeve of his pajamas, and Persephone did. Once. Twice. Three times. Until Owen took a deep breath and let it out slowly.

"Thanks," he said. "I remember again. I remember him." Persephone nodded and wrapped her arm around her little brother. She remembered too.

She thought about the host's words. No, she didn't need change to happen overnight. She just needed change to be *possible.*

~~ 13 ~~

TEA AND THE GARDEN

Two days after Levi's seizure, Persephone walked to the grocery store and bought a package of orchid food with some money she'd earned taking care of her neighbor's houseplants. And then she made her way to Mrs. McCullacutty's house. Neither of her parents had given her permission to go back. And she hadn't asked. But the memory of that dying orchid felt too important, no matter what her parents had said. She would just keep it a secret. For now.

Blue met her on the curb in front of Mrs. McCullacutty's big old white house and led her up the sidewalk onto the porch, her tail high and waving—a small but sincere welcome flag. Persephone rang the bell, and then they both waited until Mrs. McCullacutty opened the door.

She wore sparkly red heels, cuffed and ruffled ankle socks, and a blue party dress with a gauzy overlay covered in tiny pink flowers. Pretty much anyone else would have looked ridiculous in that outfit. But combined with a sweeping updo—her silvery gray hair piled high in waves on her head—and a pair of very round, very red glasses, Mrs. McCullacutty was breathtaking.

"Hello!" Persephone took a tiny step back, trying to absorb the wonder of Mrs. McCullacutty's style. "Are you going to a party?"

"Good morning, Persephone," said Mrs. McCullacutty. "I hadn't scheduled any parties today, unless you have one I could attend?"

"Well," Persephone fumbled, "my birthday's on Tuesday, three days from now. Maybe you would like to come over for that?"

"Marvelous!" Mrs. McCullacutty clapped her hands and turned to Blue. "I suppose I'll have to find something suitable to wear." She tapped her chin, thinking on the matter, and Blue continued purring at their feet on the porch. "Oh! Do come in!" Mrs. McCullacutty suddenly remembered Persephone standing on the porch and opened the door a little wider, ushering her inside. "I was just making tea. Would you like some?" Persephone didn't really drink tea, or coffee for that matter. Both felt a little too grown up. But she nodded.

"Sure. Thanks."

"Excellent!" Mrs. McCullacutty smiled brightly. "Tea for two!" She turned on her sparkly red heel and led them through the house and into the kitchen.

Black and white tiles checkerboarded their way across the floor, beneath hutches and under the legs of a tall peacock-blue table that served as a kitchen island.

A copper teapot steamed on the stovetop, and Mrs. McCullacutty gestured to a green hutch on the other side of the kitchen.

"Fetch some plates and cups from there, would you, please?"

The kitchen was just as full of beautiful and odd things as the rest of the house, but it felt more functional. A collection of copper pans hung on one wall, gleaming in the sunlight that shone through a tall stained glass window. The light streaming in fell on a towering shelf of colorful glass vases in one corner. A birdcage hung from the ceiling in another, and a small yellow bird perched inside the cage, absolutely still, studying Persephone with bright unblinking black eyes.

"That's Piccadilly." Mrs. McCullacutty looked fondly toward the bird. "Perhaps he will sing for you." At first, Persephone wasn't sure he was real, despite what Mrs. McCullacutty had just said. But then the bird gave a little shuffle of feathers and opened his beak like he was chirping or singing, though no sound came out. Nevertheless, Mrs. McCullacutty looked at Persephone triumphantly. "There!" she exclaimed. "What did I tell you?" Persephone smiled but said nothing. Piccadilly didn't make a sound.

This was such an odd house.

Persephone turned away from the bird and cautiously opened the tall green hutch, searching for plates and cups as Mrs. McCullacutty had asked. Inside she found shelves full of them. Some were delicate and ruffle-edged, some gold-rimmed and etched, some plain but so thin and fine

Persephone was certain the light would shine right through if she held them up to the window.

"Which ones do you want?" Persephone breathed.

"Whichever two seem right," said Mrs. McCullacutty. "The hutch will decide anyway." She stood at the counter preparing tea, so Persephone shrugged and carefully chose two small plates from the stack directly in front of her. One was awash with pink flowers against a pale blue backdrop—a blue summer sky full of tossed blooms. It matched Mrs. McCullacutty's dress almost perfectly. The other was green—new green, like early spring leaves—and covered with twining vines. Persephone stared at them for a moment. Like Mrs. McCullacutty had said, it was as if the cupboard had picked them specifically. Like it had known about her. She handed the plates and cups to Mrs. McCullacutty, who nodded approvingly before placing them on a silver tray she'd pulled from some other cupboard in the giant kitchen. It was already loaded with a bowl of sugar and a little pitcher of cream, the copper teapot, a tower of pale yellow cookies, and the smallest vase Persephone had ever seen, holding a sprig of red geranium.

Blue was already in the sitting room, waiting for them in her patch of sunlight on the back of a chair. A second chair had been added to the room, as if the house had expected Persephone, and Mrs. McCullacutty motioned for her to sit as she situated the tea tray.

"So," she began, settling herself in her chair and pouring tea. "What brings you back to my house today?" Persephone watched as Mrs. McCullacutty picked up her teacup and saucer and sipped with a practiced air. Persephone copied her, but everything was fragile and hot and prone to spilling. The tea was sweet, and everything felt fancy. She wished she was better at drinking it. Persephone set her cup and saucer back down on the table before trying to talk.

"Well, this brought me back to your house, actually." She pulled the little package of orchid food from her pocket and handed it to Mrs. McCullacutty. The old woman stared at it a moment before setting it aside on the table.

"Why are you so concerned about my orchid, dear? Or my yard, for that matter?" She lifted an eyebrow. Persephone was a little disappointed that Mrs. McCullacutty wasn't more excited about the orchid food. She'd spent her own money to get it. She glanced at Blue, who watched her carefully. The little gray cat's eyes were half-closed in a knowing, comforting sort of way.

"You don't need to worry," she seemed to say. *"This is a believing place."*

"I—I make things grow," Persephone said after a moment, glancing at the collection of red geraniums on the windowsill. She felt her face warm, her body a little hot and uncomfortable. The only other person, besides her family who really knew this about her was Mya. Persephone had learned that most people were just glad to have her help with their plants when they needed it—they didn't really want to know what made her different, and why.

Mrs. McCullacutty just nodded.

"Yes," she said. "I knew there was something about you."

Persephone had only been around Mrs. McCullacutty two times, including today, and not counting that first time with the open window, the lilac bushes, and the yelling. But she was quickly realizing Mrs. McCullacutty wasn't like most people.

"I've always been good with growing things," Persephone began.

Mrs. McCullacutty leaned back in her chair with a smile, making herself comfortable as Persephone told her about those cherry trees in the hospital courtyard, and about her neighbor's houseplants, and about how the lawn grew back twice as fast when she mowed. And down the hall in the kitchen, Piccadilly began to sing.

Together, Persephone and Mrs. McCullacutty opened the package of orchid food, and following the instructions, they carefully mixed it and fed the plant. And then Persephone sat, cross-legged on the window seat. She talked to the orchid, encouraging it to grow, and Mrs. McCullacutty listened for a minute or two before returning to the kitchen to put away their tea things.

Twenty minutes later, when Persephone wandered back into the kitchen in search of Mrs. McCullacutty, she found her standing at attention by the back door. She had changed out of her gauzy blue party dress and had put on what Persephone imagined was exactly the sort of outfit a woman on safari might wear. Only, from about a hundred years ago. She even had one of those wide-brimmed hats complete with a veil to keep out mosquitos and offer shade from the sun. Persephone didn't know if she should laugh or ask for a pair of binoculars. Blue sat primly at Mrs. McCullacutty's feet, serious and dignified.

"Are you going exploring?" Persephone asked carefully.

"In a manner of speaking," Mrs. McCullacutty said. "Would you consider joining me? Despite my initial reservations, Blue has encouraged me to let you have a look at the yard and the garden—whatever remains of it. It has been left to its own devices for quite some time. Too long, perhaps. You see, the house has always had a mind of its own, and over the years a considerable amount has leaked out."

A considerable amount of what? Persephone wondered.

"After listening to your story and hearing you speak of your ability to make things grow," Mrs. McCullacutty continued, "I wonder if you might be exactly the sort of person the garden needs. Perhaps you can talk some sense into it. Encourage it to consider returning to its proper job."

"Its proper job?" Persephone was confused. What kind of job did Mrs. McCullacutty's garden have, besides growing?

"My grandmother, who lived in this house before my mother, and before me, designed the grounds—the yard and garden—as an invitation to any who might care to enjoy it. A community garden of sorts. A place where people could come and be together, enjoying the beauty of the place and the beauty of one another's company. But their invitation was always more exclusive than I liked. And even as a girl it did not feel right that only certain people were welcome. The house and the garden felt the same. It caused a lot of conflict within these walls . . ." Mrs. McCullacutty trailed off. She sounded sad, just as she had when she'd told Persephone about her dying orchid. After a moment she shook her head and smiled, patting the doorframe, the way she might pet Blue. "I think it's time to air things out a bit, inside and outside these old walls. The house has taken a liking to you. I can't help but imagine the same will be true of the garden."

Persephone glanced at Blue and then back at Mrs. McCullacutty, standing there in her safari outfit.

"Okay, sure," Persephone said. "Lead the way."

Two giant maple trees stood like royal sentries at the back of the house, stretching a canopy of green over the yard, and Persephone stepped through them, like a portal to somewhere else. Their silvery bark made her feel like she was standing in the presence of two mighty women dressed for battle.

"The Queens," said Mrs. McCullacutty. "I planted them myself years ago." She touched her fingertips to each tree as she too stepped between them. Persephone wasn't sure how that was possible, as these trees were likely a century old. Then she remembered her mother's words. Were the stories Persephone had heard about Mrs. McCullacutty more than just stories?

Persephone wondered as they walked.

Unlike many of the tidy and trimmed yards in Coulter, there were no trimmed hedges, no rambling rows of colorful border flowers, or dappled green hosta leaves that

Persephone could see. At the back of Mrs. McCullacutty's house, everything felt wild. Unkept. *More.* Like anything could happen here.

Mrs. McCullacutty escorted Persephone around the grounds, which were far larger than she had imagined. "No one has come here in quite some time," said Mrs. McCullacutty, almost apologetically.

It was a tangled mess, overgrown and wild and mysterious and wonderful. Persephone could feel the garden's loneliness and desire for growth the same way she could feel her own feet anchored against the ground. It was real and alive and hungry for more than what it had been.

"Do you want to turn this back into a community garden?" she asked Mrs. McCullacutty. "A place where anyone who wants to could come and visit, and plant things of their own?" Mrs. McCullacutty smiled a slow, delighted smile.

"That is exactly the right sort of question," she said. "My grandparents and my parents envisioned a park for those who met with their approval. But this garden has always wanted to be more than that. It wants to be a part of things—part of many people's lives." Persephone laughed. It was almost a relief to hear Mrs. McCullacutty talk about the garden as if it were more than what it seemed. Because it was. Persephone understood that.

"Well," she began. "Maybe you could start by using the raised garden beds back here for vegetables and things." Persephone pointed to an open spot in the middle of the yard. "There's enough sun for tomatoes. People could plant runner beans and vining peas there. And lettuce and kale and chard could go over there. There is definitely enough room for pumpkins and squash . . . People could come with their families, and there could be music . . ." Persephone spun in a full circle, seeing it all unfurl and stretch out in her mind. In addition to flowers and vegetables there could be a meandering stone walkway with thyme growing between the stones. And over there, an elegant wood trellis could be built for grapes, or maybe fast-growing hyacinth beans with their lavender booms and deep purple pods. She could see families gathering for picnics, and maybe someone strumming a guitar in the shade . . .

Mrs. McCullacutty studied Persephone with an appraising eye. Blue rose and trotted to where she stood, rubbing herself against Mrs. McCullacutty's ankles.

"*You see?*" she seemed to say, staring at Persephone. "*I told you she was clever.*"

Persephone grinned, but then her joy flickered a bit. Before she could begin planting or pruning or raking or growing a single thing here in Mrs. McCullacutty's garden, she would have to make sure her parents were okay with this marvelous plan.

14

PLANTING LIES

Persephone walked home, her brain whirring with everything Mrs. McCullacutty had shown her in the garden. On the outside, and if you weren't paying attention, Mrs. McCullacutty's yard and the forgotten garden looked exactly like any other unkept, extremely overgrown piece of property. Tangled, messy, wild, and old. It was full of massive trees and untrimmed hedges, rambling vines, and the chaos that growing things have when they are left alone too long. But underneath all that, there was *more*. Persephone could feel it. A longing. Maybe it came from her, or maybe it came from the garden—she wasn't sure. But it made her want to bury her hands in the soft, loamy earth. She wanted to drink in the fragrance of forgotten flowers, trim back the hedges until they stood tall and straight again, and find out what might happen if the garden started to imagine what it might become.

By the time she had said goodbye to Mrs. McCullacutty,

Persephone had made a promise to herself: She would come back, as often as possible. She would return Mrs. McCullacutty's garden to its original glory, and more. It would be a community garden where anyone and everyone could come and grow things, enjoy the beauty of the place, or just rest. Then, when *Small Town Revival* came to Coulter, because they would, *they must,* they would see what she had done. How beautiful it was. They would want to feature it on the show, and perhaps Mrs. McCullacutty's garden would be the winning project. One hundred thousand dollars for Persephone and her family. For her brother. There would be money for medical bills and money for Levi's treatment and therapy. It would be a *miracle.*

But visions of gardens and television shows and money and miracles flickered out like a birthday candle wish as Persephone walked down the driveway and found her mother waiting on the step. The look on her face made it clear that Persephone was in a lot of trouble.

Persephone's heart sank.

"*Where* have you been?" Mom's arms were folded tightly across her chest.

"I—I was walking around town." Not a lie. But not the whole truth either.

"Do you know how long you were gone, Persephone?" Her mother's voice trembled, and Persephone slowly shook her head. "Two and a half hours! I had no idea where you were. You didn't leave a note! You didn't tell anyone where you were! You just disappeared!"

Persephone stared at her feet.

"I was worried," her mother continued. "No—I was *frantic*. I didn't know if you had decided to go swim laps— I didn't know if something happened at the lake . . ."

Persephone looked up as her mother's voice broke, suddenly understanding. She hadn't known where Levi was either, that day. Not until the paramedics called.

"I'm sorry," Persephone whispered. "I wasn't at the lake. I'd never go there without telling you." Tears felt close.

Mom's lip trembled, and she nodded. "Good." Her mother took a deep breath and let it out slowly, collecting herself as the silence settled between them. And then Persephone stood up a little straighter, an idea dawning.

"Mom," she said carefully, "as I was walking around town, I started thinking . . . Do you remember how you said that you and Dad wanted to get to know Mrs. McCullacutty a little better?"

"Still thinking about her garden, huh?" Her mother arched an eyebrow.

"Yeah, I guess I am." Persephone grinned. "Well, I saw Mrs. McCullacutty today, and I invited her over for my birthday." Persephone let words roll off her tongue. Guilt plucked at her heart. But she needed to make it all okay when Mrs. McCullacutty showed up. She *had* invited her. But it had happened accidentally. While she was at her house. Where she had been forbidden to go.

"You invited her over?" Her mother sat back, a bit dismayed.

"Yes." Persephone nodded. "When I saw her in town, today." Another partial truth—her house *was* in town, after all. "I thought you and Dad wanted a chance to get to know her better, so this seemed like a good time." Persephone's heart was racing.

"Well, we *do* want to get to know her better," her mother said, exasperated.

"And isn't my birthday a good time to do that?" Persephone tried to keep her face open and hopeful. "I'm sorry I didn't ask you first." Guilt sat heavy in her stomach as her lie settled. "Do you—do you want me to tell her not to come?" She offered it up sincerely, but she knew her mother would never withdraw an invitation.

"No." Her mother shook her head and Persephone gave her a small smile. "It will be fine." Her mother sighed.

"She's a nice person, Mom." But it didn't feel like this was *fine*, even though Persephone had gotten what she wanted.

"I'm sure she is," said her mother. "And now your dad and I will get a chance to meet her for ourselves."

Persephone nodded. Her stomach felt tied in knots. Everything she was doing, even improving Mrs. McCullacutty's garden, she was doing to ultimately help her family. So why did it feel so messy?

15

FIFTEEN LAPS

"How far this morning?" Persephone's mother asked. She stood on the dock staring at the quiet water of Galion Lake on Sunday, sipping her coffee.

"Fifteen," Persephone said after a minute.

"Do you want me to count?"

Persephone nodded and then sat on the dock, dangling her feet in the water. This was the hardest part. Getting in. Getting started. Not because she didn't think she could do it, or because the water was that cold, but because her mind got loud before it got quiet. And it was hard not to listen.

What's the point, Persephone? her mind asked in a hard-to-ignore voice. *Even if you swim a mile, it doesn't change anything. You can't go back. So what if you do? What if you do actually manage to swim a mile? Then what? What does it prove?*

Persephone gritted her teeth and jumped off the dock.

"One," her mother counted. Persephone touched the edge of the dock and reached for handfuls of water. She said "one" all the way across the swimming area, touching the rope and buoys on the other side before making her way back.

Reach—Pull—Breathe.

She kept swimming.

Reach—Pull—Breathe.

She watched as each lap matched the number of fingers her mom held up before completing a flip turn against the side of the dock and heading back, repeating the number in her head. *Four . . . Four . . . Four . . .* Then *Five . . . Five . . . Five . . .* And *Six . . . Six . . . Six . . .*

Nine left. Then eight.

Reach—Pull—Breathe. Reach—Pull—Breathe.

Persephone's thoughts drifted to Tuesday and her birthday. To Mrs. McCullacutty, who was coming. The old woman's orchid. Her community garden. Her thoughts snagged on the application paperwork and letter she'd sent to Mr. Francis Graham at Epiphany Television. It had been one week, and she still hadn't heard anything back. Not a word. Not that she could really expect a response that quickly, but she couldn't help feeling disappointed anyway. She'd been checking the post office box every day; only more bills greeted her.

Ten . . . Ten . . . Ten . . .

Reach—Pull—Breathe.

And then, as Persephone surfaced for air, she found that Mya had appeared and seated herself on the dock beside her mother, just like she'd done a week ago. Persephone fixed her gaze on her once-best-friend just until she pushed herself forward in the water—and then ignored the blurry, fogged-over version of a girl who refused to leave.

Why couldn't Mya understand that it was easier when she wasn't around? That what had happened that terrible day last summer—the blood spreading into the sand around her brother's head, the wail of ambulance sirens, the *thump-thump-thump* of an approaching medical helicopter's propeller, her mother's hands hovering over her brother's body as the paramedics worked—it was all easier to shut out when Mya, or her brother, or anything associated with them, were not around. And yet, here she was. Again. And the memories washed over Persephone in waves.

If *only* she had been there.

Thirteen . . . Thirteen . . . Thirteen . . .

Persephone hadn't invited Mya to her thirteenth birthday. This would be the first year since kindergarten she would eat strawberry cake and ice cream without her. Mya wouldn't be there to sit beside her on the couch as Persephone opened presents.

Fourteen . . . Fourteen . . . Fourteen . . .

Reach—Pull—Breathe.

The last lap was the hardest.

Persephone's arms ached. Her legs burned. Her memories latched themselves to her heart like an anchor. The water no longer made room for her. Instead, it seemed to push back. She fought.

Reach—Pull—Breathe.

Persephone's mother flashed ten fingers plus five. Fifteen. Persephone reached for the edge of the dock and caught it, air filling her lungs with no pauses in between. Mom clapped and Mya smiled. But Persephone felt no joy. Only relief.

She hauled herself out and up onto the dock, taking the towel her mother handed her and wrapping it around her shoulders.

"I came to give you this," Mya said as Persephone struggled to catch her breath.

It was a small gift box.

"You could have just left it on the dock," she panted. The words left her mouth before she could stop them— harsh and short. But maybe Mya had been ready, because she just blinked and then shrugged.

"Yah, I guess. But I wanted to give it to you myself." She handed Persephone a small package wrapped in strawberry-printed paper. Persephone's wet fingers left darker pink splotches where they touched. Her mother began filling the silence with words about Mya's kindness—how thoughtful she was to come down to the dock and give Persephone a birthday present. And she was right.

"Thanks," Persephone mumbled.

"Open it," Mya insisted. And while Persephone would have rather waited until she was home by herself, she did. It was a package of flower seeds. Forget-me-nots. Tiny blue flowers that grew in clouds over the ground, their centers as yellow as the sun.

In medieval times, people would wear the little blue flowers as a sign of faithfulness to someone they cared about. Persephone had told Mya all about them one summer, when the two of them were playing and came upon on a patch of the flowers. They'd picked some, sticking them in each other's hair until they wore blue-and-yellow crowns.

Forget-me-not. No matter what.

And now Mya was saying it again. The promise made in seed form—the hope of a thousand flowers. The words repeated a thousand times: *Forget-me-not. No matter what.*

Persephone stuffed the package of seeds into her bag, mumbled another thanks, and stumbled up the dock toward home.

The only nice thing about being dripping wet when your once-best-friend gives you a gift like that is that no one can tell if the water streaming down your face is lake water, or tears.

16

BOVISTA PILA

Persephone dropped her wet towel into the laundry basket, shed her swimsuit, and hopped in the shower to rinse off the lake water. Then she found a fresh T-shirt and a pair of shorts. She was rummaging under her bed for sneakers when her mother knocked loudly. Persephone stared at the door. And then stood up and took a deep breath.

"Come in," she said. She knew what was coming. She knew because she'd felt it when her harsh words had sailed into the morning air as Mya handed her the package wrapped in strawberry paper. Persephone had seen the brief blink of tears in Mya's eyes as her mother had tried to fight the sting of her words with gentler ones. She'd seen the slump of Mya's shoulders as Persephone stuffed the package of seeds into her backpack and walked away, leaving her on the dock.

"We need to talk," her mother said.

"About what?" Persephone crossed and then uncrossed her arms.

"I've let this thing between you and Mya go on long enough." Her mother sliced a line of finality through the air with her hand. "I keep telling myself to give it time, to stay out of it. You two have been friends for a long time and you are old enough to work through some of this on your own." She took a breath and ran her hands through her hair before continuing in a slightly softer tone. "I told myself you needed time after Levi's accident to sort out how you felt. We all did! But this"—she gestured in wordless exasperation— "this has to stop." Her voice was rising. "What I saw last week and then again this morning is proof that you're not going to sort this out. Not because you can't, but because you *won't*."

Persephone's heart pounded. She felt hot. Anger was funneling up inside her. She did not want to talk about this. Not with Mom. Not with Dad. Not with anyone. Not ever.

"If you decide to let your friendship with Mya fall apart, that's your choice. But you do not get to let it end because of misdirected blame and your own stubborn unkindness. What happened to Levi was an *accident*." Her mother's voice was clear and certain. "Joseph is not to blame. Mya is not to blame. Mr. and Mrs. Lowry are not to blame. If anyone is to blame, it's Levi!" Her voice snagged on the edge of her tears.

"How can you *say that*?" Persephone gasped. She felt like someone had struck a match in her chest. "And how do you really know it's not Joseph's fault? You weren't there, out on the lake, out on that boat! Everyone is taking Joseph's side, but how do we even know he's telling the truth? Maybe Joseph just let Levi fall! Maybe he even pushed him!"

"No." The word was ice-cold and cut into Persephone's rant like a knife.

One word. But there was such power in it. Such certainty. Her mom took a shaking breath and continued. "True, we weren't there. Out on the lake or the boat. But I arrived just after the emergency crew, Persephone. You didn't see Joseph's face that afternoon or see him on his knees in the water with Levi. You did not hear him crying, talking to your brother—*talking and talking and talking*—telling him everything was going to be okay, to just *hang on*. You did not hear the EMTs praising the work he'd done, keeping your brother from going under—refusing to give up. Joseph was exhausted! He couldn't even stand up out of the water on his own. A few more minutes out there and they both would have drowned." Her voice broke and she stood inches from Persephone, her body shaking. "Joseph gave everything he had to try to save your brother. The only reason Levi is still alive at all is because of Joseph. The only reason I'm able to hold on to the hope that Levi could possibly make some sort of progress, someday, is because of Joseph. The only reason I can go into Levi's room just down the hall"—she pointed—"and talk to him—tell him I love him—and know he hears my voice, is because of Joseph. So I refuse to stand here another minute while you treat the Lowrys as if they are to blame." Tears streamed down her mom's face.

"Well then"—a sob escaped Persephone, anger turning the deep ache of her sadness into something sharp and ugly—"maybe you should just adopt Joseph. Like a replacement son!"

There's a ground mushroom called the *Bovista pila*, that, when bumped or stepped on, cracks open and releases a cloud of spores—like smoke. They were commonly called puffballs, and Persephone and Mya used to stomp on them over and over until there was no smoke left. They populated future puffballs one stomp and a hundred million spores at a time.

She felt like one of them now, a *Bovista pila*. Like someone had stomped on her and she'd released spores of smoke—a fog of dark words that landed all over her mother.

She thought her mother might slap her. Her eyes blazed and her face was white, her lips were pressed tightly together. Her mother's hands shook. But instead of leaving a mark on Persephone's face, her mother lifted her hand and wiped tears off Persephone's cheek.

And then, before Mom could stop her, Persephone walked out of the room past her mother and ran.

17

IN THE RIGHT DIRECTION

Persephone didn't stop. She couldn't. She kept going—

Out of the house and down the block. Past the water tower and mailboxes, old houses, and crumbling curbs. She ran past the post office, where she knew more bills waited— bills her family couldn't pay. She ran across Main Street, where she tripped over the corner of a bike rack and tore her knee against the pavement. But she was too sad and angry to care. She was up and running down First Avenue, Second Avenue, then Third, her sneakers pounding against the cement sidewalks, echoing the beat and boom of her heart.

By the time she got to Fourth Avenue, she was breathless and jogging, and her knee had started to ache. By Fifth, she slowed to a walk. Blood ran down her leg from the gash in her knee. She'd probably have a scar. *Good.* This day felt like it should be marked by a scar.

She limped down the street after running out of sidewalk,

and then finally sat down on a curb and closed her eyes, taking deep, shuddering breaths under the hot sun.

Birds sang overhead.

Insects rasped from hidden places in the tall grass ditch across the street.

A car horn honked several blocks away and then went silent.

"You're getting blood on my grass," said an old man's deep gravelly voice.

Persephone opened her eyes.

A small vine with heart-shaped leaves curled around the mailbox post beside her.

"Oh," Persephone said, looking up into the man's wrinkled brown face. "I'm sorry."

"You look as though you've come a long way." The man eyed Persephone from under the brim of a straw hat. "Did you get where you were going?"

"I don't know," Persephone said miserably.

The man nodded, his eyes thoughtful. "Well," he said, "you may either keep sitting there, bleeding on my grass, or you can get up and we will do something about that knee. Either way, I'll be over there on the porch in the shade. It's hot enough to boil frogs out here." He gestured to the house behind him and left, walking across the lawn. Persephone heard his footsteps on the porch stairs and then the rhythmic creak of a porch swing settling into motion.

She listened to the *creak-crook, creak-crook* of the swing against its chains for a minute and then she stood up, sweat trickling down her back. She limped across the yard, climbed the porch steps, and stood in front of the swing, waiting.

"Right then," said the man. "Let's do something about that knee." He stood up and opened the screen door. "Malachi!" he called. Persephone started. *Malachi?* She only knew one person with that name. There was no reply from inside the house. "Malachi!" called the man, a little louder.

"Here!" said a familiar voice. "What's up, Gramps?" Persephone heard bare feet against linoleum and then a boy stood in the doorway. His brown eyes widened at the sight of Persephone.

"What are you doing here?"

"What are *you* doing here?" Persephone retorted.

"I live here! What happened to your knee?"

"I see you two already know one another." Malachi's grandfather chuckled, clearing his throat. "That's marvelous." Then he looked at them both with a calculating expression and gestured for Persephone to come inside. "Malachi, perhaps you'd like to offer this girl some lemonade while I find the first aid kit." Malachi eyed Persephone warily, and it suddenly dawned on her—he probably thought she'd come to tell on him. About the graffiti that he supposedly had permission to paint.

"I didn't know you lived here," she said, hoping he would understand. He didn't look like he believed her. "I was just, um, running. And I fell. Your grandfather offered to help." She shrugged helplessly.

"*Lemonade*," said Malachi's gramps with emphasis, and Malachi blinked and turned, pulling a glass from the

cupboard. "So, you two know each other from school?"
Persephone and Malachi both nodded.

"And do you have a name?"

"Persephone," said Malachi and Persephone at the same time. The kitchen suddenly felt a little too small.

"That's an awfully big name," said the old man.

"Yes," Persephone agreed. "Some days it feels too big."

"Like today?" he asked, and Persephone nodded.

"Like today." She glanced at Malachi, who was filling two glasses with lemonade from a pitcher in the fridge. He was pretending not to listen. She wished he wasn't there. If she'd known he lived here—that this nice old man was his grandpa—she never would have come inside. Sometimes it was just easier being hurt and tired and embarrassed and sad in front of people you didn't know.

"I'm Terrance Rathmason," the old man introduced himself, "Malachi's grandfather. Now. Let's get you cleaned up." He gestured to a chair, and then began rummaging through a first aid kit. Malachi set the glass of lemonade down beside Persephone and lifted himself onto the kitchen counter, perching there like an oversized bird, watching. His face was full of questions. But he couldn't ask, and she couldn't answer without giving them both away. The water tower and the alleyway graffiti, Mrs. McCullacutty, and Persephone's argument with Mya sat between them like a mountain of trouble neither of them wanted to climb.

Persephone looked around. Honey-oak cabinets hung on the walls, and off-white linoleum stretched across the floor. A refrigerator door full of notes and pictures and a couple of beautiful pencil drawings. She glanced at the boy on the counter, the charcoal drawing pencil in his pocket. His fingers stained with pencil lead. Malachi was an artist. He met her gaze, and she quickly glanced away and around the rest of the room.

Most remarkable, and completely out of place with the rest of the kitchen, were the flowers—orchids in every window and on every surface—and all of them were blooming.

"Oh! They're alive!" Persephone said, astonished. And forgetting her knee, she lurched to where a pot sat on the sill. Delicate white blooms hung on the thinnest filaments of green attached to a stem that arched and bent under their weight. They reminded Persephone of pearls dripping from the lobe of a movie star's ear.

"Well, yes," said Malachi's grandfather. "Keeping houseplants alive is typically the goal." Persephone flushed.

"I know— I just mean, I've never seen orchids bloom-ing like this." She gestured around the room. "My friend has a huge orchid"—Persephone stretched out her arms to demonstrate—"but it's dying, and I don't know what to do for it. I fed it, it gets plenty of light, I've talked to it quite a lot, and I was running out of ideas and people to ask for help because I didn't know anyone else who grew them! But here you are!"

"Here I am," said Malachi's grandfather with a smile, and he pointed to the chair. "Come and sit. We can talk about your friend's orchid while I patch up your knee." He pulled out cloths and Band-Aids and ointment, and while he carefully cleaned the gravel and dirt from Persephone's cut, they talked about orchids.

He explained to Persephone that in the wild, orchids feed on the decaying bodies of birds and reptiles, insects and other plants, so they need quite a lot of nutrients when they're not in their natural environment. He told her how he made his own orchid food out of milk, tea, molasses, dried and crushed chicken bones, eggshells, and Epsom salt. It sounded like a magical potion, and the recipe was clearly working. He pointed out each variety of orchid to Persephone, naming them as he went.

"*Phalaenopsis*, or moth orchid, as they're commonly called," he said. "Pink varieties, and white." And then he moved on. "*Dendrobium*—green, purple, and yellow." He pointed to pots and flowers with smaller greenery and larger, more prolific blooms. "Those beauties are the easiest to grow," he said. "And then there's my favorites, the *Paphiopedilum*—slipper orchids."

"Oh!" Persephone recognized the familiar shape. "These grow here in the wild, don't they?" She studied the pouch-shaped pink-and-white bloom. They looked a little like a small pair of shoes with trailing leaf-ribbon laces.

"Yes, they do grow wild here," said Malachi's grandfather. "Funny, isn't it? How sometimes you can find the most valuable and rare things right under your nose?" He carefully peeled the paper off the adhesive part of a large Band-Aid and smoothed it neatly over the cut on Persephone's knee. It was clean, dabbed with antibiotic ointment, and bandaged. He leaned back to study his work. "That should do."

"Thank you," said Persephone. "You should be a doctor!"

She traced the edge of the Band-Aid with her fingertip, relieved that it felt so much better already.

"Actually, I was a doctor," said Malachi's grandfather, straightening. "I still remember a few things." He winked at Persephone.

"Well, I bet you were a good one." Persephone grinned.

"I was," he said. "But the thing about being a doctor, or a gardener"—he gestured to the orchids—"is that all you can do is help. In the end, bodies, plants, everything, really, have to grow in the right direction on their own."

18

A BARGAIN

Malachi and his grandfather followed Persephone out the screen door and onto the porch, watching with matched expressions of concern as she limped down the stairs.

"Wait," Malachi said. "I could give you a ride home." He suddenly looked a little embarrassed. "I mean—if you want?"

"Okay, sure," Persephone said. "That would be great. It's kind of a long walk back."

Malachi smiled. "I'll grab my bike." Then he disappeared inside. Persephone watched him go and then turned to his grandfather.

"Do you think"—she hesitated—"if you have time, that you could come and look at my friend's orchid? Maybe you could figure out what's wrong with it? Help it get better?" Dr. Rathmason frowned. He suddenly seemed like the kind of person who didn't easily agree to things. "Maybe we could make a trade or something," Persephone suggested, looking around and thinking quickly. "I could come and help you around here, if you want? Mow the lawn, or something, in exchange for your help?"

He rubbed his chin and studied Persephone with the same calculating expression he'd worn earlier. Not unkind, but like he might be making plans.

"I appreciate your willingness to help," he said, "but Malachi does an excellent job mowing the lawn." Persephone's heart sank. "However," Dr. Rathmason continued, "my grandson has been wandering around the house lately like a fish out of water. One of his friends recently moved away and the other is off at camp for the summer. Boredom is setting in. Perhaps you could help me out with that?"

"You—you want me to hang out with Malachi?" Persephone frowned. "Like, as friends?"

Dr. Rathmason smiled and shrugged a shoulder.

She would have done that anyway, maybe, if Malachi had wanted. Now . . . now it felt weird.

"Well, we—we're already friends," she said. "So . . ." She let her words trail off. She could tell Dr. Rathmason that she was bored too, but the truth was, she *wasn't* bored. Not even a little. She had *a lot* of plans. And she wasn't sure how Malachi Rathmason would fit into them. But helping Mrs. McCullacutty's orchid and transforming her yard into a community garden for when *Small Town Revival* arrived were too important for her to back out now.

"So . . . ?" Dr. Rathmason asked.

Persephone gave a small smile. "So, yeah, we can hang out."

"Excellent," the old man said. "I'll tell you what. I'll mix up a batch of my special orchid food once a week. That store-bought stuff is rubbish. We will start there. I have a feeling your friend's orchid is just a bit malnourished. Let's see if that helps, all right?"

"All right." Persephone smiled. "Thanks!" But her enthusiasm faded a bit as Malachi hauled open the garage door and wheeled out a BMX bike. She glanced at Dr. Rathmason, who gave her a conspiratorial wink. Orchid food in exchange for friendship. She frowned. It felt tricky. Messy.

"You ready to go?" Malachi sat on his bike, holding it steady.

"Yep," she said, stepping up on the pegs and hanging on to his shoulders. And they set off.

Levi used to haul her around on the back of his bike. To the lake when they went swimming. To school in the fall before snow fell. To town for candy and pop at the corner store. Malachi was smaller than Levi, his shoulders narrower under Persephone's grip, but his balance was steady, and they didn't fall.

"Where do you live, anyway?" Malachi asked.

"You know, I'm not quite ready to go home just yet," Persephone said. "I want to show you something first." She hadn't planned any of this, but now that she was in the middle of it, it felt right.

Malachi braked slowly and came to a stop at the corner, turning to look at Persephone.

"Oh. I know that look," he said, frowning a little.

"What look?"

"That one." He pointed to Persephone's face. "That's the one you have when you're going to do dangerous, foolish, brave stuff."

"How do you even know I have a look?" Persephone laughed.

"I pay attention," Malachi said, and Persephone felt a stab of guilt. *Not quite well enough,* she thought. The deal she'd made with his grandfather was already beginning to feel heavy the way her lies were. Malachi trusted her. Her last friendship had ended badly, and this one was off to a rocky start. She should just steer clear of friends altogether! But she wanted to help fix Mrs. McCullacutty's orchid. The life of that flower felt like proof of her ability to make things grow. Mrs. McCullacutty had offered to let her revive her forgotten community garden! But it was even bigger than that. Persephone knew that once *Small Town Revival* arrived in Coulter, all it would take was one look at her work in Mrs. McCullacutty's garden and she'd be the winner of that one-hundred-thousand-dollar prize.

Just down the street, Persephone's house sat ordinary and full of heartache on the curb. Somewhere inside, her mother would be waiting—their unfinished argument still hanging in the air.

But down the street in the opposite direction, Persephone could just glimpse the corner where the next street began. Mrs. McCullacutty's house and her garden sat just two blocks beyond—curious and strange and full of possibility.

"That way," she said to Malachi, pointing in the direction of Mrs. McCullacutty's house. She could feel the garden tugging at her heart, as if it knew how much she wanted to be there, working on it, making it beautiful again.

Mrs. McCullacutty had told her to come to the back gate if she ever wanted to visit the garden. *"It will open for you,"* she had said, and then amended, *"Or perhaps it won't. It really depends on the garden."* She had smiled at Persephone as if this made complete sense, and Persephone had nodded as if she understood. But now, as she and Malachi stood at the back gate with the forgotten, wild, mysterious, once-and-future community garden on the other side, she felt a little nervous.

"Is this a good idea?" Malachi asked. "I mean, is it *safe*?" Persephone glanced at him, remembering what Mrs. McCullacutty had said last time they were both here, about the house and unexpected visitors. Was the garden expecting either of them? She grinned.

"I guess we'll find out," she said, and the gate swung open beneath her hand.

Last time she was there, Mrs. McCullacutty had explained that some of the wildness from inside the house had leaked out over the years, whatever that meant, and while Persephone didn't quite understand, it explained why she felt the way she did as the gate closed firmly behind them.

"What is this place?" Malachi whispered.

"This is what I wanted to show you," Persephone said. "This is Mrs. McCullacutty's garden."

Wild grape vines had clamored over one another until a tangled arch formed above them, forcing Persephone and Malachi to duck and crawl their way through. The vine tunnel opened into a shadowed stretch of ground dotted with yellow and blue violets. This was bordered by fruit trees, which hadn't seen the edge of a pruning knife in decades. A small white shed sat farther off, and two giant silver maple trees—the Queens—reigned over the back of Mrs. McCullacutty's old white house. A low stone wall ran into the woods along the other side of the garden—sturdy and sound in some places, but crumbling in others. And dispersed throughout, the edges of old flower beds poked out from beneath overgrown grass and shrubs, like the partially submerged bones of some massive creature, moldering in the quiet wildness of the place.

"What are we doing here?" Malachi whispered, and Persephone glanced at him, surprised to find his face had gone a little pale. She looked around, trying to see things as he might be seeing them, and then shuddered a little. If she couldn't *feel* the garden, whispering and hoping to be seen and loved despite everything it had become, she might be scared of it too.

"It's okay," Persephone said quietly, but Malachi's eyes were wide. He didn't look like he believed her. Persephone reached out and squeezed his hand. *You're not alone.* It was as much reassurance as she could offer. His hand was cold, but he squeezed back.

"I visited Mrs. McCullacutty the other day and she took me back here and asked if I'd be willing to help bring this place to life again," Persephone explained. She released Malachi's hand. "I'm pretty good at making things grow." She hadn't intended to tell him that, but it seemed like exactly the right thing to say, now that they were both here.

"So, you're what, like, a budding botanist or something?" Malachi grinned at his own play on words and Persephone laughed.

"Something like that," she said. But Malachi's smile faded as he watched Persephone run her hands through the leaves of a small plant nodding beside the low stone wall. The leaves grew and reached for her fingers, just enough to be barely noticeable, but Malachi saw and leaned close with wide eyes.

"Are you doing that? Or is it this place?" His voice was a little shaky, and Persephone suddenly felt nervous.

"Maybe a little of both?"

"How?" Malachi breathed, watching as a leaf uncurled before his eyes and fluttered against Persephone's fingers.

"I don't know, exactly," she said, her voice quiet. "But I think it's kind of like your art."

"My art?" Malachi frowned.

"Your street art and the drawings you do." Persephone glanced at the first two fingers on Malachi's right hand, always stained with pencil lead and ink, and remembered the drawings hanging on his grandfather's refrigerator. They were good the way Levi's architectural drawings had been good. Lovely and interesting and clever. "It's like a way of seeing the world—differently than anyone else—and whatever it is inside you that makes you really *feel*, just comes out. I want to see things grow, and change . . ." Persephone frowned, trying to make him understand. "I don't know *how* it works—like the science of it, or whatever." She shrugged. "But things grow for me. They always have."

"And Mrs. McCullacutty knows?" Malachi asked. Persephone nodded. "And she asked you to help her with . . . this?" He swept an arm over the tangled garden that stretched out before them. Persephone nodded again. "And you just said *yes* to fixing up someone else's garden all summer? Why?"

Persephone sighed, untangling her fingers from the plant. Malachi didn't understand. He leaned against the rock wall, frowning, his hands shoved deep into his pockets.

Being here was making Persephone tell him more than she'd planned. But maybe—maybe that was why the garden had pulled at her today as she stood on the back of Malachi's bike. Maybe she *needed* to tell him. Maybe she was *supposed* to. She sat down and patted the grass beside her. Malachi sat down awkwardly.

"Have you ever wanted something to change so bad you'd do almost anything?" He was quiet for a moment and then nodded. "Well," Persephone continued, "last week I found something my brother started, before his accident." She swallowed hard, plucking at the grass, afraid to look at Malachi.

This was a truth she hadn't told anyone, and here she was telling the one person who already knew more about her than she liked. It felt dangerous, trusting a friend. But he hadn't said a word about the water tower. And maybe that meant something. Maybe friendships could be built on the stuff people kept safe for you. "He was working on an application to a big television network in New York," Persephone said, her voice low. "Levi had been planning to submit Coulter to the show *Small Town Revival*." Malachi's mouth fell open.

"I've watched that show!" he said.

Persephone nodded. "Me too. Levi and I used to watch it together all the time. I mean, we still kind of do. It's just different now." She shrugged. "I know it's a long shot, to hope that our town could be picked for something like that. But there's a huge cash prize awarded to the person who completes the winning project. I think that's one of the reasons Levi was submitting Coulter. He needed money for school." Persephone plucked at the grass. "Now my family could really use that money for other things. So, I mailed in the application."

"And this garden?" Malachi asked, looking around. "Is this going to be your winning project?"

"Hopefully," Persephone said. "The show always highlights projects and people who are working to make things better for the town. Especially projects that restore or revive something. I think they'd be interested in a community garden this massive—"

"And possibly *magical*—" Malachi interjected.

"And possibly magical." Persephone smiled. "There's so much history here. It was built and designed for the community to enjoy a long time ago. It's just been forgotten. Levi was the one who started this whole thing. It only seems right to finish it for him." She shrugged. "Besides, I'm not sure how else to get the kind of money we need for his bills and treatments and stuff. Unless you have a pile of money lying around somewhere that I can have?" She grinned, but the need was too real to joke about. And it was getting harder not to be discouraged because it had been one week, and she still hadn't heard a thing from Mr. Francis Graham. How much longer would she have to wait?

Malachi saw through her smile and gave her one of his own.

"If I had a pile of money, Persephone," he said, "I'd share it with you." He was so sincere, she had to swallow back the lump rising in her throat. She wouldn't cry. Not now. Not in front of him.

"Maybe I could help you here instead. In the garden," Malachi said. "You know, get things ready for when *Small Town Revival* chooses Coulter."

"You would do that, Malachi?" Persephone blinked back her tears, looking around at the overgrown chaos that had almost forgotten it was ever a garden. It was going to take a lot of work to help reimagine this place and make it what it could be.

"Sure." Malachi grinned. "And you can just call me Mal, if you want. All my friends do." He carefully tied a blade of grass into knots. "Besides, I really don't have anything else going on this summer." Persephone chewed her lip, remembering what his grandfather had said. Malachi was just as alone as she was. "Plus, I kinda want to see what happens when you start using your powers and making things grow." Malachi wiggled his fingers and Persephone laughed.

"I don't have powers, *Mal*," she said, trying out the nickname he had offered. "It's just a . . . skill. But you have to promise you won't tell anyone about any of this. Not a word! If anyone finds out, especially before I hear anything back from *Small Town Revival*, I'll be in so much trouble."

"I promise I won't say a word to anyone." Malachi crossed his heart, twice. Persephone smiled. But the ache of guilt twisted her insides. Her friendship with Malachi already felt like more than just part of some silly bargain. So she had to make sure he never learned the truth.

19

BIRTHDAY CELEBRATION

On the evening of Persephone's thirteenth birthday, pink balloons hung from the light fixture above the table in the dining room, and strawberry cake with strawberry ice cream sat, reigning in pink splendor, on the kitchen counter. And at precisely six o'clock, Mrs. McCullacutty rang the doorbell. Persephone ran to get it, stomach butterflies twirling.

She had thought about inviting Malachi over too, especially after their conversation in the garden, but decided that might be a little awkward. Besides, if Malachi accidentally said anything about what they were doing, her parents might overhear, and then she'd have to explain why she'd been at Mrs. McCullacutty's house without their permission. Persephone couldn't risk it. Things with her mother still felt messy.

Persephone had apologized for running off after their fight, and had told her about Dr. Rathmason and how he'd helped her knee. But things didn't feel quite the same as they had before.

Persephone squared her shoulders and opened the door for Mrs. McCullacutty. The old woman stood on the porch holding a small box wrapped in purple tissue paper and tied with a gauzy green ribbon that matched her gauzy green silk dress. It was definitely a dress fit for a party, but Persephone wasn't sure her birthday was the right occasion. A party at an opera house, or a ball thrown in honor of a prince, perhaps. Persephone's own yellow sundress—pulled from the back of her closet—paled in comparison. In fact, everything felt a little pale today. Shadowed. She tried not to think about the fact that this was the first birthday she was celebrating without Levi, but it wasn't something she could ignore.

"Happy Birthday, dear!" cried Mrs. McCullacutty as Persephone opened the door. She was magnificent. "How is my young gardener this evening?"

Persephone's eyes widened. She glanced over her shoulder at her mother, who was coming down the hall.

"I haven't actually had a chance to talk to my parents about working in your garden yet," she whispered hurriedly, twisting her hands in the skirt of her dress. Mom had been very clear about her going back, actually. Mrs. McCullacutty gave her a funny little look, but then nodded.

"*Thank you*," Persephone mouthed. "Please come in, Mrs. McCullacutty," she said cheerfully, perhaps a little too loud, holding the door for the woman and her green dress. Persephone's mother appeared in the doorway.

"It's good to see you, Mrs. McCullacutty," she said. "What a stunning dress!"

"Oh, please, call me Jane," said Mrs. McCullacutty. "And thank you! It is, isn't it?" She examined herself, almost as if she were as surprised by her dress as the rest of them. "It was a gift from a French dignitary. I didn't expect it to still fit, as I was much younger the last time I wore it. But it appears to be the sort of garment that allows for the changing human form." Persephone's mother didn't seem to know what to say to this, so she just murmured something about how nice it would be to have clothes that did that.

Dad coughed, attempting to smother a chuckle when he walked into the room, and both Mom and Mrs. McCullacutty looked at him sharply. He bowed slightly in response. *He bowed.* And then took Mrs. McCullacutty's hand in his.

"It's very nice to meet you," he said. "Persephone speaks highly of you and it's an honor to have you in our home." Everyone was acting like she was the queen or something.

Persephone winced a little as Mrs. McCullacutty studied her dad's hands. He had showered and scrubbed and shaved, but there was still the memory of soot buried in his skin. If Mrs. McCullacutty noticed, she didn't comment.

Persephone was proud of her dad. For the work he did. For the difference it made to so many people in their town. Without him, a lot of people in Coulter wouldn't be able to heat their homes. In fact, Persephone would be surprised if there was a roof in Coulter her dad hadn't been on, a chimney he hadn't cleaned or repaired. Clean chimneys and clean fireplaces meant safe, warm houses all winter long. And that was especially true in northern Wisconsin, where the winters were long and cold. But she wondered sometimes what it would be like to have a dad who dressed in a suit and went to work at a nice clean office. She wondered if their bills would be more manageable if her dad did that kind of work instead.

"You have a lovely home," Mrs. McCullacutty said to Persephone's parents. "I've been in Coulter for quite some time, and your house has been here almost as long as I have. It's been owned by several people, but none quite so lovely, or as interesting, or as hardworking, as your family."

"How long have you been in Coulter?" Dad cleared his throat, slightly uncomfortable with her praise.

"Oh, about a hundred and fifty years or so," she said lightly. "It depends on who you ask." They all laughed. Because of course she was joking. Wasn't she?

Owen walked over from where he'd been standing in the corner of the room then. "Do you want to see my scar?" He pushed himself between Persephone's parents to show Mrs. McCullacutty. He was set on having a scar ever since his friend Sam got stitches in his forehead the week before school let out. His recent injury at the park was making him hopeful. Mom looked horrified and hurried to intervene, but Mrs. McCullacutty indicated that indeed, she did wish to see Owen's scar.

"I have quite a lot of scars myself," she told Owen, bending over to see the Band-Aid he revealed under one rolled-up pant leg. "Pirates, you know." Owen's eyes widened and she winked. "Ah yes." Mrs. McCullacutty acknowledged the bandaged injury on his small knee. "Yes, that certainly has scar potential." Satisfied, Persephone's younger brother rolled his pant leg back down and grinned up at her. "I'm Owen," he said. "I'm seven."

"Indeed," she replied, "I loved being seven, though it has been quite some time since I've been that age." Owen scrunched his nose and looked to Dad for a proper response. But Dad just laughed and ruffled Owen's hair.

"You have another son," she said to them.

Persephone's heart lurched, and the room went quiet. She looked at Mom, feeling a little panicky. Most people didn't ask about Levi. They already knew. But Mrs. McCullacutty wasn't most people.

"We do have another son," Mom said after a moment, glancing at Dad. "But he was in a terrible accident last summer. He isn't able to get up and greet visitors."

That's one way of putting it, Persephone thought. A weight was building in her chest. She tried to push away the shadow of Levi's absence.

"Yes, I know about the accident, dear." Mrs. McCullacutty let her gaze fall first on Persephone's mother and then her dad. "I'm tremendously sorry. But—I wonder . . ." She hesitated. "Would you mind terribly if I met him anyway?"

In the year since Levi's accident, no one had ever asked that before. People asked how he was doing as a courtesy, and then Levi was dismissed. Like he was a non-person— made of lost days and memory. But not Mrs. McCullacutty. The weight in Persephone's chest was so heavy she thought she might need to sit down. Even Owen looked worried. Mom smiled carefully, and extended a hand in the direction of Levi's room.

"Please," she said. "Come and meet Levi."

They were all quiet as they walked down the hall, Mrs. McCullacutty's swishing and whispering skirts the only sound. And then they stood in the doorway of Levi's bedroom.

"Levi," Mom said quietly, "there's someone here who would like to meet you."

Persephone's older brother made no response. No motion to turn his head or move. He didn't smile or acknowledge that he'd even heard. He just half lay half sat in bed, his head lolling to one side. Persephone went in and straightened the blankets that lay across his lap, and her mother followed, adjusting his head.

"May I?" Mrs. McCullacutty gestured, and Mom nodded. And then she walked right up to Levi's bed and gently patted his hand. "It's nice to meet you, Levi Clark," she said politely, like he was wide awake and shaking her hand. "You were an excellent lifeguard," she said. "I always appreciated that you were watching whenever I would come down to the lake. When you were guarding, I never felt like I needed to keep an eye on all those children in the swimming area. You were good for this old lady's nerves." She patted his hand again and then turned back to Persephone's mother, who was standing there with tear-filled eyes.

"My late husband slipped into a coma for several weeks before he passed," she said, her voice calm and steady. "Brain cancer. I'm not sure he ever heard my voice, or if he knew it was me, but I always felt that it was important to keep talking."

"I'm sorry for your loss," Persephone's dad said, his voice a little ragged.

"And I am sorry for yours," said Mrs. McCullacutty frankly. "We never get to choose when we say goodbye, do we? Only how."

"Only how," Mom echoed.

"Now, then," Mrs. McCullacutty said, turning to Owen and Persephone. "I heard there might be strawberry cake and ice cream, and I am rather fond of strawberry cake and ice cream."

So with that, the tension in the room fell away as they slipped back out into the hallway, and the weight in Persephone's chest lifted like a pink birthday balloon.

Persephone sat on the back patio as the sun began to set, slapping at an occasional mosquito and eating pink cake with pink frosting and pink ice cream that kept threatening to melt and drip everywhere. Owen sat beside her, licking melted ice cream off his plate. Mom and Dad and Mrs. McCullacutty talked, and Persephone thought nervously about all the ways she could explain herself if Mrs. McCullacutty said something about her visits.

Soon, Dad switched on the string of lights that hung over the patio to welcome the end of day. And then Mrs. McCullacutty retrieved the gift she'd brought for Persephone.

"Your love of plants and growing things has been in clear evidence from the moment I met you," Mrs. McCullacutty said, handing the brightly wrapped box to

Persephone. "I thought these would suit your inclinations."

Hesitantly, Persephone tugged off the gauzy ribbon and then peeled back the paper. The lid lifted easily, and under the crisp white tissue sat a small packet of seeds. Owen crowded close to get a better look. Persephone lifted the packet from the box and opened the flap, peering inside. They looked like ordinary seeds, but unlike the packet of forget-me-nots Mya had given her, this one was not labeled. She had no idea what sort of plants or flowers would grow.

"Thank you!" She smiled at Mrs. McCullacutty and then faltered. "What kind of seeds are they?" Mrs. McCullacutty folded her hands in her lap.

"I'm afraid we won't know until you plant them, dear," she said. "That is why seeds are so wonderful. They are an entire world of potential—secret, hidden away, and forced to endure the struggle of growth before they reveal themselves."

She smiled at Persephone and then turned to her parents. "I wonder if you would allow me to issue an invitation to your daughter." She paused, offering Persephone a reassuring look. "You see," she continued, "I have a rather old and curious garden that used to belong to this town—a community garden as it were—and it needs a bit of attention. It has become clear to me, after a conversation I had with your daughter, that this remarkable girl of yours has a knack for making things grow. I wonder if you would permit me to call upon her skills over the course of the summer. I could use someone with her particular gifts. I would pay her for her time, of course."

Persephone glanced between her parents and Mrs. McCullacutty. This was an unexpected turn of events.

"She is remarkable, isn't she?" Dad smiled at Persephone. "We're flattered by your request, and I'm sure Persephone would be very helpful." Persephone nodded eagerly. "But if you will give us a little bit of time to talk it over, we will let you know later this week. We've tried to make decisions together as a family, especially since Levi's accident, and I want to make sure we talk with Persephone about this before we decide anything."

"I would expect nothing less," Mrs. McCullacutty said. Persephone felt a small sinking feeling in her chest. Why couldn't they just have said *yes*?

"Thank you for the seeds," Persephone said quietly. *And for not telling about my visits, and for asking my parents if I could come and work in your garden . . .* But the last part she said only with her eyes. Mrs. McCullacutty nodded slightly, understanding.

"You're quite welcome, dear," she said. "Thank you for the invitation to join you and your lovely family. It's been quite some time since anyone asked me to a celebration. I've enjoyed myself greatly." Mrs. McCullacutty cleared her throat. "This has been a most enjoyable evening." She stood, sweeping her gauzy green skirts behind her. "But I think it's time I say good night."

"I'll walk you out," Persephone's mother said, standing.

"Can I offer you a ride home?" Dad asked. It was truly dark now, but the heat and humidity from the day still made everything feel damp and close. Owen was chasing fireflies in the yard, releasing them as soon as he'd had a chance to study their glowing bodies inside his cupped hands.

"Oh, thank you for the offer, but no." Mrs. McCullacutty paused. "I quite enjoy walking in the dark." She reached out and patted Persephone's hand with her own wrinkled one. "I'll see you soon," she said. Persephone's heart jumped. It felt like a secret message. Like Mrs. McCullacutty was magical, and with a wave of her wand, she might simply rearrange the mess Persephone was making with all her secrets and half-truths, weaving it into something hopeful. Mrs. McCullacutty waved to them all as she made her way down the walkway and into the gathering darkness.

Mom, Dad, Owen, and Persephone stood on the front step waving back until she was out of sight. And then they blinked. Persephone felt like she was waking from a dream or spell, edged in gauzy green silk.

"What a strange, no, eccentric—" amended Mom.

"Thoughtful—" said Dad.

"Wonderful—" Persephone added.

"—fancy lady!" finished Owen.

And they were all right.

20

ONE-YEAR ANNIVERSARY

On Friday morning, a week after Persephone's birthday, the sky stretched low and gray with clouds, their dark underbellies hanging heavy over the horizon. It had finally rained sometime during the night and Persephone and her mother tried to avoid the puddles as they walked to the lake.

They had all tried to pretend that they didn't remember what today was. But each member of Persephone's family had looked at the calendar that morning. The day had been marked permanently in their hearts and memories, even though it would have been a relief to forget.

Were there cakes for days people started being not-alive-but-not-dead? Like birthday cakes in reverse? Persephone ran her hands through her hair, tying it back in a ponytail and trying to shake off her sad thoughts.

"We need to remember *all* of Levi today," her mother had said after they'd sat in silence for several long minutes at the breakfast table. "Not just his accident. He wouldn't want us sitting here thinking only about the sad things. We need to make today about how he laughed and teased us, the things he liked, the way he loved others—" Mom's voice caught on her tears, even as she tried to smile, and Persephone's dad planted a kiss between her eyes where the crease there had deepened since Last Year's June.

Once they reached the dock, Persephone's mother took her usual spot with her umbrella folded up beside her, just in case. The air was warm, and Persephone didn't mind if it rained while she swam. There was something wonderful about water falling on you and the lake suspending you between ground and sky. It was the closest thing to being a fish she could imagine. Water everywhere, but she could still breathe.

On her third lap, Persephone paused at the dock, catching her breath and blinking up at her mother through the big heavy raindrops that had started falling.

"Do you want to go home?" Persephone panted. "Are you getting wet?" Her mother was curled under the canopy of her red umbrella, a perfect dry circle forming around her on the dock. The red umbrella drew Persephone's eyes to the red lifeguard chair, and she suddenly wondered if it was hard for her mom to sit on the dock, watching her. Especially today. She'd sat with Levi too, watching as he learned to swim, and then later watching as he watched others—keeping them safe. And here she was, watching again.

"I want to be here today," said her mother. "I want to sit here, help you count, and remember." Her smile was steady despite the rain and the memories. "You go ahead and finish your laps." A drop of rain fell off the edge of her umbrella and into her coffee cup with a *plop!* She pulled the cup out of the rain's reach. Persephone stood up in the water and stretched on her toes. Her mother met her halfway, and Persephone planted a rain-and-lake-water kiss on her cheek.

"Thank you," she said softly, sliding back into the water, which was warmer than the air and somehow comforting.

"Lap four?" her mother asked.

"Lap four." Persephone smiled. And she went back under.

Last night after dinner, Persephone's parents had sat her down in the living room and told her she was allowed to help Mrs. McCullacutty with her garden. But there were a few conditions.

"We are so glad we had the opportunity to meet Mrs. McCullacutty," Dad had said. "She seems like a nice person, though a little odd . . ." He'd frowned, trailing off like he was still trying to wrap his mind around the whole idea of Mrs. McCullacutty. Persephone had been too excited to sit still a moment longer and jumped to her feet to thank them both, but Dad held up his hand, and Persephone slowly sat back down. "Mom spoke with Mrs. McCullacutty on the phone, and the three of us have reached an agreement: You are allowed to visit and help her with her garden, but you need to let us know when you're going over there, and how long you think you'll be gone. No more running off and letting us worry."

It was all Persephone could do to contain her joy and relief.

"I promise," she'd said, throwing her arms around them both.

She would go over to Mrs. McCullacutty's as soon as the rain stopped. She wanted to be in the garden that would change things for Levi. Especially today.

Reach—Pull—Breathe. Reach—Pull—Breathe.

And while she waited for the rain to let up, she would swim eighteen laps. One lap for each year her brother had been himself. Today, this would be her way of remembering.

21

FOLLOWING BLUE

Saturday afternoon was chore day. Persephone and her family were busy collecting laundry and sweeping dust from corners, wiping out bathroom sinks and removing fingerprints from the entryway window, when Persephone glanced outside and found Blue waiting expectantly on the front step. Had the cat been taller, she probably would have rung the doorbell. Persephone opened the front door, a roll of paper towels under one arm, and smiled at the small gray cat.

"Hello, Blue," she said. "What are you doing here?" Blue stood, meeting her outstretched fingers before turning with a flick of her tail and traipsing down the sidewalk. An invitation to follow.

"It's chore day." Persephone held up the roll of paper towels as proof. Blue twitched her tail the way a person might have shrugged.

"*So,*" she seemed to say. "*Obligations haven't stopped you before.*"

The cat wasn't wrong.

"I'm going outside for a minute!" Persephone called into the house. "Blue is here." She waited for a response.

"Blue is here?" Her mother came down the hallway, her phone in one pink-rubber-gloved hand as though she'd just finished a call. She wiped hair out of her face with her forearm.

"Yes," Persephone said. "Mrs. McCullacutty's cat."

"Oh. How nice." Her mother wasn't quite sure how to respond to finding Blue on the front step. She held up her phone. "I just heard from Dr. Rathmason. He wanted to let you know that he has more orchid food for you." Her mother raised an eyebrow. "Mrs. McCullacutty's orchid?" Persephone nodded as her mother followed her to the front door.

"Dr. Rathmason helped me with my knee that day . . . remember?" Persephone said, and her mother nodded. "Well, it turns out he's really good at growing orchids, and Mrs. McCullacutty has a giant one that's dying. I don't know how to help it. So I asked Dr. Rathmason if he had any suggestions."

"I see," Mom said, sliding her phone into her pocket. "And he has a special kind of orchid food?"

Persephone nodded. "And this is Blue." Persephone gestured to the cat, who was still waiting patiently on the front step. Another unusual friend. She felt a little silly introducing her mother to a cat. But Blue had always felt like *more* than just a cat. "Blue, this is my mom," Persephone said. Blue blinked at Persephone's mother and Persephone's mother peeled off a pink glove.

"Kitty—kitty—kitty—" She stretched out her hand. But Blue wasn't impressed, or she didn't care for the smell of bleach, and simply stared before looking to Persephone as if to say, *"Right, then. So, can you come now?"*

Persephone's mother put her glove back on.

"It's chore day," she said to Blue. "Have her back in an hour." Blue flicked her tail and then stood up and headed down the sidewalk, looking back to make sure Persephone was following. "One hour," her mother reiterated, and then shook her head. "I can't believe I'm talking to a cat."

"One hour," Persephone agreed.

Blue led the way down the street, her tail high in the air. Once she was sure Persephone was there, they started off, and the cat didn't turn back again.

She led them to the alley behind the Coulter Lumber Yard, where they found Jerry Gilbert, the lumberyard manager, operating a forklift. He waved and Persephone waved back. Her dad worked with Jerry all the time, ordering brick and building materials.

Jerry stopped the forklift and waved Persephone over.

"Jane McCullacutty called me this morning and said you might show up." He took off his bright yellow hard hat and scratched his head and then put his hard hat back on. He squinted at Persephone, his eyes an indistinguishable color, face brown and wrinkled from the sun. And then he squinted at Blue, who sat at her feet. "She said you might be needing some lumber."

"She did?" Persephone glanced down at Blue, who met her gaze with half-lidded eyes.

"Mm-hmm." Jerry shifted the ever-present toothpick he chewed to the other side of his mouth. "She opened an account for you. Said to make sure and help you with whatever you might need."

The absence of a response from Mr. Francis Graham snaked itself around Persephone's heart. She was staking a lot of hope on *Small Town Revival*'s celebration of her work in Mrs. McCullacutty's garden. Of *course* her suggested improvements for the garden would cost money—the repaired beds, new pathways, a trellis, even dirt! Why hadn't she thought about that? Mrs. McCullacutty clearly had. And she'd done something about it too, knowing Persephone didn't have money for any of those things. Would she be angry when she learned Persephone had ulterior motives and additional plans for her garden that she knew nothing about?

Blue stood up, unconcerned with moral dilemmas. She slipped between a broken slat in the alley fence without a backward glance. And just like that, she was gone.

"So, is there something I can help you find?" Jerry asked. He was watching Persephone watch the place in the fence where Blue had vanished. A small vine with heart-shaped leaves had rambled up and over the broken slat.

"Um. No. Not yet." Persephone looked up. "Thank you though. I'll let you know when I'm ready to get some— um—wood and stuff." She didn't even know what she'd need, exactly. Jerry nodded, and the forklift roared to life as he turned the key in the ignition.

Persephone glanced once more at the hole in the fence. She waved goodbye to the man in the yellow hard hat and then turned to go, and nearly collided with Mya as she came out of the alley.

Mya was on her bike, coming down the sidewalk. The surprised look on her face matched the surprised look on Persephone's, and Mya swerved to avoid hitting her, rolling sideways off the edge of the curb. She and her bike were suddenly a tangle of limbs and wheels.

"Oh my gosh! Are you okay?" Persephone was pulling the bike off Mya and kneeling beside her before she remembered they weren't friends anymore.

Mya groaned and pulled herself to a sitting position before examining her elbow, which was bleeding.

"Oh! You're hurt!" Persephone exclaimed.

"Why'd you jump out of the alley at me?" Mya snapped.

"I didn't!" Persephone rocked back on her heels. "I was just talking to Jerry about wood for Mrs. McCullacutty's garden, and Blue wandered off, and I was in a hurry because I only have an hour, and I just remembered I need to tell Mrs. McCullacutty about Malachi's grandfather's orchid food!" It all came out in a jumbled mess, and by the look on Mya's face, Persephone realized just how much was going on that she would have told her all about, had it been before Last Year's June. She chewed her lip. It wasn't so long ago that *she* had been bleeding, sitting on a curb, and someone had been unexpectedly kind. Persephone remembered how that felt. "You can come with me," she said. "If you want? Mrs. McCullacutty will have Band-Aids."

Mya studied Persephone's face for a minute, her eyes narrowing as if she were waiting for Persephone to change her mind or say something mean. But then she nodded, getting to her feet and righting her bike. The front wheel was a little more crooked than it should be. Mya unsnapped her helmet and hung it over the handlebars, and then she and Persephone just stood there for a minute, not quite sure what to do next. Here they were, a whole year between them, and a lot of hurt that Band-Aids couldn't fix.

"So, Mrs. McCullacutty, huh?" Mya raised an eyebrow.

"Yeah." Persephone nodded and started walking, and Mya fell into step beside her, wheeling her bike. "Where were you going, anyway, before we crashed?"

"I was following this gray cat," Mya said. "It just appeared out of *nowhere* and sat down in front of me on the sidewalk and I—"

"—and you followed," Persephone finished, laughing. Mya nodded and Persephone laughed again, the sound strange and bright between them. "That was Blue," Persephone said. "She's Mrs. McCullacutty's cat, sort of. But she's not a normal cat. I'm not actually sure she's a cat at all. Sometimes I think she's something *more*." Persephone watched Mya out of the corner of her eye, and despite the bike accident, and her bleeding elbow, she was almost smiling. Not at Persephone, but at *them*. At the two of them. "The first time I followed Blue," Persephone said, "I climbed the water tower to rescue her."

A shared truth. It felt like hope.

Mya's steps faltered, and she stared at Persephone

with her mouth open. She glanced across town where the rounded top of the water tower was just visible between the trees.

"That water tower?" she asked.

Persephone nodded.

"Tell me," Mya said, like she would have if Last Year's June had never happened. And Persephone did.

22

AN ODD INTRODUCTION

Mya stood beside Persephone on the porch in front of Mrs. McCullacutty's house, her shoulders straight. She knew the stories about Mrs. McCullacutty as well as anyone. In fact, Mya and Persephone used to tell them to each other, like ghost stories, when they had sleepovers, each tale bigger and more bizarre. And now that Persephone knew Mrs. McCullacutty, she wished they had never told them. She rang the doorbell.

"This is nice," she said, taking a deep breath.

"Yeah," Mya said, clearing her throat. "Nice."

Persephone rang the doorbell twice more. By the third ring, she was feeling a little strange. Mrs. McCullacutty always opened the door the first time she knocked, or the first time she rang the bell. Sometimes even before. Maybe she wasn't home?

But Mrs. McCullacutty opened the door at last, dressed in a soft gray pantsuit, her silvery gray hair done up on top of her head. And she looked very normal. Even more odd, was the cane she leaned on. A *cane*. She looked very un–Mrs. McCullacutty-like. Where were the red glasses or the yellow rain boots? Where was the gauzy blue party dress or the umbrella? Something wasn't right. Persephone already knew the house and the garden behaved in peculiar ways, but did the house affect Mrs. McCullacutty more than she'd realized?

As Mrs. McCullacutty stood in the doorway, the air inside the house rushed out to greet Mya and Persephone—a little colder and quieter than usual. Persephone took a step back.

"Why, hello, Persephone," the old woman said, as though nothing at all were unusual. "And you must be Mya," she said, turning to greet her. Even though Persephone had never talked about Mya with Mrs. McCullacutty, she wasn't surprised she knew who she was. That, at least, felt very Mrs. McCullacutty-like.

"Hello," said Mya. "It's nice to meet you."

"Please come in," said Mrs. McCullacutty, "I just put the teapot on."

"That sounds great," Persephone said. "I can't stay very long today, but Mya hurt her arm." She gestured at Mya's elbow. "Do you have any Band-Aids?" Mrs. McCullacutty's face wrinkled with concern.

"Yes," she said. "Yes, of course. In the kitchen. I'll show you."

They followed her inside. It was all as odd and amazing and curious as the first time Persephone had seen it, and it was just as odd and amazing and curious watching Mya see it. Her once-best-friend ran her fingertips over the chipped paint of a carousel horse's ear and studied the faces of the people in blue. It seemed like the entryway art collection had grown. She and Mya stared at each other's reflections in the massive gold mirror. Mya's blue eyes met Persephone's gray ones, and she smiled.

They walked past the open door of the piano room and Mya sucked her breath between her teeth at the sight of the lion and the ostrich; let out a tiny cry of wonder at the butterflies and moths in their cases as they passed the library; and just kept shaking her head after that.

"This is unreal," Mya said under her breath.

"Right?" Persephone nodded.

It was strange, having her here. Nice, but strange. She wasn't quite sure what to say or do. Everything felt different. More fragile. Like they were holding their breaths. Meeting each other again, for the first time.

Mrs. McCullacutty led them into the kitchen where the teapot whistled on the stove. She turned it off and talked with Mya, asking questions about school and her family and things she was interested in while Persephone rummaged through a first aid kit for ointment and a Band-Aid. Finding what she needed, Persephone cleaned Mya's scrape for her, because it was hard to reach one-handed.

Mrs. McCullacutty didn't act as though anything at all were amiss, but things felt less wonderous than they usually did, as though the house seemed at odds with itself today.

Plus, there was Mrs. McCullacutty's cane. Persephone

had never seen her use one before. It made her seem less like herself—or at least, less like the version of Mrs. McCullacutty Persephone was familiar with. The last time Persephone had seen her was the night of her birthday. She remembered the gauzy green dress and how she had walked home in the dark, alone and unafraid. She seemed like an entirely different person now.

Mya helped set up the tea tray for Mrs. McCullacutty, getting cookies from a jar on the counter and setting them on a plate. Persephone went to the green cupboard in search of plates and cups for tea.

She reached for the top of the stack, standing on her toes, when suddenly Piccadilly squawked a warning note from his cage. Persephone turned just in time to watch Mrs. McCullacutty sway slightly, and then with a small cry, crumple into a kitchen chair. A cool breeze raced down the hall like a door had suddenly been thrown open at the back of the house, and it ruffled Mrs. McCullacutty's hair and the tablecloth and the curtains that hung over the window above the kitchen sink.

"Oh—!" she breathed. "Oh dear. The house hates being ignored." She laughed lightly, and gave Persephone a confiding look, as if she might understand and agree. "Please, dear." Mrs. McCullacutty gestured to Persephone. "Let's open some windows, shall we? I think we could all use a little fresh air." She pointed to the kitchen window, and Persephone rushed over and tugged on it, trying to slide it open, but it was stuck. Mya helped, and together they finally slid the window open with a bang. The girls moved from window to window, struggling to open each one as if the house were fighting them. But gradually, with some fresh air blowing down the hall and into the kitchen, Mrs. McCullacutty took several deep breaths and seemed to collect herself.

"Is she okay?" Mya whispered, and Persephone frowned.

"I think so," Persephone whispered back. But that didn't feel quite true. Something was up. But she wasn't sure if it was Mrs. McCullacutty, or her house. Or both.

"I'm terribly sorry, girls," Mrs. McCullacutty said, smiling tiredly, "but I'm afraid I'm feeling a bit indisposed this afternoon. This old house is rather bossy sometimes, and I could use a nap." Her voice was calm and cheerful, but Persephone suddenly felt like she was somewhere she didn't belong. Mrs. McCullacutty stood, with effort, leaning on her cane. She looked . . . fragile. Persephone's stomach twisted.

"Are you all right?" It seemed like the wrong question, but Persephone didn't know the right one.

"Yes, of course," Mrs. McCullacutty said. But Persephone didn't quite believe her. "It's not an easy task arguing with forces out of your control! Makes this old lady tired. Perhaps you could come back tomorrow? We can have tea then. I imagine you would like to show Mya the garden?"

"Do you think you'll be feeling well enough tomorrow?" Persephone asked.

"Yes. Yes, I'm quite certain of it." Mrs. McCullacutty smiled.

"Okay. I'll see you tomorrow then."

"It was lovely to meet you, Mya," Mrs. McCullacutty said as the girls turned to go.

"It was great to meet you too," Mya said.

The house ushered them out and closed the door with a resounding *click* behind them. The girls stood on the step in silence for a moment.

"Well, that was weird," Persephone said quietly.

"So, Mrs. McCullacutty is different, normally?" Mya asked.

"Yes." Persephone's chest felt tight. "The house is different normally too. I don't know what's wrong."

"The *house* is normally different? You act like it's alive or something!" Mya laughed. Persephone laughed too, a little nervously.

"Well, maybe she'll be more herself tomorrow," Mya said.

"Yeah. Maybe."

"I should probably go." Mya looked away, down the street toward where her house sat on the other side of town. "I told Joseph I'd meet him later for ice cream—" She broke off, her gaze snapping to Persephone as she realized what she'd just said.

The words hit Persephone like a slow fall. She could see the ground coming, but there was no way to brace herself against the impact.

She took a deep breath.

And then another.

Mya was having ice cream with her brother this afternoon.

Levi might never have ice cream again.

And Persephone would never have it with him.

She stared at her once-best-friend for a second as they both tried to decide what to do—with their faces, their words, their hearts.

"I have to go too," Persephone said after a long pause. "I can't be late." Her voice came out hard and pinched. It was taking everything she had to keep from crying.

"Okay," Mya said quietly, nodding. "See you tomorrow?" It was a question. Hope hung on the end of it like someone drowning.

"I don't think so." Persephone blinked rapidly. Mya stared at her, and then turned on her heel without another word, collected her bike from where she had leaned it against a tree, and walked away. Persephone watched her go.

Mya would go home, and she and Joseph would have ice cream, and everything would be normal. Joseph would go to college in the fall, and grow up, and have a whole life.

But Persephone would go home, where her brother would be in bed, the same place he'd been since Last Year's June. And she and the rest of her family would try to pretend like they were okay. At the end of the summer, Levi would stay right where he was. And that's all his life would ever be, unless she could do something to change it.

23

OLD ACQUAINTANCES

Much to Persephone's relief, Mrs. McCullacutty's cane was gone the next day, and so was the gray outfit she'd been wearing. Instead, she wore powder-blue slacks and a white sweater with sequins all over the front. She seemed more like herself. And so did the house. Persephone heaved a sigh of relief—and confusion. Something was up. She could feel it—the way you could feel a storm brewing on a hot day in the middle of August. But what kind of storm could a house make?

"So your friend wasn't able to come today?" Mrs. McCullacutty asked as she prepared tea. Persephone shook her head and pulled two plates and two cups from the green hutch, handing them to Mrs. McCullacutty. A plate of scones joined them on the tea tray. She didn't really want to talk about Mya.

"No, she had plans." A lie. "But I finally brought you something I've been meaning to share—" Persephone pulled a small jar from her pocket and held it up triumphantly.

"This is a jar of Dr. Rathmason's miraculous orchid fo—"

CRASH.

Mrs. McCullacutty dropped the tea tray to the floor.

"My goodness. I'm so sorry, dear," Mrs. McCullacutty said.

"Are you okay?" Persephone asked.

"Yes." The old lady took a pause. "Did you say Dr. Rathmason?"

Persephone watched Mrs. McCullacutty carefully and nodded as she began cleaning up the mess.

"Yes," she said. "He's Malachi's grandfather."

"Yes. Yes, of course. I know who he is. I just didn't realize you were friends with Terrance. How . . . interesting." Mrs. McCullacutty pressed her palms to the sides of her powder-blue slacks and sat down carefully in one of the wingback chairs in the study.

"I'm not sure we're friends exactly," said Persephone, "but he's very good with plants. Especially orchids. I thought he might know how to help yours and so I told him about it one day a couple weeks ago. He suggested his special orchid food." Persephone almost mentioned the friendship bargain she'd made, but decided to keep that part to herself.

"Did he know it was *my* plant he was mixing up his miraculous food for?" She took the jar of orchid food from Persephone and held it almost tenderly.

"Well, I'm not sure," Persephone said after a moment of consideration. "I don't think I ever actually told him whose orchid needed help."

"I see," said Mrs. McCullacutty sadly, setting the jar of orchid food on the counter. "He *is* good with plants," she said. "Especially orchids. He gave me the orchid you're trying to save, you know."

"Dr. Rathmason gave you that giant orchid?" Surprise and curiosity felt like an electric current under Persephone's skin.

Mrs. McCullacutty nodded "He did. We used to be— quite close. But things didn't go as planned, and I made choices that hurt him terribly. Sad, though I'm afraid there's nothing to be done about it now. It was years and years ago."

What was years and years ago? Persephone wanted to ask. But Blue looked at her with a note of warning in her eyes as she hopped down from Mrs. McCullacutty's lap. So Persephone kept her questions to herself.

Mrs. McCullacutty filled Persephone's cup with tea and handed it to her. "Never let anger destroy something you care about," she said, her voice firm. "Sometimes, anger is just sadness wearing a suit of armor." She met Persephone's gaze, and Persephone felt like Mrs. McCullacutty knew things again—things she hadn't told her, the same way she had known her name the day they first met.

"Would you care for a scone, dear?" Mrs. McCullacutty held out a pile of scones, and Persephone reached for the plate the green cupboard had given her. It was covered in a delicate spray of blue forget-me-nots.

∼ 24 ∼

QUESTIONS

The thing about swimming was that it made Persephone focus on things she normally did automatically. Like breathing. It made her count, searching for natural rhythms she couldn't remember unless she put everything else aside and listened to the beat of her own heart—how it synced up with her lungs.

Reach—Pull—Breathe. Reach—Pull—Breathe.

She broke the surface, gasping for air.

Dad sat on the dock with her that evening. Mom had been too busy with work to come to the lake earlier and was too tired by the time she was done, so Dad had come with her instead.

He stretched his legs out on the dock, the length of the week—of the past year—weighing on him like the ever-present stain of chimney soot. But after she swam a few laps, Persephone noticed the lines in his face relaxing, and by the time she hit lap eighteen, the weight of bricks, mortar, hospital bills, and a son who would not—could not—come back, looked like it had slipped off him a little.

Water will do that. You can't sit beside it or swim in it for very long before it starts to take things from you. Fear, worry, anger. Water is a gentle thief.

Persephone held on to the edge of the dock, catching her breath.

"That was twenty, kiddo," Dad said. She looked up at him, his face haloed by the soft light of a dying day at the end of June.

"Two more," Persephone said, panting. "Just two more." He squinted at her for a moment and then nodded.

"Two more," he agreed with a quick smile. Persephone dove back under the water.

Dad was quiet on their walk home, the evening light gathering close around them and collecting in deeper shadows under the trees.

"You're really becoming quite the swimmer, Persephone. But . . . why a mile?" he asked at last, pausing to pick up the end of her towel that she'd dropped, and wrapping it back around her shoulders. Persephone pulled her towel closer and looked up at him.

"Because that's the goal Levi and I set." She shrugged and her dad smiled, but Persephone knew by the softness around his eyes that there was more to his question.

"I can see why that would be important." He nodded. "But is that all there is to it? The fact that Levi helped you set that distance? Don't get me wrong, your mom and I are so impressed with all your hard work and your dedication. I've never seen you so committed to your swimming goals as you've been this summer. It's amazing, and I can tell you feel strongly about it." He paused. "But what happens when you reach a mile?"

Persephone swallowed hard and twisted a loose thread from her towel around and around her finger. *Why* and *then what.*

"I don't know. It's just . . . important that I do this," she said. It wasn't an answer, exactly, but Dad just nodded and wrapped an arm around her shoulders in a quick hug.

"Well, I'm proud of you," he said.

But his questions haunted her.

She knew the *why* part. Not that it would change or fix anything. She had to do it anyway. For Levi.

But she didn't know what happened *after* she'd swum a mile. Maybe she would swim it again. *Again and again and again.* Until she knew.

25

NOT ALONE

Just after breakfast the next morning, a knock at the front door had Persephone racing to answer. To her surprise, Malachi Rathmason stood on the front step, a look of alarm on his face.

"Hey, Malachi," she said, opening the door. "What's up?"

"I need to talk to you," he said urgently.

"Who is it?" Mom called, stepping into the hall before Malachi could say anything else. He shoved his hands in his pockets, and Persephone had the sudden desire to grab his hand—to keep him from hiding.

"Malachi," said Persephone. "My friend from school." She gestured to the boy on the step.

"Oh—I thought I heard you say hello to Mya," her mother said. "Hello, Malachi. What are you up to today?"

Persephone was wondering the same thing.

"I just—uh—needed Persephone's advice about—um—a *letter* I'm working on," Malachi said, struggling to find the words. He flushed. "Is it okay if she hangs out for a little while?"

Persephone's mother raised an eyebrow.

"It's a summer project," Persephone said quickly. "For school. An optional summer project." She didn't look at Malachi. "I told Mal I'd help him, if he wanted." The lie slid out and she tried not to squirm under her mom's gaze. She wasn't sure why she felt the sudden need to cover for Malachi, but they were getting pretty good at keeping each other's secrets, and that felt like something worth protecting. Her mother nodded, and Malachi grinned.

"Great! Thanks! We're just going over to my house for a little bit." He thumbed in that general direction and then glanced at Persephone. "You ready?"

"Ready." She nodded. "I'll be back soon." Persephone offered her mother a smile, but she couldn't decide if it was suspicion or something else that filled her mom's eyes as she waved them off.

Malachi waited until they reached the end of the driveway and Persephone's mother had gone back inside before he explained.

"I just came from the hardware store," he began, his voice low. "I was getting more paint for a project I'm working on. Mrs. Perry was standing behind the counter, going on and on about how she'd just heard the most amazing news. She was saying Coulter was going to be on television—" Persephone gasped and halted on the sidewalk.

"I know! That's what I thought too, because you were pretty clear about it being a big secret the other day in Mrs. McCullacutty's garden."

"It *is* a big secret!" Persephone whispered. She stared at him, the question snaking its way around her heart. "Did *you* tell someone?" Mal recoiled and shook his head, hurt by her question.

"No! I'd never tell anyone when you asked me not to!"

"Okay, okay! Sorry!" But Persephone hadn't told anyone else. "What am I going to do?" This was not good. *How did Mrs. Perry find out? And does she know something I don't? Had Coulter been picked?*

"Okay, hang on— Let's not freak out yet." Malachi pulled his hands out of his pockets and met Persephone's gaze, determination squaring his shoulders. "You haven't heard one way or the other yet, right, about Coulter being accepted?"

Persephone shook her head. She hadn't heard anything.

"Okay," Mal continued, "but a letter from Epiphany TV could be in the mail right now—official acceptance and notification that Coulter had been chosen for *Small Town Revival*. Maybe that's how word got out. Maybe some kind of official announcement arrived, and people started talking? Maybe, instead of coming to you, the letter went to the mayor or something? Her mailing address and city information were part of the application your brother filled out, right?"

Persephone's heart had started pounding as she considered the possibilities. Mal was trying to make her feel better, but he was also right. It was *possible*. There was only one way to find out.

"Let's go see," she said, a little breathless. A strange lightness had begun filling her chest. Mal grabbed her hand and squeezed.

And they set off at a run for the post office.

26

A RESPONSE

Mrs. Rosalyn Howard looked up from the mail she was sorting as Persephone and Malachi rushed into the post office, the bell over the door jingling wildly.

"Persephone!" she exclaimed, waving her hands. "I'm so glad to see you! Some rather *important* mail arrived for your *family* today." She stumbled over the words slightly as she glanced toward Mr. Grove's open office door and slid the envelope across the counter.

It was a thick white envelope. Epiphany Television and *Small Town Revival*'s logo were embossed in the corner. It was addressed to Levi. Persephone's hands were shaking, and she pressed them flat against the cool post office counter.

"I'll need you to sign for this," Mrs. Howard said.

"What?" Persephone blinked.

"You'll need to sign for the letter," called the postmaster from his office. "It was sent certified, so the sender could be certain it was received by the intended recipient. That can be anyone in your family." Mrs. Howard nodded in confirmation. "And as Levi can't sign for it, I need you to sign for him," she said gently.

Persephone's breathing hitched in her chest as the weight of Mrs. Howard's words settled. For a moment she wondered if Mrs. Howard knew that she had forged Levi's signature on the letter she sent to Epiphany TV too.

She snatched the pen off the counter. "Should I sign Levi's name?" she asked.

"No, dear." Mrs. Howard smiled. "You go ahead and sign your own. Signing someone else's name on official documents is forgery."

Persephone swallowed hard and hastily signed her own name before clutching the envelope to her chest.

"Mrs. Howard," Persephone asked, "does anyone else besides you and Mr. Grove know about this letter?" Mrs. Howard suddenly seemed *very* interested in the contents of one of the mail bins.

"I can't imagine so," she said. "Save perhaps for my dear friend, Mavis." Mrs. Howard glanced at Mr. Grove's office door again and lowered her voice. "She was in here just a little while ago while I was sorting mail and that letter might have been on the counter. It's possible she got a look at it and assumed the rest?"

Persephone nodded, a panicky feeling swirling in the pit of her stomach. It wasn't hard to imagine Mrs. Howard sliding this envelope across the counter to Mavis while she stood there chatting. Persephone could almost see their faces. Their eyebrows rising into their freshly permed hair. Questions and speculation filling the air like a swarm of bees. If Mrs. Howard enjoyed a bit of town gossip now and then, Mrs. Mavis Lynch enjoyed it twice as much. All it would take is one glance at the *Small Town Revival* logo for them to pull all kinds of possibilities from her unopened envelope.

"Well, now we know how word got around town," Malachi muttered under his breath.

"I'm sure Mavis will keep things to herself," said Mrs. Howard. But her certainty seemed to falter, and she picked up the phone behind the counter. "I'll call her right now and ask her to do just that!"

"No—no, it's all right," Persephone said, trying to force a smile. It was already too late for that. If people at the hardware store were talking, then the whole town already thought *Small Town Revival* was coming to Coulter, thanks to Mavis Lynch's eager sharing. But the truth was, they didn't even know what kind of news the letter held!

"It will be fine." Persephone took a shaky breath, running her fingers across the envelope's smooth surface.

"You don't look very good, dear. Are you *sure* everything is all right?" Mrs. Howard leaned forward, concerned, and Persephone smiled widely.

"I'm fine!" she said. "I'll just grab the rest of the mail before I head home." She began fishing for the mail key in her pocket, only to realize that she had left it on the kitchen counter in her rush to get to the post office.

"Don't trouble yourself. I'll get it for you!" Mrs. Howard

was eager to be helpful. She returned a moment later, sliding the stack of bills across the counter. OVERDUE was stamped in bright red letters across the one on top, and Persephone stared at it for a moment before snatching it off the counter and shoving through the post office door, Malachi on her heels.

Persephone stood outside in the bright sunshine staring at the mail. In one hand, an envelope so large and white and crisp that the glare of the sun off the paper and the embossed logo hurt her eyes. And in the other hand, a stack of bills.

"Open it! *Open it!*" Malachi rocked from one foot to the other, almost dancing beside her on the sidewalk. But her hands were shaking too hard. What if this envelope held nothing more than a fancy rejection?

"I can't! *What if—*"

Malachi laughed and tugged on her arm.

"*What if* is a terrible way to live," he said. "Come on. Let's not stand on the post office steps any longer or Mrs. Howard will be trying to get a look through the windows!"

They walked all the way to the lake and sat on one of the benches that overlooked the swimming area. Persephone's racing heart knocked around in her chest, and Malachi didn't say a word as she finally opened the envelope. With shaking hands, she pulled out the top sheet of paper and began to read.

Dear Levi,

I am delighted to inform you that after careful consideration, my team and I have reviewed your application and have selected Coulter, Wisconsin, as one of our picks for our forthcoming season of **Small Town Revival.** *Congratulations!*

We always send out a formal acceptance notification, but moving forward, we will be in contact more informally through email and over the phone.

As you can imagine, there are countless details to orchestrate as we set plans in motion. I will be connecting you with my production lead—Rebecca Mathews—for an initial interview, at which time you'll be able to voice any questions you have about the process. I look forward to working with you!

Sincerely,
Francis Graham
Production Exc.
Small Town Revival
Epiphany Television Inc.
"A little change can start a big revival!"

Persephone leaned back, the hard frame of the bench digging into her back as she stared out at Galion Lake. Her head buzzed.

It was almost too much to believe.

This whole thing had started with a lie. With her brother's name signed in *her* handwriting. And now *Small Town Revival* had picked Coulter! It was everything she could have hoped for. But what was she supposed to do now? And why hadn't she thought this through more? She closed her eyes.

Reach—Pull—Breathe. Reach—Pull—Breathe.

Mal didn't say anything. He just scraped his shoes back and forth, back and forth in the sand under the bench. He didn't try to fix anything. He just sat there with her, their shoulders almost touching, and it was nice not to be alone. Gradually Persephone's racing heart slowed, and her breathing calmed.

"Are you okay?" asked Malachi. "Just in shock?"

Persephone turned to Malachi. "*Small Town Revival* is coming here! They actually picked Coulter! But *Levi* is supposed to be their lead contact for the show. *He's* the guy who's supposed do all the interviews and everything! He would have been *amazing*."

Tears were rolling down her face, and she dashed them away angrily. What had she *thought* would happen? That she could just pretend to be her brother? She'd gotten exactly what she wanted, and now everything was way more complicated than she ever could have dreamed. Had her parents heard the news yet?

Mal jumped to his feet. "I'm sure it's bittersweet, but you did it!" He couldn't contain his excitement a minute longer. "Do you know what this means? You could actually win that money! You have a real shot at getting those treatments for your brother!" He shot both fists in the air and spun in a circle in the sand. "This is going to be so amazing!"

"But what am I supposed to do now?" Persephone lurched off the bench and held up the letter, the sun glancing off the white paper. "I am not Levi! And I'm definitely not eighteen!" She waved the letter in the air and then slumped back into the bench. "I don't know how to do this."

Malachi's face fell and he slowly sat back down on the bench.

"Right. Yeah. Okay." He leaned forward, resting his elbows on his knees, his forehead scrunched in thought. "Well, how about this: What if, after the production lead emails *Levi*, you respond from your brother's email account and ask all your questions or whatever, until you're certain that it absolutely *can't work*—and then you tell them what happened and back out. *Or*, maybe you decide that it *could work*, and then you can tell your parents what happened and get them to help you. At least then you'll have a little more time to think about everything?"

Persephone chewed her lip and then nodded slowly. That made sense. Perfect sense, actually. And it would be enough for now.

"Hey. Why are you helping me?" she asked suddenly.

"Because that's what friends do," Malachi said, surprised by her question. Guilt rolled around in the pit of Persephone's stomach.

Friends. She didn't think he'd still call her that if he found out about the bargain she'd struck. He would hate her.

"I like your plan," Persephone said slowly. "Any idea

what I should tell people if they start asking questions?" She rubbed her forehead. "Thanks to Mrs. Howard and Mrs. Lynch, I bet people will want to know when the film crew will arrive."

"Well," Mal said, "if people ask, just tell them you don't know all the details yet." Mal shrugged. "You can always go back and explain what happened after you decide what you're going to do . . ." Persephone nodded. What other option did she have? But somewhere in the middle of nervous doubt, hope flickered in Persephone's chest.

"So, it's a plan?" Mal offered her a fist bump.

"It's a plan." She bumped her knuckles against his, but neither of them smiled. "Just until I have some questions answered and I decide what to do about all of this," Persephone said.

Malachi agreed. "Just until then."

27

WHAT FRIENDS DO

Despite the weight of the overdue bills in her back pocket, plus what Persephone was about to let everyone believe, and the not-yet solution to her there-but-not brother, Persephone felt less alone than she had in a long time. Malachi matched her steps as they walked home, hands swinging at his sides, his backpack over one shoulder. At least the excuse they'd given her mother about their mutual "summer school project" hadn't been entirely fabricated. They *had* worked on a "letter." Sort of.

"Wait, you never told me about your art project," Persephone said suddenly. "The one you were getting paint for, at the hardware store this morning."

"Well, you've never been real excited about my work before." He quirked an eyebrow. "Pretty sure you called it vandalism the first time I showed you something, so I figured you didn't want to know," Malachi said.

"Oh. Right," Persephone said. "I'm sorry."

"I don't want to destroy people's property, you know." Mal was sincere. "Most of the places I paint are falling down, broken, ugly places that no one ever notices until I paint them. And when I can figure out who owns the buildings, I always ask permission first. But, man, I'd give anything for a big clean wall somewhere important—a giant blank canvas!"

Persephone remembered the painting he'd done of the sunflower in the alley behind the hardware store—how good it had been. She thought of the drawings on his grandfather's fridge. And how the first two fingers on his right hand always seemed to be smudged with pencil lead, like he was constantly in the middle of an art project.

"I think art is a kind of invitation," Mal said.

"An invitation?" She didn't quite understand. But she wanted to.

"Like—permission to look at things differently." Malachi had started talking with his hands, animated and excited. "Art can make people see the world in a completely new way. It can make you think and feel new things! And I want to be part of that. You know what I mean?"

"You want to change the world—make it more beautiful by opening people's eyes in a way—with art," Persephone said. He glanced sideways at her.

"Yeah," he said.

"I know exactly what you mean." Persephone smiled. They climbed up the porch steps and Persephone pushed open the front door, the relief of cool air-conditioning greeting them. But that relief was short-lived as Owen ran and threw his arms around her in a frantic hug, burying his face against her. She glanced up and met her neighbor's gaze from across the kitchen as her little brother began crying, mumbling something indistinguishable, his words muffled in Persephone's shirt. Owen's best friend, Sam, stood beside his mom, Mrs. Lin, in their kitchen, but her own mom was nowhere to be seen.

"Hello, Mrs. Lin, what—what's going on?"

Through his tears, Owen told her. "Levi had another seizure! A really bad one! The ambulance people came and took him away!"

Persephone glanced up at Mrs. Lin, and she nodded.

"Your mother asked if I would keep an eye on Owen until you came home. She went to the hospital with Levi. Your dad is on his way there as well."

"Oh—um, all right," Persephone whispered, her arms tightening around her little brother.

"Your mom will be back tonight," Mrs. Lin said, crossing the kitchen and squeezing Persephone's shoulder. "I'm so sorry, sweetheart. Do you want to come over? Or I can keep an eye on Owen at my house?" Owen peered up at Persephone, his face sad and full of questions she couldn't answer. Persephone shook her head and hugged her little brother.

"Thank you," she said quietly. "But I think we'll be okay here, together."

Mrs. Lin nodded, and after a few minutes and kind goodbyes, she and Sam walked back home.

Malachi stood in the entryway, his hands deep in his pockets again.

"Do you want me to go?" he asked. Persephone shook her head.

"No. Please stay?" she said, pulling three glasses from the kitchen cupboard for lemonade, desperate for some small, normal thing she could do. Mal nodded and took his glass of lemonade wordlessly. Persephone held hers in shaking hands, trying to decide what to do next. Everything was falling apart. Again. No matter what she did, no matter what plans she made, things just kept getting worse.

"Now what?" Owen asked. She stared down at him. She had no idea. But Mal pulled out a stool and sat down at the kitchen counter, patting the empty seat beside him. Owen came around the counter and climbed up beside Mal.

"Hey," said Malachi. He stuck out his hand. "I'm Mal." Owen studied his hand for a moment and then shook it firmly.

"I'm Owen," said Owen.

"Yes," said Malachi. "I've heard of you."

"You've heard of me?" Owen asked, his eyes growing wide. Mal nodded and took another sip of lemonade.

"Your sister told me about you," Mal said. Persephone hadn't. Not really, but it was perhaps the kindest lie she'd ever heard, and she smiled at Mal over the rim of her glass. "She told me you were a great helper," continued Mal. "We were actually looking for someone who might help us with a project."

Mal raised his eyebrows at Persephone. *Okay to invite him?* And she nodded.

"What kind of project?" Owen asked.

"A garden," Mal said, his voice dropping to a whisper. "A magic garden." Owen rolled his eyes and Persephone laughed. "What?" Mal asked, pretending to be offended. "I'm serious!"

"Really?" Owen asked, skepticism in his voice, but Persephone nodded.

"Really!" She took another sip of lemonade and smiled at Mal.

Thank you.

He smiled back and gave her a little nod.

That's what friends do.

28

CONFESSIONS AND LIES

Persephone, Malachi, and Owen spent the rest of the day working in Mrs. McCullacutty's garden. The muscles in Persephone's arms ached and sweat ran into her eyes. She raked, hauled branches and debris into the woods, gathered up dead leaves, trimmed the grass, and worked to get everything ready for what would eventually become a revived community garden. Owen helped, talking Mal's ear off the whole time. And occasionally, when Persephone stopped to catch her breath, she'd glance up and meet Mal's gaze across the yard. Butterflies flipped in her stomach. *It's probably just because he's keeping so many of my secrets,* she told herself. But it was strange. She hadn't expected him to be, well, to be *himself.* Kind and genuine and funny.

When the sun began dipping below the tree line, the three of them gathered up their tools and put them away.

"See you tomorrow?" Mal asked, wiping his face on his sleeve.

"And the day after that, and the day after that, and the day after that," Persephone said emphatically. Mrs. McCullacutty was paying both of them for their work—twenty-five dollars a week, each—but even if she hadn't been, Persephone was pretty sure Mal would have kept showing up to help.

"Deal." Malachi grinned and then glanced at Owen, who was sitting cross-legged in the grass, Blue in his lap. The cat had wandered into the yard as they were finishing up, eager to inspect their work. "I'm sorry about Levi," Mal said. Persephone watched her little brother and the small gray cat.

"Thanks," she said after a minute. "I'm sorry too. He would have liked you."

"I think I would have liked him too," Mal said.

As Owen and Persephone walked home later, one of their neighbors, whose houseplants Persephone had nursed back to health, stopped them on the sidewalk.

"Persephone and Owen!" she said excitedly. "I heard some interesting news while I was in town this afternoon!" Persephone glanced down at Owen, who looked up at her, his eyes full of questions. "A friend of mine told me the television show *Small Town Revival* was coming to Coulter, and that you had something to do with it!"

"Oh— Really?" Persephone cleared her throat, and Owen's eyes grew wide.

"Persephone, is that true?" he asked, tugging on her hand.

"I—no—I mean—" She looked at the woman. "I sent in

some information—just for, you know—just to see if a town like ours might be a good fit for the show . . ." Persephone stumbled over her words.

"And have you heard back? My friend said you'd had confirmation or something?"

"*No.* I mean, yes—I mean, I got a notice in the mail that my, uh, *information* had been received. That's all." Persephone shrugged and then smiled cheerfully, tugging Owen with her as she tried to make her way around the woman on the sidewalk.

"Oh. Well, how interesting. And exciting! I guess I misunderstood . . ." The woman frowned slightly as Persephone gave her a little wave.

"It's okay. It happens," she said over her shoulder. "Um— have a nice day!"

"Yes, you too!" the woman called after her, and Persephone ducked her head and tried to quiet Owen's questions and ignore his suspicious looks as they made their way home.

Persephone's mother came home late that night—long after Persephone had tucked Owen into bed. She couldn't sleep, and had curled up with a book instead, pillows and blankets piled up around her.

The front door opened and closed softly as her mother entered. She tiptoed down the hall and leaned against the doorframe for a moment before lying down beside Persephone with a heavy sigh.

Persephone didn't need to ask to know that Levi was not okay. Of course, her brother hadn't been okay for a while now. But the seizures weren't just changing him; they were changing all of them—pressing fear into places they thought they'd guarded. Punching holes where there were already too many. Casting shadows where it was already dark.

"Dad will stay at the hospital with Levi tonight," Mom said tiredly. "Hopefully, your brother will be able to come home in a day or two. They're running some tests to make sure he's stable." Persephone just nodded. "Did things go okay with Owen here at home?" Mom asked.

"Yeah." Persephone smiled. "He and Malachi and I worked on Mrs. McCullacutty's garden for a while this evening after Mrs. Lin and Sam went home." Her mention of the garden seemed to spark something, and her mother sat up.

"I heard the most interesting rumor today," she said hesitantly. Persephone's heart started pounding. "It seems Epiphany Television Incorporated—the production company behind *Small Town Revival*—is coming to Coulter. And my very own daughter is behind it all." Her mother stared at Persephone, waiting.

"Word travels fast, I guess," Persephone said nervously, thinking of the woman who had stopped her and Owen on the sidewalk. Besides Levi's seizure, this was what had bothered her the most all day. How was she supposed to explain this to her parents? Mom cleared her throat.

"Did you know Levi was planning to submit Coulter to *Small Town Revival*?" Mom's voice was quiet. Persephone froze. She *knew.* Mom knew about the application Levi had filled out and the forms he had completed.

"Was he?" Persephone whispered.

"Did you submit Coulter, Persephone? On Levi's behalf?"

Persephone couldn't seem to make her words work, so Mom continued.

"Levi talked to Dad and me about his plan," she said carefully. "We weren't entirely comfortable with the idea, so we discussed it for quite a while. There is a lot that goes on behind the scenes when it comes to these types of shows. People's lives become just another piece of information served up for the viewer's entertainment. Things can be misrepresented."

Persephone nodded. She remembered Levi saying something like that to her too.

"Levi reached out to a past show participant and was able to ask them a bunch of questions about what it had been like, being on the show, and what it was like after. That person had some really great things to say about the production team and the show's desire to help people and small towns. But he told Levi the truth too—about what it was like to be on display. Your whole life available for people to watch and judge and speculate about without ever getting to know you for real. And about how the show edited things for television that really upset some people in the town."

Persephone thought about the speculations Mrs. Lynch and Mrs. Howard had made about the letter today, and how their speculation had felt like an intrusion. How just the presence of the letter had already begun to spread rumors around town.

"In the end, Levi decided it wasn't something he wanted," Mom said. "As much as he liked the idea of winning money and doing something big for Coulter, he worried about the impact it could have on our town in the larger sense. And he didn't want to sacrifice the relationships he had with his friends and neighbors."

"So, he *didn't* want to do it?" Persephone asked. Something like dismay curled around her heart and started to squeeze. "After all the work he put in, he changed his mind?"

"Yes. He decided *not* to send in the application," Mom said.

Persephone swallowed. She had been so certain that sending it in was something Levi wanted that she hadn't even stopped to consider she might be wrong.

"Persephone, did you send in Levi's application?" Mom asked.

"Yes," Persephone whispered. "But I haven't heard back yet!" The truth and the lie somersaulted out of her mouth before she had a chance to think about either one. "What I mean is—what happened, I think, is that the rumors started today because I got a letter back from Epiphany TV saying that my application had been received and thanks for sending it . . ."

Lies, lies, lies. Mom's face was incredulous. Skeptical. Persephone felt sick to her stomach.

"Mrs. Howard saw the logo on the envelope," she

continued, scrambling for a way to explain the rumors. "Maybe she just assumed . . ." That much was true at least.

Lies mixed with truth. Truth mixed with lies. It was all perfectly plausible.

Persephone trailed off and her mother frowned. Mom knew Mrs. Howard as well as anyone, and it wasn't the first time she'd heard a rumor that turned out to be little more than gossip. Mrs. McCullacutty herself was proof of that.

It all reminded Persephone of the game "Telephone." A group of friends sits in a circle and one person begins by whispering something in the next person's ear. Person after person, that sentence is whispered around the circle until the last person has to say what they heard out loud. But by the time the sentence arrives, it's nothing like the original. Persephone felt like she'd whispered a simple line of hope into someone's ear, and now she was hearing her words again—but they sounded much different.

"Persephone, you mailed something that wasn't yours to mail—something very important that affects a lot of people, including your family—without talking to Dad or me about it first." Her mother rubbed a weary hand over her face.

True. But Persephone wasn't ready to give up. Levi might have decided not to mail the application last summer, but a lot had changed since then. She frowned, fighting back tears and guilt. And her mother didn't even know about her signing Levi's name! That she had done all this for *them*. To make things better for her family. Instead, it felt like she was only making things worse.

"Do you think I should email them?" Persephone asked quietly. "Tell them that I changed my mind? Withdraw the application, like Levi would have wanted?"

"I think that's a good idea." Her mother nodded, closing her eyes. "I'm too tired to think about this anymore tonight. I hope we will have some better news from the doctors tomorrow about your brother. Once we know what's going on with Levi, then Dad and I can talk about this more."

Persephone just nodded, wrapping her arms around herself.

"I'm very glad you haven't actually heard anything back yet," Mom said. "It will make it much easier to stop all this before it even gets started."

Persephone swallowed hard and looked down.

"It's not about the rumors, Persephone, it's about telling the truth. Doing the right thing for everyone involved. Including Levi, who can't make choices for himself anymore."

Exactly, Persephone thought. If her mother only realized why she'd really submitted Coulter in the first place.

"I'll email them," she lied. "I'll tell them no." Persephone almost couldn't get the words out around the lump in her throat. "Mom, I'm really sorry . . ." *That* was the truth. She truly was sorry, but right now, this was the only way she knew how to make change happen.

Her mother closed her eyes and stood up.

"I know, sweetheart," she said. She bent over and planted a kiss on Persephone's forehead. "We'll talk about it more tomorrow." Her mother switched off Persephone's light and closed her bedroom door on her way out.

But Persephone couldn't sleep. She tossed and turned, her stomach twisted with guilt and worry. It was too late to go back. She'd planted seeds she couldn't dig up and now she didn't know what to do. What kind of flowers would bloom if all the seeds were lies?

29

REVELATIONS

Persephone's unfinished conversation with her mother didn't happen the next morning, or the morning after that. Levi wasn't able to be released like they'd all hoped. Her parents rotated between home and the hospital—Mom leaving in time for Dad to come home exhausted and fall asleep on the couch for a few hours before he had to get up and go to work. And so, Persephone was left to continue thinking things over on her own.

It didn't get any easier when Persephone—no, *Levi*—received an email from the production lead, Miss Rebecca Mathews, just as the letter from Mr. Francis Graham had said she would. Miss Mathews outlined a few details and asked if there was a good time to set up a phone call. She needed an answer from Persephone by July 27.

Persephone read and reread that email, wondering what Miss Mathews would say if she could see her family right now. If she knew how much they needed the money that *Small Town Revival* was willing to bring to Coulter, and the prize they'd award the winning project.

She thought about the hope of that money with every bill she collected from the post office over the next several days. She thought about it every time her parents switched places at the hospital to sit beside her brother while doctors ran expensive tests. And she thought about it every time she looked around her town and people smiled and waved, thinking that she, Persephone Pearl Clark, was making something amazing happen for their town.

Mrs. Perry had stopped her in front of the hardware store just yesterday.

"So, what can you tell us about all of these television show rumors, Persephone?" she had asked, throwing her arm around Persephone's shoulders and leaning in conspiratorially, as if Persephone was about to tell her everything.

"Well, you know—" Persephone stumbled, trying to remember what Mal had suggested she say, searching for something believable. "Schedules are still up in the air—"

"Wait—you've talked with a production crew!" Mrs. Perry gasped and gave Persephone a little hug. "Won't it be wonderful! There is so much to be excited about!" She beamed and Persephone nodded as Mrs. Perry's assumption settled like a stone in the pit of her stomach. "So much to be excited about," she echoed half-heartedly, saying nothing to explain the truth.

Mrs. Perry wasn't the only neighbor who had asked Persephone questions about *Small Town Revival*. With each *yes* she shared, each question she answered, the more the rumors circulating around town began to sound like facts. She overhead people saying things . . .

"Small Town Revival *is coming to Coulter!*"

"Scheduling is underway!"

"Production crews will be here soon!"

So she didn't tell Rebecca Mathews the truth. She *couldn't*. She sat at Levi's desk, her hands resting on his computer as she stared at the blank screen and blinking cursor. It was impossible to make herself send an email that would throw all hope away, for everyone, even after what her mother had told her about Levi's decision. Things were different for him—for all of them—now. Now they were all stuck in ways they hadn't been before, and she finally had a chance to do something about that.

So instead of withdrawing her application and telling Rebecca Mathews *thanks but no thanks*, Persephone filled the next several days with sore muscles, blistered palms, a tired back, and sweat. *Small Town Revival* didn't need a response for four and a half more weeks. For now, she would do what she could to make change happen somehow.

She pruned overgrown hedges, piled rocks and bricks, and pulled out what felt like miles of rambling Virginia creeper from Mrs. McCullacutty's garden.

The old woman often came out and sat in the garden as Persephone worked, telling stories from when she had been a child—how people had come to this very garden to admire her family's collection of beautiful plants and unique trees, to be together, and to share one another's lives under the spreading branches and watchful presence of the Queens.

One afternoon when Persephone needed a shovel and a fresh pair of gloves, Mrs. McCullacutty pulled a key from her pocket and led her across the lawn to where the little white shed sat at the edge of the yard, tucked away like it didn't want too much attention. Mrs. McCullacutty unlocked the doors and then stood back as they swung open.

"I'm not exactly sure what's in here *now*," she said, gesturing to the interior. She said "now" as if sometime between this afternoon and the last time the shed had been opened, things might have changed inside. "But I think you'll find everything you need." She smiled. "And perhaps some things you don't. But that's usually the way of it."

"The way of it?" Persephone asked, peering inside, a little nervous.

"Well, yes—you open a long-closed door and potential rolls out," Mrs. McCullacutty explained. "But sometimes spiders hide in the more shadowy corners. Be brave."

Persephone shuddered a little.

The shed, like Mrs. McCullacutty's house, was full of oddities. But it all seemed to be mostly yard and garden related. Tools were everywhere, and garden furniture, and flowerpots—none of it matched. Instead, it seemed as though each item had been collected for its uniqueness.

There was a stone birdbath covered in stone starfish partially hidden behind an old gate, its iron latch shaped like a flowering vine with heart-shaped leaves.

Several dusty crates on a shelf against the far wall contained hand tools—trowels and spades and rakes—their painted handles chipped with age and use. There were garden gloves, and plant markers, a small stone rabbit with black glass eyes that glittered in the shadows, and a small stone tortoise with thinly sliced and polished agates fixed to its shell. Persephone fished a pair of gloves from a crate on the shelf, and found a shovel leaning in one corner. She was careful as she took them from the shed, because of spiders. And potential.

Sometimes, as she worked, it felt to Persephone like the garden was helping—shrinking back overgrown hedges in places, and straightening up the crumbling rock wall when she wasn't looking. Other times it felt like it was making things even harder—trailing vines where they didn't belong, and erupting new clumps and tufts of grass where she didn't want them. She never actually saw any of it happening, of course, but the garden was never completely still or quiet like normal gardens were; it was always *more*. Persephone drew her own conclusions.

On the Sunday before the Fourth of July, Mal skipped up the three cement stairs into Mrs. McCullacutty's yard on his bike, wheeling to a stop as he bumped against the front wheel of Persephone's wheelbarrow. A fist bump—but with tires.

"I have something to show you," he said by way of greeting. He leaned his bike against a tree and dropped into the grass. Persephone sat beside him, curious, as he pulled an envelope from his pocket, yellowed around the edges and brittle with age.

"A letter—" Persephone said, reaching for it, but her hands were filthy, so Mal held it up for her to inspect without touching.

"This is just one of many," Mal said. "I found them."

"You found them?" Persephone stared at him.

"In my gramps's old stuff," Mal said.

"And you opened them?" Persephone gasped.

"Nah, they were already open," Mal said, rolling his eyes. "And I put them all back after I read them."

"Who are they from?" she asked, curiosity getting the better of her.

"That's what's so wild. They're from Mrs. McCullacutty—to my gramps!" Mal said, lifting the envelope flap and pulling out the fragile letter. He unfolded the paper so she could see the signature at the bottom. Jane McCullacutty. "She must have written them many years ago," Mal said. "They're love letters!" He waved the sheet of paper in front of Persephone and waggled his eyebrows. "And it gets even stranger! She and my gramps were planning to get married!"

"Wait. Really? But why is that strange?" Persephone frowned, confused. Malachi looked at her skeptically.

"Because! Wisconsin never had an official law preventing interracial marriage back then, but it would have been really frowned upon for them to get married, or probably even be seen together!"

"For real? There were actually laws that said people couldn't be together if their skin colors were different?" Persephone felt her mouth drop open. She'd thought she'd done her history homework well enough, but she'd honestly never considered how all that history might have actually affected people's lives. People she knew. People she cared about. Her neighbors. Friends.

Mal stared at her like he couldn't believe she didn't know this.

Persephone glanced at the letter in his hand. "I guess that helps explain why she acted so strange when I told her about the orchid food your grandpa made . . ."

"Gramps mixed you up some of his miraculous orchid food, huh?" Mal grinned. "You're lucky! He doesn't share that with just anyone."

Persephone tried to smile but it felt a little crooked.

"Yeah, lucky," she said.

"So, what do you think?" Mal waved the letter in front of Persephone, waiting for her to be as excited as he was about the discovery, but it just made Persephone sad.

"I think it's sad and terrible and unfair," she said, "that whoever or whatever happened all those years ago forced them apart, and that even after all this time, they still live this close to each other and aren't even friends."

Mal frowned and then nodded slowly.

"Yeah, I guess you're right," he said, carefully folding the letter and sliding it into his backpack. "But it has to mean something—that Gramps kept these letters, even after all this time."

"Either way, it's none of our business," Persephone said. "You should put that letter back where you found it."

"Okay, I will! Sheesh. Calm down." Mal was a little defensive. "It's not like I'm going to go tell the world."

"You told me," Persephone said.

"Well, you're not the world," Mal said. "You're my friend. You tell me stuff, so I figured I could tell you stuff too."

"Oh." Persephone felt her stomach do a little flip. "Well, you can." She smiled. "And I'm glad you did."

"Yeah?"

"Yeah."

They were both quiet for a minute, and Malachi suddenly seemed a little embarrassed and in a hurry to change the subject.

"Need any help in the garden today?" he asked. "Please tell me there's no more Virginia creeper."

Persephone grinned. "I think we got it all," she said. "Unless the garden wants us to deal with it a little longer." She eyed the garden suspiciously and Mal laughed.

"You're starting to sound like Mrs. McCullacutty!" he said. "Talking to gardens and houses and cats as if they weren't just gardens and houses and cats."

Persephone laughed. He had a way of making things feel lighter—better.

"Well, I was going to mow the lawn. Do you want to help me with that?" Persephone asked, examining the length of the grass instead of the color of Mal's eyes—a beautiful shade of brown. Darker around the edges. Not that she'd been studying them or anything.

"I'd *love* to mow the lawn," Mal said, jumping to his feet with feigned enthusiasm. "Lawn mowing is my *favorite*. Is there a mower around here somewhere, or do we have to cut it with one of those blades?" He made a swinging motion, like he was swiping a long blade through the grass, felling it in great swaths.

"Well, Mrs. McCullacutty probably has a scythe or two around here somewhere, if you really want . . ." Persephone said.

"Maybe next time." Mal laughed. So Persephone led the way through knee-high grass to the small white shed at the edge of the backyard and pulled open the doors.

"What in the world . . ." Her words trailed off as she stood in the open doorway. Because inside, everything was different. It had all been rearranged. Not like someone had shuffled things around, but like the *walls* had shifted. The built-in shelves on the left wall had moved to the back wall instead. The tools hanging where the shelf used to be were now hanging on the left. And there were new tools in addition to the old. There was a collection of tall thin stakes with curious decorative hooks leaning in an orderly row against the wall, along with several strings of lights, neatly coiled and dusty, like they'd always been there. Except that they hadn't. Garden lights, Persephone realized. The stakes could be set into the ground and lights hung between them—it would be beautiful, strung and lit along the rock path she was creating for the garden in her mind.

"What's the matter?" Mal had come to stand beside her in the open doorway, staring at what probably looked like a completely normal garden shed.

"*I'm not exactly sure what's in here* now," Mrs. McCullacutty had said. And now Persephone understood what she meant.

"Nothing." Persephone looked at Mal and grinned. "Just, you know, *potential*." Mal looked a little puzzled but followed Persephone inside and brushed dust from the top of an old lawn mower.

"Let's see if it works." He pushed it out into the yard and pulled the rope a few times, but the engine just groaned. "Hmm." Mal opened the gas tank and checked the oil, fiddling with this and that while Persephone poked around inside the shed.

She didn't understand how it worked. This shed, Mrs. McCullacutty's house, the garden, any of it. But it all felt alive somehow. Knowing and seeing in a way that sheds and houses and gardens shouldn't be able to. She couldn't decide if it scared her or made her feel awake. Seen. Unstuck. And it was then that her eyes landed on a can of paint. Lifeguard-chair red. She gasped, picking it up, along with the paintbrush that lay beside it. She remembered the faded and peeling paint on Levi's lifeguard chair at the beach, and she ran the soft bristles of the paintbrush against the palm of her hand.

Maybe there were places like this filled with potential in forgotten corners all over the world, just waiting for someone to make use of them, no matter how improbable, or unusual, or difficult it might be to believe.

And like a confirmation Persephone couldn't dismiss, the old lawn mower, covered in dust and almost forgotten by the world, suddenly roared to life.

~~ 30 ~~

FIREWORKS

The nearly inaudible whine of a launched rocket, followed by the sudden explosive *BOOM* over Galion Lake marked the first of a few practice fireworks the night of July 4. Persephone whirled to catch a glimpse. The show wouldn't begin until ten p.m., but she wanted to hurry and get there before the last of the good spots were taken.

Their family had bounced between parades, and Music in the Park, the kiddie carnival, and the brat sale fundraiser put on by the Lions Club. Everyone was a little sunburned and tired, but excited for the fireworks.

"All right, you guys have fun," Dad said, ushering Mom, Owen, and Persephone outside. "I want a full explanation of every firework when you get back. Color, size, noise level, all of it." Levi had come home from the hospital a couple days ago, and neither of her parents were willing to leave him. So Persephone had agreed to take Owen to the carnival today. Honestly, she didn't mind. Levi had arrived .

back home in an ambulance, hooked up to more machines than usual, and even after the efficient ambulance crew had left, and Levi was settled in his own room, everything still felt strange and uncertain.

He was in the hospital for three days while tests had been run and reports made, old assessments updated, but ultimately, there was no new diagnosis. Levi just continued slipping further and further away from them, leaving less of himself and more memories of everything he had once been. Dad would stay home with him tonight, and Mom would go with Owen and Persephone to the fireworks. It felt like they were all caught between the way life used to be and the way it was now, and trying to find some new "normal" in between.

Once the paramedics left, Persephone had needed to see Levi. But as she'd stood in the doorway and watched him sleep, she couldn't stop the tears from coming. He was so changed from the brother she used to know.

Returning to her own room, she'd sat at her desk, Levi's email open on her computer and her fingers poised over her keyboard. She'd promised her mom she would tell the show they were no longer interested, but she couldn't make herself do it. Levi had decided not to send that application himself. But she couldn't help but wonder: *Would he send it now, if he knew how bad things were?* It was a question she couldn't answer. All she knew was that she couldn't give up the hope of one hundred thousand dollars. Not when Levi needed it now more than ever.

Eventually, Persephone had just turned off her

computer. She had three weeks left to respond to Miss Mathews—and figure out what to do.

A sea of picnic blankets and lawn chairs stretched down the beach as Persephone and Owen and Mom reached the lakefront. A few more practice fireworks had been launched overhead as they walked, and Owen was nearly bursting with excitement. Persephone scanned the crowd looking for familiar faces. The red lifeguard chair rose over the heads of everyone gathered onshore.

"Hey, you guys," said a voice Persephone hadn't heard in almost a year. She looked up and met Joseph Lowry's hesitant smile.

Persephone had done her best to avoid Mya this past year, but she'd tried to avoid Joseph even more. It wasn't that hard; Persephone had just made sure she wasn't around when the two families were together. It was easy to come up with an excuse to disappear, and no one questioned it. But now, it was even harder to watch her mother hold out an arm as Joseph gave her a familiar one-armed side hug. Owen, never shy, wrapped both arms around Joseph's waist and hugged him tight. Joseph laughed. It was a strange sound, bringing back a hundred memories.

"Mom and Dad said to watch for you." Joseph gestured to a blanket where Mr. and Mrs. Lowry and Mya were sitting. They waved them over. Persephone's mother hesitated, and Persephone shook her head the tiniest bit. Her mother avoided her gaze, set her shoulders, and smiled at Joseph.

"Thanks." She nodded. "We'd love to join you."

No, we wouldn't! Persephone screamed in her head. *We want to sit far away. We don't even want to be here anymore!*

"I'm going to go find Malachi and—" Persephone turned, looking for an excuse to disappear, but her mother wrapped a surprisingly strong hand around her shoulders.

"No." She was firm. "Not this time. You can join us." She released her hesitantly, as if Persephone might bolt at any moment. Joseph studied her warily, meeting her gaze and refusing to look away. Persephone stared right back.

He was taller than she remembered. He'd started wearing his dark hair a little longer. And he had grown broader—while her brother's body had begun to atrophy. But there was something missing in Joseph too. A lightness. His easy grin. It was gone. Maybe it had left the day Persephone's brother did.

Mya patted a spot beside her on the blanket her family had spread on the ground. And so, Persephone sat. Unwillingly. Her once-best-friend offered an uncertain smile, but Persephone's heart was hammering too hard against her ribs for her to return it. She could feel the weight of tears and anger threatening to rise.

Mr. and Mrs. Lowry made small talk with Mom, asking questions about work and their summers. They laughed together. They asked about Levi.

How could they all sit here together on the same blanket under the cover of a warm July sky, only one year after Levi's accident, and *laugh*?

The sudden explosion of a firework overhead was so

loud and so unexpected, that something in Persephone's chest felt like it cracked. She jumped and scrambled to her feet, trying to get out from under the sky.

Mya stared at her with wide eyes, and Persephone's mother reached for her, her face worried. But the effort it had taken to sit on that blanket with all of them had transformed into something that shoved fire into Persephone's arms and legs. She couldn't sit back down. Not here, at the lake. Not beside Joseph or Mya or any of them. She couldn't pretend to enjoy the night. Or that everything was just totally fine and normal.

Persephone shook her head, slowly backing away as another firework whistled overhead and then exploded in a teeth-jarring roll that echoed across the water, reverberating in her chest.

She whirled around, then broke into a run. She ignored Mom's calls to come back, tripping over people on picnic blankets and the legs of lawn chairs in the dark. Twice she stumbled, and then she hit the ground. The palms of her hands, already raw from the handles of rakes and the press of garden sheers, tore open against the asphalt in the parking lot beside the lake's picnic area. Persephone hissed against the pain, crouching close to the ground. She tried to take deep breaths. In, out. In, out.

Then an ambulance siren blared. Lights flashed as the fire department and local paramedic team tested their equipment, preparing for the possibility of an emergency during the night's fireworks show.

And something inside of Persephone broke.

Memories from Last Year's June washed over her. Sounds and images that lived in the shadowed corners of her mind pushed past the walls she had built around them.

Blood pooling in the sand from the gash in Levi's head.

The medical helicopter blades reverberating *thump-thump-thump-thump-thump-thump-thump* as the aircraft lowered, then landed.

The jerking and heaving of Levi's body with rib-breaking chest compressions during CPR.

Joseph kneeling beside them in the water as they waited for Levi to be airlifted to the hospital in the city.

She wasn't supposed to have these memories. Persephone wasn't supposed to have been there. She'd ignored her mother's instructions: *"Stay at home and wait for me!"*

No.

Persephone had followed anyway and just stood there, watching everything fall apart. Her life. Her family. Her friendships. Her brother. She'd just stood there, hands clapped over her mouth, keeping her screams inside.

And now something inside of her couldn't stop screaming. She couldn't catch her breath. Tears were hot on her skin, and she tucked herself close to the ground as sirens shrieked in the air all around her . . .

Again.

And again.

And then Joseph was there, kneeling on the pavement, his face shadowed by the flickering light of a dying firework.

For a minute Persephone didn't know what was happening. But then he gently pulled her hands from her ears so she could hear what he was saying.

"It's okay, Persephone," he said. "I've got you."

She scrambled back.

"It's okay," he said again.

And the part of her that had been stuck in that awful memory just a second ago, suddenly somersaulted and shifted into something else. Something sharp and terrible. The anger, the heat of it, narrowed and focused until it was just Joseph and his assurance that it would all be okay. It felt like the worst kind of lie. Everything in her life was exactly the opposite of okay. Because of him.

"Get away from me!" she hissed, getting to her feet. Tears ran down her face. "This is because of you! You and your stupid boat!" Persephone's voice was loud as she fought to be heard over the fireworks.

Joseph took a step back, flinching like she'd hit him, and for a second, she thought she had. But her hands were still by her sides, her palms bloody. She didn't feel as if she belonged to herself anymore—her words just tumbled out like the whir of noise from a box fan on high.

"What were you even doing that day?" She clenched her hands into fists, and barely noticed when her nails pressed into the cuts on her palms. "When he hit his head, did you do *anything*? Or did you just stand there? Did you push him—"

Her words broke off as Joseph came toe-to-toe with her, his face so close that his breath blew strands of hair off her forehead. He shook his head, his expression twisted with anger and something else.

Grief.

"Don't you *dare*." His voice was low. "You have no idea."

"Oh yeah?" Persephone took a step back, her words coming too fast. Too raw. "Then tell me! Tell me you didn't do it! I saw you two fighting the night before the accident! I couldn't hear what you were saying, but I was watching through the window and I saw Levi yelling, waving his arms around, and then I saw you get in your truck and slam the door before you drove off!"

She was breathing hard, like she had been running, and she watched a look of surprise cross Joseph's face. "Levi stood in the street for a long time after that, and when he came inside, he shut himself in his room and didn't come out for the rest of the night. So tell me about that, huh? And tell me I have no idea what it's like, now, to stand beside his bed and talk to him and wait—for nothing. *Nothing.* Tell me how he can't smile, or eat, or move, or say my name. How he can't say anything at all. Tell me, Joseph! He's my brother and—"

"He's my friend!" Joseph threw open his arms, reaching into the dark. "And I love him too."

Persephone stared at him, searching his face, waiting for the explanation that would make everything make sense. But he shook his head slowly, something inside him closing back up.

"No matter what I say, it's never going to be enough." His face crumpled. "You've been avoiding me for an entire year. Running away. And nothing I tell you about that day is going to make any difference. You don't want the *truth*, Persephone. You want something that doesn't hurt, or make you uncomfortable, or leave you with questions! Well, I can't give you that. Because the truth is this was all Levi's fault."

Persephone turned and ran.

31

A TRUE TRUTH

The following day, Persephone doubled her efforts in the garden.
Her mother wrapped her hands in gauze, and she wore
gloves, but her palms still hurt, reminding her of a truth
she didn't want. A truth that hurt. She worked anyway, grit-
ting her teeth as she fought with a garden that seemed set
against her that afternoon. But Malachi showed up to help,
which made things a little easier—just knowing he was
there, knowing she didn't have to do the work alone. Even
if the garden was stubborn. Even if her hands hurt, and her
heart ached almost more than she could stand.

Then, close to dark, Mya showed up too. And the
memory of Persephone's words, the accusations she'd
thrown at Joseph the previous night, felt like broken glass
inside of her. Sharp, and cruel. She didn't know what to
believe anymore, but it felt good to hang on to her anger.
The thought of being anything else was almost too much to
think about.

Malachi glanced uncertainly between the two of them, and then anchored his hands in his pockets.

"Hey, Mya," he said. He looked at them both and then squinted at the sinking sun. "You know, I think I need to split for today. I'll see you tomorrow, yeah?"

"Yeah." Persephone nodded, trying not to care that he was leaving. But she did. Because now she would be alone with Mya and the truths and lies that were wild and raw inside of her. She watched Mal go, riding his bike down the sidewalk, skipping all three cement stairs in a graceful arc of tires. And then it was just Mya. Her once-best-friend.

Mya surveyed their work with wide eyes, a pair of gloves gripped in one hand, and then met Persephone's gaze. Steady. Determined.

"Hey," she said.

"Hey." Persephone tried to smile, but she couldn't. Had Joseph told her what she'd said to him?

"Your mom said you'd be here."

Persephone nodded and looked around. "I've been working on this . . . garden." She shrugged a shoulder. It didn't look much like a garden. It still looked like a rather overgrown *idea* of a garden. It seemed to be fighting her efforts. For the last couple of days, it had felt like the work she'd done had to be done all over again. There were still no flower beds or paths. No trellis or climbing wall or fence. No strings of lights, or welcoming gates to swing wide for gardeners or visitors. But Mya walked around, looking at everything anyway. The trimmed hedges, the mowed lawn, the ordered piles of materials Persephone planned to use—bricks and stones for the path, containers for flowers.

"So—what are you doing here?" Persephone asked. Once the words were out, she knew she could have said them differently. "I mean—" She paused, not sure how to fix things. Her words. Their friendship. The past year.

"I'm here to help." Mya held up her gloves as proof.

"But—but why?"

"Because I'm your friend." Mya let that truth settle between them. A tiny seed.

Persephone swallowed hard. She was suddenly more tired than she'd felt in a long time. Tired of fighting— Mya, Joseph, her parents, herself, the truth . . . She still didn't know how to answer Rebecca Mathews at Epiphany Television, and she couldn't delay a response much longer. But there were also a few things she *did* know: Her brother wasn't getting any better. His seizures weren't improving, and the bills wouldn't stop coming. But there was this: Mya kept showing up.

"Thank you," she said finally, blinking back tears. "Thank you for coming."

Mya was her friend. And Persephone needed her.

It was a true truth. One Persephone hadn't been able to change, no matter what she'd said and done, or hadn't said and done, since Last Year's June. It felt like a miracle. She wrapped it around herself and held on tight.

~~ 32 ~~

RENEWED FRIENDSHIPS

That evening, Persephone couldn't stop thinking about the way Mya had shown up—the way she refused to give up, even though Persephone had. And as she swam her laps the next morning—twenty-eight of them—an idea began to bloom. She wasn't the only one who needed a friend.

Mrs. McCullacutty was having tea at a small table that had been set up beneath the shade of the Queens when Persephone walked through the gate later that morning. She took a deep breath and sat down beside her.

"Good morning," she said, just as she'd practiced in front of her bedroom mirror. "I've been thinking, and it's time you write a letter to Dr. Rathmason."

Persephone watched Mrs. McCullacutty's teacup tremble slightly in its saucer as she considered that. Blue lay in the garden between them in a patch of sunshine. Her tail twitched. It was the only sign the small gray cat was listening.

"Good morning to you, my dear. And may I ask

why you think I should write a letter to the esteemed Dr. Rathmason, maker of orchid food?" Mrs. McCullacutty set her teacup and saucer down and smoothed her shaky hands over her dress. Plumb taffeta, crinkly and shimmery. She wore blue heels with lace overlay decorating them from heel to toe, and a hat. One of those small brimless ones with a mesh veil. She had the veil turned up and a peacock feather broach held it in place. Maybe she *had* been an actress once. She certainly had the clothes for it.

"Because if you don't, then nothing will ever change," Persephone said. She hadn't told her about the letters Malachi had found. But she knew there was an old ache inside of Mrs. McCullacutty where her friendship with Dr. Rathmason used to live. She had seen a glimpse of it on that very first day she had stepped inside Mrs. McCullacutty's house, with the orchid, before she even knew who had given it to her. *Thip-thip-thip*, her sad words like rain on wet pavement.

Persephone clutched her hands tightly in her lap. Her own words about change were almost the same ones her mother had said—the smell of watermelon bubble bath heavy in the humid bathroom air. They nearly choked her now. A red rose wrapped bright petals around the bowl of the teacup in her hands. The lip and handle were painted with thorns. No vines. No leaves. Just thorns. *Were her words thorns? Was she? Is that what the green cupboard was telling her today?*

"My dear girl," Mrs. McCullacutty said after a moment. "I have to wonder if we are talking about *my* particular story, or *yours*." Persephone picked up her cup and saucer again, taking a careful sip. She met Mrs. McCullacutty's gaze.

She'd never told her about Mya and Joseph and Last Year's June, but anyone who'd lived in Coulter for more than two minutes knew about her family and the Lowrys. And Mrs. McCullacutty was remarkably good at knowing things. Blue opened a pair of sleepy green eyes and looked at her.

"Mya kept telling me it wasn't Joseph's fault." Persephone took a steadying breath. "Levi's accident, I mean." Mrs. McCullacutty nodded.

"And yet you have not wanted to believe her," Mrs. McCullacutty said. "Is Mya in the habit of lying to you?"

Persephone shook her head. "No." She felt miserable. "But I guess it just seemed easier if it were someone's fault." She struggled to find the right words. "Because then I could be mad. Instead of just sad all the time."

"Ahh." Mrs. McCullacutty nodded. "Sad is terribly difficult, is it not? There is almost no one to show us how to do it. We are all very good at showing one another how to be angry. Sometimes it can even make you feel strong." She sipped her tea. "Conversely, it can make you feel like something inside of you is broken. Or weak. But it's not."

Overhead the Queens rustled green and silver leaves in agreement. Mrs. McCullacutty stared up at them for several long moments, listening, and then set her teacup back on the table. "If you'll excuse me for a moment, I have something I want to show you." She rose from her place in the garden and walked back into the house. When she returned, she carried a framed photograph and handed it to Persephone. There were two young people in the black-and-white picture. They stood close together, their arms thrown over each other's shoulders.

"That's me, and that's Terrance—Dr. Rathmason—long before he was a doctor," Mrs. McCullacutty said. "Back then he was just Terry." She settled into her chair. Persephone blinked, startled by the childish face of young Mrs. McCullacutty. The girl in the photograph smiled back, frozen in time. She had changed, of course, but she also hadn't. "I was twelve in that photograph," said Mrs. McCullacutty. "Terry was fourteen and my best friend in the world. We grew up together."

Persephone studied the face of the boy—his bright smile. Malachi's smile. Mal looked like his grandfather.

"Terry's father worked for one of the iron mines my father owned, and I don't think either of our fathers realized how close we were until it was too late for them to change our minds. Of course, our friendship looked much different than the friendship you have with Malachi," Mrs. McCullacutty said gently. Persephone looked up as her voice changed. She sounded angrier than Persephone had ever heard. "When we were children, the world was happy to shout about its hate and brokenness. It pretended everything was okay while insisting my friend drink from a separate water fountain." Mrs. McCullacutty clenched her teacup so tightly that Persephone was afraid the fragile porcelain might break. "These days, the hate and brokenness might look a little different, but they're still there."

Persephone frowned and studied the photograph of the two friends again. There was a cat in the left-hand corner of the picture. Small. Dark. Blurry. As if it had moved at the last moment and marred the exposure. She glanced at Blue. Her eyes were half-lidded against the light that filtered through the trees overhead. *Not possible.*

"So, you were still friends in this picture." Persephone looked at Mrs. McCullacutty and she nodded. "But you aren't now?"

"We were best friends," she said. "We had lovely, grand adventures together."

"What happened? That you aren't friends anymore?" Persephone's question felt big and loud in the quiet beneath the Queens, and she stumbled over her words. "I mean—if you don't mind telling me?"

"I think it all began when we fell in love." Mrs. McCullacutty settled back into her chair, resting her teacup on her knee. "Though, perhaps we were always in love. You couldn't help being in love with Terry." She laughed. "Even when he was young"—she reached over and tapped a finger on the boy in the picture—"he had a sharpness about him. Always was so alive. You wanted to be close to him and stand in his glow." Persephone nodded and smiled. Malachi was like that too. "When Terry turned twenty, he asked my father for permission to marry me, as boys did in those days. Of course, my father refused." Mrs. McCullacutty shook her head.

She sighed. "He risked a lot, asking my father. But he insisted it was worth it. To do the honorable thing. Unfortunately, things like honor and justice only work when everyone follows the same rules." Mrs. McCullacutty went very quiet for several long minutes as if she were remembering something she'd rather forget. "Both Terry and I discovered too late that my father followed his own rules," she said finally. "And those rules did not include the equal treatment of the man I loved. I was never allowed to see Terrance again."

"How could your father do that?" Persephone gasped.

"Powerful men have done whatever they pleased for a great while, my dear. My father was no exception." Persephone felt her hands begin to shake and she wrapped her fingers around the photograph a little tighter. "So I listened," said Mrs. McCullacutty. "It was the only way I could protect Terry from my father and men like him. Even when Terrance sent me a letter asking me to elope, I said no. I didn't even answer his letter. I didn't know what else to do."

"He asked you to run away and get married?" Persephone leaned forward in her chair.

Mrs. McCullacutty nodded. "But I was too afraid of what my father would do. It was too high a price for either of us." Persephone glanced around the garden. *Did the garden remember this too? Did it remember them all? Did it feel their heartaches and hold the weight of their questions?*

"After that, I was heartbroken, as you can imagine. My father sent me away to a women's college in Chicago," said Mrs. McCullacutty. "I suppose so I couldn't follow my heart. And then one afternoon, I met a young man named Everett. An art collector. Rich, handsome, and from a white family. I was lonely, and homesick, and as unfair and selfish as it was, I let myself imagine a life that invoked my father's approval, rather than his hatred."

Blue leaped up into Persephone's lap while Mrs. McCullacutty talked. A silent witness. Persephone stroked her ears, imagining young Mrs. McCullacutty and Terrance Rathmason, both full of heartache because of what others had decided for them.

"So, you and Everett fell in love?" Persephone asked.

"We did." Mrs. McCullacutty smiled, a little wistfully. "We got married and were happy and had many adventures before Everett got sick. He collected and sold rare and beautiful art all over the world. He became quite renowned. My father was delighted, of course. But I was never able to make things right with Terrance. I had betrayed him. He had been willing to give up everything, and I hadn't even been able to stand up to my father. He had every right to be angry—still does. And yet, somehow, we both managed to stay right here in Coulter. Even so, part of me still hasn't given up hope that someday we will have the opportunity to reconcile. Even after all this time. Especially now."

"Why especially now?" Persephone looked up from the photograph in her hands to Mrs. McCullacutty's face. She looked quiet. Reflective.

"Because it's almost time for me to leave. I've been putting it off for as long as I can, but I can't stay much longer—things to do, you know." She smiled, as if her words were a secret joke.

"But—where are you going?" Persephone put the photograph down, afraid she might drop it, and stood up, suddenly unable to sit there.

"Just—away, for a time." Mrs. McCullacutty studied her teacup, refusing to look at Persephone. "I have a grandnephew who recently lost his father. I'm his only living relative, and I've agreed to go and look after him for a while."

"But you'll be back?" A panicky feeling was rolling around inside Persephone. Mrs. McCullacutty couldn't leave! *She couldn't!*

"Of course, dear." Mrs. McCullacutty smiled.

"When will you go?" Persephone wasn't sure she believed her.

"I don't want you to worry." Mrs. McCullacutty reached over, patting her hand. "Everything will be exactly as it should be," she said. "I won't leave for a little while yet, and you can help me get ready. I must settle this old house for while I'm away. And there is the garden of course! You've made such wonderful progress—"

"But I'm not finished yet," Persephone said quickly. "You can't leave until the garden is finished!"

Mrs. McCullacutty nodded and patted her hand again.

"I'll do my best, dear," she said. "I wonder if you'd be willing to look after Blue and Piccadilly in my absence? I usually leave Blue in charge of things, but I'm sure she wouldn't mind the help." Persephone ran her hand down the cat's soft warm back and Blue purred happily, opening one green eye as if waiting for Persephone's response.

"Yes, of course," Persephone said. She blew out a breath, trying to ease the uncertainty. *It would be fine. Everything would be just fine.* And Persephone would be here waiting with Blue and Piccadilly and the garden and her magnificent old house when Mrs. McCullacutty got back.

So why did it suddenly feel like things were unraveling?

~ 33 ~

CONVERSATION WITH LEVI

Thursday night, Persephone got the popcorn and slipped quietly into Levi's room.

She hated to admit it, but she'd been avoiding him since he got back from the hospital. She'd even missed watching *Small Town Revival* with him last week.

After this last seizure, Levi felt different. More gone, if that were possible. Like he'd gone deeper inside himself, further away from them.

Persephone stood over her brother for a minute, watching him. Wanting him to open his eyes, wanting a slow smile to creep over his face as he realized she was standing there.

But there was nothing.

She turned on the TV and tried to let the old eagerness roll over her as the familiar theme song jingled in time with *Small Town Revival*'s introduction clips. She tried to imagine Coulter, Wisconsin, on the screen. But she couldn't focus. The magic had faded. Even her popcorn tasted stale. She sighed and finally turned off the TV, sitting in silence at the foot of her brother's bed.

"Levi? Can you hear me?" Her voice sounded too loud in the quiet hum of his bedroom. She hadn't expected a response, of course, but that didn't stop her from wanting one. Terribly. "I'm going to pretend you can hear me, okay?" She turned around, frowning at the quiet figure on the bed. "Hang on a second, I have an idea." She got up and rummaged through her brother's dresser drawers until she found what she was looking for. Once she had, she unfolded the sunglasses and gently placed them on Levi's face. If she looked past the feeding tube in his nose, Persephone could almost imagine her brother cracking a grin behind those shades. She climbed back up on the foot of his bed, folding her legs beneath her.

"I had a fight with Joseph," she said, picking at the blanket. His words still haunted her. "At the fireworks on the Fourth of July. It was the first time I talked to him since your accident."

"Wow. You haven't talked to Joseph in a whole year? Sheesh, Pip! That's a long time to wait to argue with someone!" She imagined Levi's voice, his tone, the way he would pull himself up in bed and cross his arms.

"I know." Persephone glanced up, imagining the crease between her brother's eyebrows. "I said some really mean things."

"Well, did he deserve them?"

Persephone smiled. He had always been willing to believe her. To believe *in* her. And then her face fell. This time she hadn't earned that.

"No." She shook her head. "He didn't deserve anything I've said or done this year, Levi." She felt tears rising. "I've been mean to Mya too."

"*To Mya?*" Levi would lean forward, maybe, his face confused. "*Why?*"

"Because I thought it was Joseph's fault somehow. Your accident. Maybe I even *wanted* it to be his fault."

"*Why would you want that?*"

"Because if it's his fault, he can be punished or something. And that would make it more fair, or like he was getting what he deserved." The words were the exact truth of how she felt, but they tasted like smoke and ash in her mouth. Sometimes the truth does.

"I just wanted it to be someone's fault so they would hurt. Like—like *I* hurt."

"*Oh. I see.*" Levi's shades slipped down his face and Persephone leaned over and pushed them back up.

"Joseph told me, '*You don't want the* truth*, Persephone. You want something that doesn't hurt, or make you uncomfortable, or leave you with questions!*'" Persephone twisted her fingers in the blanket.

"*Well, I don't really want this to be the truth either.*" Her brother gestured to himself in her imagination. "*But . . . what if this is what we get, Pip?*"

"No. This can't be it. There are these treatments . . ." Persephone bit her lip to keep it from wobbling.

"*Oh?*" The brother who lived in her memory quirked an eyebrow.

"Yeah, but everything is really expensive and there's

no money, and I'm trying to do something about that, but I think I'm making a real mess of things."

"*Really? Did you rob a bank or something?*" She imagined him leaning back against the pillow, a smirk on his face.

"No." She rolled her eyes. "But I did something. Something big. And I think you're going to be pretty mad about it." Persephone ran her hands through her hair.

"*I'm not going to be mad, Pip. You already told me you were trying to help, remember?*" Her brother waited quietly in her imagination, and so she told him about the application she'd found on his computer, about submitting Coulter for *Small Town Revival*, and how she'd signed his name to the bottom of the letter he'd written. She explained about how Coulter had been accepted and about the possibility of winning one hundred thousand dollars.

"Also, because of the way rumors spread, the whole town basically thinks they are going to be on TV." She paused. "But you thought about that, didn't you? You didn't want everyone to be part of a public display. That's why you didn't send the application yourself."

"*Yeah. It was exciting at first, but in the end, it just didn't feel worth it. Even if the show could have helped revive Coulter or whatever, it would have cost too much—family and my friends were too important. Our lives were too important. The change, or at least the possibility of it, didn't feel like a fair trade.*"

"What am I supposed to do now, Levi? The whole town is going to hate me and never trust me again if I tell them that Coulter was never picked in the first place, which isn't even true, plus I still have to write that woman Rebecca Mathews back and explain *why* Coulter can't participate; Mya is still trying to be my friend even though I don't know how to do that exactly; I think I might have a crush on Malachi Rathmason, which is the worst because he'll hate me if he finds out about the deal I made with his grandfather; and despite everything, I still don't know how to answer that question you left—I don't know how to change the world. For either of us. Oh, and I've been lying to Mom and Dad. A lot." Persephone buried her face in her hands.

"I wish you were here." Her voice was barely a whisper in the quiet bedroom. "I miss you."

"I miss you too, Pip." She could almost hear the words as if they were his own. *"And I wish I was here. But even if I was, I'm pretty sure I couldn't fix this for you. Besides, I think you already know what you need to do."*

Persephone pulled her hair back and put it into a ponytail. Then she sat down at Levi's desk, and opened his computer. Logging into her brother's account, she read through Rebecca Mathews's email again, and then leaned back, chewing on her thumbnail and staring out the window. A vine with heart-shaped leaves had crawled up the corner of the house and was nodding gently at her through the glass.

"Are you stuck?" she imagined her brother asked from the bed.

"Not exactly," Persephone whispered. "This is just hard."

"You can tell them about me," Levi said, and in her imagination, he took off the sunglasses she had placed on his face. *"You can start there, Pip. Just tell the truth."*

And so she did. Haltingly at first. And then faster and faster until it sprawled across the computer screen. An honest account of Last Year's June and all that it had come to mean for Persephone and her family. And because of the accident, all that it could never mean for *Small Town Revival*. Climbing back up on the end of Levi's bed, she read it aloud to him. And in her imagination, he gave his approval.

"That sounds good, Pip. Nice work."

She hovered over the send button for just a moment and then clicked on it, listening as the email flew away, along with the hope of one hundred thousand dollars, paid medical bills, new treatments, and improving things for Levi, her family, herself, and her town. She shook her head.

No. She wouldn't think about that right now. This was what Levi had wanted.

She stared at her quiet brother, hoping and hoping and hoping it was still true.

"So, what are you going to do about Joseph?" he asked in her imagination. *"You're kind of on a roll with this truth-telling stuff tonight."*

"Joseph hates me," Persephone said. "I'm sure of it. He'll never talk to me again. Not after the things I said. And what would I even say to him now? I can't tell him what I just told you! He'd make sure I got arrested or something!" Her brother laughed somewhere in her memory.

"Nah. He'd never do that." And then his voice went

serious. *"But I think you need to tell him you're sorry. Tell him you were wrong. That would be a good place to start."*

"But what if he won't talk to me? And besides, shouldn't he have to pay for what happened to you?"

"What do you mean?"

"I mean, he was there. Shouldn't he be held accountable?"

"Pip, don't you think Joseph is already holding himself accountable?" Her brother's voice was heavy in her mind.

Persephone blinked back tears. This was too hard. She couldn't do it. She wasn't brave enough.

"Write him a letter, Pip. Start by putting your words on paper. Can you do that?"

She nodded slowly. "Yes. Okay. I think I can be brave enough for that."

"I know you can do this. When you're ready." In her mind, Levi grinned. *"Hey. Good talk, Pip."*

Persephone smiled through her tears. "Yeah. Good talk."

34

ICE CREAM

Persephone made garden plans in her head on the way to the post office the next morning. She had written and rewritten a letter to Joseph about 473 times before finally sliding it into an envelope and stuffing it into her pocket.

Owen and his best friend, Sam, were messing around, elbowing each other and laughing as they made their way down the sidewalk in front of her. Mom had asked her to keep an eye on them today, but she could really use some help in the garden. She couldn't quit thinking about Mrs. McCullacutty leaving. It would be wonderful if the garden were finished before she left.

"Hey!" Persephone called. "I'll buy you each a double-scoop ice cream cone if you come help me at Mrs. McCullacutty's garden today." The boys probably wouldn't be a ton of help, but at least Persephone could get some work done. Mal had been out of town for the last couple days and she hadn't seen or heard from him. She kicked a rock into the gutter.

The dirt for the raised garden beds was supposed to be delivered today, and she wasn't sure how was she was going to get it all into the garden beds on her own. She'd unearthed and rebuilt most of them. They had probably been decorative, years and years ago, filled with seasonal bulbs, cut flowers, and ornamental plants. But Persephone and Mrs. McCullacutty had agreed that they should be more than that now—open to friends and neighbors who might want to plant some vegetables. And the garden seemed to agree. It pulled back branches where the shade was too heavy for tomato vines and runner beans, and offered a bit more shade for lettuce and radishes, kale and chard. There were eight garden beds now, thanks to the account Mrs. McCullacutty had opened at the lumber store, the work Persephone and Mal had done, and the plans for raised garden beds she'd found online. And now, each one had to be filled with soil— rich and loamy and heavy. It would take her forever, one wheelbarrow load and shovelful at a time, but with Owen and Sam's help, it might go a little faster.

The three of them marched the rest of the way to Perry's Hardware Store; it was a little like a general store where you could find pretty much anything you needed, including eight flavors of ice cream. But they weren't the only ones searching for cool treats on a hot day, and Persephone's stomach fluttered when she saw who else was there.

"Hey, Malachi!" Owen said.

"Owen!" Mal grinned at her little brother and then looked around, searching for—for *her*. Her stomach did another flip twist. "Hey, Persephone!" Mal said. "What's up?"

"Hey! You're back!" She was happier about that than she thought she'd be.

"Yep! You miss me?" Mal was trying to be funny, but Persephone felt her face heat up a little. She *had* missed him.

"So, good day for ice cream, right?" She gestured at the cooler, changing the subject. Owen and Sam were pressing their noses to the glass case and peering inside. "I bribed them," she added.

Mal raised an eyebrow. "Into what?"

"Hard labor." She shrugged. "The dirt is coming today." The words sounded a little like an invitation, but she didn't want Mal to think he *had* to help if he didn't want to.

"Cool!" he said. "I totally forgot the dirt was coming today!"

Mr. Perry handed two double-scoop ice cream cones to Sam and Owen from behind the ice cream counter while Mrs. Perry waited to check them out at the register. The boys instantly began working on their ice cream cones as they headed for the front door.

"Sam and I will be outside!" Owen called, and Persephone nodded.

"So how was Madison?" Persephone asked, peering into the ice cream cooler and trying to decide what flavor she wanted. Malachi spent a week every summer with his mom in the city.

"It was good." He shrugged. "I went to basketball camp for the week, my mom and I ate out at this one corner deli I really like, and I played a bunch of video games while she was at work. It was fun."

"Are you going to play ball again this year?" Persephone suddenly remembered sitting on the bleachers after school with Mya, watching the boys' basketball team practice. Malachi had been one of the better players.

Mal shrugged. "I don't know. I mean, I like playing and I really like winning, but I'm not sure basketball is my thing. A lot of the guys take it super seriously, and sometimes that just feels like a lot of pressure."

Persephone nodded. "Who has time for basketball when there is art to create?" She grinned, remembering the drawings on the refrigerator at his house, the ever-present rattle of paint cans in his backpack, and the lure of street art—Mal's invitation to the world.

"Yeah! Exactly!" Mal laughed, and Persephone felt her stomach flip-twist again.

And then the front door swung open, and they forgot about ice cream, basketball, and random stomach flip turns as Sam rushed in. His face was pale and scared.

"Hurry!" he yelled. "Come quick!" His voice snagged on a sob. "Owen fell!"

35

OWEN

For a split second, Persephone forgot how to breathe. And then the weight of Sam's words hit her like a gut punch. She tore out of the hardware store, ice cream forgotten, and ran after Sam. Her heart pounded as she followed him around the corner and into the alley.

Owen lay crumpled on the tar under a ladder that ran up the side of the building. The view from up there was great—you could see most of Main Street, and she'd often thought it would be a great place to watch the Fourth of July parade. Persephone had climbed up there with her dad once before. But Owen had climbed it alone. And Persephone hadn't been there to stop it from happening.

"Owen?" Persephone crouched down beside him, her hands on his chest. "Owen?" His body was still. Blood ran down the side of his face and onto the tar.

"Don't move him!" Malachi had raced out right behind Persephone. "You can't move him until we know he doesn't have a spinal injury." He pulled his phone out of his pocket and dialed 911. Persephone had the vague sense of him talking somewhere behind her. She knelt, because she was shaking too hard to do anything else, and gently touched Owen's face. She wanted to force him awake, but she knew Mal was right. Moving him could make it worse.

And then she couldn't hold on to any thoughts that made sense. There were just words inside her, all strung together by her racing heartbeat. All she could get out was "please—" over and over.

"Please—Please—Please—Please—"

And then Mr. and Mrs. Perry were there, kneeling beside Owen and Persephone. Mr. Perry reached out and pressed two fingers against Owen's neck, just under his jaw, checking for a pulse. He found it, and a small measure of relief settled in. He nodded to his wife, who breathed a deep sigh of relief and knelt beside Persephone, one arm wrapped around her shoulders. She was saying something about help coming soon and how Owen was going to be okay. But people had said things like that before, and Persephone knew they weren't always true.

She searched Owen's face, *please* still echoing in her mind. Owen's chest rose and fell, and now Mr. Perry was talking. She could see his lips moving and his earnest face, but she couldn't focus on what he was saying.

"Please—Please—Please—"

There was blood in Owen's hair. On his face. On the pavement. He was breathing, but maybe he would never wake up. Maybe he would never be the same.

No. Not again. Not. Again.

"Please—Please—Please—"

And then the ambulance was there.

Not again.

And people were moving with calm efficiency. But Persephone wanted them to run. *RUN.* She wanted them to hurry faster!

"Please—Please—Please—"

A gurney was hauled from the back of the vehicle and two paramedics lifted her brother onto it, putting an oxygen mask over his small face. They said things like "head trauma," "unconscious," and "stabilize" in calm, efficient voices. Persephone wondered if they made you practice calm emergency voices when you trained for this job.

"Please—Please—Please!"

A police officer appeared out of nowhere, asking her what happened in a calm, efficient voice. But she had forgotten how to speak actual words. Someone led her to the hardware store's porch steps and away from the smear of Owen's blood on the tar. A blanket appeared around her shoulders. Sam was crying. Mal was gesturing to the ladder, explaining, and she focused on the shadow of pencil lead that always seemed to stain the first two fingers of his right hand. He must see the world in such detail to be able to draw and paint it the way he did . . .

"Please—Please—Please—"

And then her mother was there, pulling her toward the car.

Not again.

"We'll meet your dad at the hospital." Her face was white as paper.

And the ambulance, with Owen in the back, left in a rush of noise and urgency.

"Please—"

36

GROWING EACH OTHER

Fortunately, Owen's injury was not as terrible as Persephone had feared. By the time her little brother arrived at the hospital, he had regained consciousness. The doctor decided to keep him overnight due to some swelling, but Owen was more interested in the number of balloons Mr. and Mrs. Perry sent to his hospital room and what flavor of shake the hospital cafeteria had, than anything else.

The next afternoon, Persephone and her parents stood beside Owen's hospital bed as his nurse bustled around, readying him for discharge. He was coming home with seven balloons and three plastic wrist bands, eight stitches in the side of his head, and strict instructions to rest and not engage in any excessive physical activity, watch screens, or read until the swelling had gone down completely. Three weeks at the very least. Concussions were nothing to mess around with. As if Persephone and her family didn't already know.

"You think I'll have a scar?" Owen asked the nurse as she stood in his room, her clipboard and the discharge papers ready for Mom and Dad to sign.

"You, sir, are going to have a fantastic scar," she said, giving him a level gaze. "But let's keep it to just this one, all right?"

"All right." Owen nodded slowly in agreement. Mom and Dad smiled and Persephone laughed, but it came out a little wild and crooked at the end. It felt strange, to laugh when relief and hope and guilt made her feel like crying.

Once Owen was home and settled, Persephone crept into his room and pulled back the corner of the blanket that hung from the top bunk over his bed. His fort was tidy— Mom had made his bed and tucked him into it with plenty of pillows. He looked very small. Too small.

"Hey," she whispered.

"Hey," he whispered back. It was the middle of the afternoon, and it felt wrong for him to be here. Now she had two brothers in bed.

"I'm gonna be okay, Persephone," Owen said matter-of-factly, and Persephone nodded, suddenly realizing she was crying. He was only *seven*. She should have taken better care of him. Not just two days ago, but *always*. Instead, she'd been a little relieved when he was out of the way, not asking questions, not bothering her, not making her remember how things used to be. She could have lost him forever— she could have lost *both* of her brothers. And no amount of laps could change that.

"I'm sorry, Owen." She knelt beside his bed, the blanket

from the top bunk draping around her shoulders like a cape. But she was no hero.

She wanted so badly to make things better for her family. And things only seemed to get more stressful and scarier all the time.

The truths she had been avoiding since she sent that email to Rebecca Mathews began to settle over her.

Hope for Levi—*gone*.

Hope for Coulter—*gone*.

Hope for answering that question for Levi—*gone*. And she had sent it all away with the push of a button. Even her little brother had almost been lost.

"It's not your fault," Owen said.

But Persephone didn't believe him.

She felt herself sinking. Sinking and sinking and sinking. She was stuck. Maybe she would be stuck forever. Just like Levi, only worse because she would *know* she was stuck and be unable to do a thing about it.

What was she going to do?

The rumors about *Small Town Revival* were still circulating around town.

How was she supposed to change things? How could she ever answer that big question for Levi? She couldn't even answer it for herself! Every time she tried to help, she just made a bigger mess!

"I'm sorry I can't help you in your garden now, Persephone." Owen reached up and wrapped one wiry arm around her neck, pulling her close for a tight hug. It was like he had sensed her tangle of questions and heartache and thought it was his fault somehow. A sob caught in the back of Persephone's throat.

"The *garden*? Who cares about a garden when my little brother *almost*—" She shook her head, trying to dislodge the terrible thought of him gone forever. "You almost got really hurt! I was so worried about the garden and everything else that I wasn't taking care of you like I should have." She squeezed him tighter. "I'm really sorry, Owen. I should just forget that garden altogether."

Owen disentangled himself from her grip.

"No, Persephone!" His small face was determined and fierce. "You can't forget the garden! You can't quit! That's *your* garden! It's only growing because of you—if you stop, everything will be sad again." His lip started to quiver. *"You'll* be sad again."

Persephone sat back, staring at him.

"I'll be sad again?"

"You've been sad." He nodded. "And mad too. But the garden is changing that."

She took a deep, shaky breath.

And then another.

She thought about how good it felt being in the garden. Making friends and making things beautiful. Together. Maybe the garden was changing things . . . changing her.

And she could still make things grow.

She could do that much.

"It's okay, Owen," she whispered. "Don't cry. I won't quit."

"Promise?" He sniffed.

"Promise," she said.

"I love you," her little brother said, wiping tears off his face with the back of his hand.

"I love you too." Persephone planted a kiss on his forehead.

Then she grabbed her gloves and made her way to Mrs. McCullacutty's house.

All the way there, she couldn't get Owen's words out of her head.

It's only growing because of you—if you stop, everything will be sad again. You'll be sad again.

Had working on Mrs. McCullacutty's garden truly changed something in her? Maybe they were growing *each other*. She started walking faster, and then jogging, determination forcing speed into her steps. She *had* to get back to work! The garden needed her, and she needed the garden. She wouldn't waste another minute.

But as she rounded the corner and Mrs. McCullacutty's house came into view, she heard someone whistling. The dirt wasn't in a pile in the middle of the yard like it was supposed to be. Persephone stumbled to a stop on the sidewalk, watching as Malachi emptied a wheelbarrow-load of rich black soil into one of the raised beds. He was sunburned, sweaty, and covered in dirt.

"Hey!" Malachi called, waving a gloved hand as he caught sight of Persephone. But she could only stand there on the sidewalk with her mouth open.

"You—you're here! And look at everything you've done!"

"Are you surprised?" Mal laughed, brushing dirt off his hands and wiping his face on his arm. He left a smear of dirt on his forehead and Persephone couldn't stop staring at it. "I hope that's okay." He suddenly looked a little uncertain.

"It's wonderful! *You're wonderful!*" Persephone forced her eyes somewhere besides Mal's face. Forced herself to ignore the butterflies that were tumbling and twirling around in her stomach. "But—why would you do all this?"

"Because I'm your friend, Persephone," Mal said, grinning. "And you needed help. And this is your garden—" He shrugged. "Well, I guess technically, it's Mrs. McCullacutty's garden. But it's growing for *you*. Come see."

Persephone hurried up the stairs into Mrs. McCullacutty's yard and followed her friend through the gate. Then she had to stop and catch her breath because *something* had happened to the garden while she was gone, only she didn't think it had anything to do with her ability to make things grow. This felt different. This felt like more. This felt like— like a *miracle*.

Over the course of the last several weeks, Persephone, and often Malachi too, had been working hard to tidy up the chaos time had wrought in the garden. They had cleared and cut away dead growth from the trees and shrubs, hedges, and vines. They trimmed and pruned the fruit trees, they unearthed garden beds, picked up and carefully piled stones where the wall had collapsed, and encouraged forgotten perennials back to life. They mowed and raked, tore out encroaching plants and weeds that threatened to choke the life out of more delicate plants, and made space for new plants that Persephone intended to add to the garden.

But in her absence, the garden had begun working its own miracles, adding to the effort she and Mal had made. Delicate green moss and lichen had crept over the broken places in the stone wall, covering over the crumbled spots. The fruit trees had suddenly decided pruning was exactly the sort of thing they needed and now burst with blooms— filling the air with apple- and pear- and plum-blossom perfume. Ferns threw massive, variegated green and gold fronds into the shade. Tiny white daisies bloomed in a carpet of yellow and gold across the grass, and at the very edge of the tree line, where sunlight and shade were in a constant dance with each other, slipper orchids had erupted into bloom.

Persephone turned in a slow circle, trying to take it all in as tears snuck out and ran down her cheeks. Those tears were for a lot of things, really—Owen's fall and a scar to prove it; Mrs. McCullacutty, who would soon be leaving; Mya, Joseph, Levi, and of course, Last Year's June. It was swimming laps, and a green cupboard full of plates and cups that echoed people's hearts; it was overdue bills, and the unexpected, undeserved, impossible kindness of friends; and this garden full of miracles . . .

"Are you crying?" Mal asked.

"No!" Persephone wiped the tears off her face with the back of her hand. "Well, *yes*." She laughed. "Thank you," she said at last, looking around the garden again, and then at her friend. "I don't know what else to say!"

"You're welcome," Mal said with a grin, "though all I did was shovel some dirt. I think something else is responsible for this garden." He threw an arm over her shoulders. And Persephone didn't care that Mal was sweaty and dirty. Or that his grandfather's bargain still hung over her. She threw both arms around him in an awkward, happy, fierce hug.

37

RUMORS AND TRUTHS

The following afternoon, Persephone hurried up the three stairs to Mrs. McCullacutty's house and knocked on the door. She carried a little jar of orchid food from Dr. Rathmason. The wind whipped her hair around as she stood on the porch, and she glanced nervously at the sky. The heat and humidity had been building for days. It felt like a storm was coming.

Once, twice, three times, Persephone knocked. The door finally swung open on its own, and Persephone stepped back as Blue sat primly in the entry like a gatekeeper.

"Oh, hello, Blue." Persephone felt the cool, quiet air of the house rush out around her. The house was being bossy again. "Is it okay if I visit? I brought food for her orchid."

"For you, girl, the door is always open," Blue seemed to say as she stood and twined around Persephone's ankles before leading her into the house.

They walked down the hall, past rooms full of strange and wonderful things, and stopped at the orchid on the window seat. It was barely alive now. Just a few leaves clung to drooping stems. Persephone stared at it, wishing she knew what was wrong. Wishing she knew how to fix it. But she didn't touch it, because Blue had made it clear she wasn't supposed to from the moment she'd first laid eyes on the impressive plant. Instead, Persephone shook the little jar of orchid food, unscrewed the lid, and emptied it onto the roots. And then, reaching out both hands, she closed her eyes, trying to hold the space around the plant, and invoke whatever growing powers she might have.

Grow. She spoke the word inside her head. *Please grow.*

Persephone opened her eyes. Nothing had changed. She didn't think it would, but she had hoped.

Blue sat on the floor, watching her with bright green eyes. Persephone dropped her hands and followed Blue down the hall.

She thought they would find Mrs. McCullacutty in her study, red geraniums in the window casting their rosy glow around the room. But they walked on, past the study. And then through the kitchen, toward the back of the house.

Persephone had never been here before. Blue led her down a short hall where doors opened into quiet rooms, decorated simply. They came to a door that led to a sitting room that seemed to double as a kind of dressing room.

It was a mess—like a windstorm had blown through, tossing clothing everywhere. Mrs. McCullacutty was hurrying around the room, almost frantic as she gathered up various articles of clothing—hats, scarves, broaches, a fur cape, even a tiara—and placed them into a trunk that sat near an open wardrobe. It was a giant old cupboard reaching almost to the ceiling, filled with even more clothes. *Beautiful* clothes. Fur coats, fabrics Persephone didn't have names for. Colors she could imagine only Mrs. McCullacutty wearing.

"Hello, dear," said Mrs. McCullacutty. She seemed as bright and cheerful as always, but on the outside, she reminded Persephone of a fading, wilting flower. It seemed like Mrs. McCullacutty and the house—or whatever magic lived inside of it—were in a disagreement of some sort, and the house was winning. Could houses make decisions for the people who lived in them? Could they boss you around? Persephone wasn't sure, but she had realized long ago that Mrs. McCullacutty's house was anything but ordinary.

"Come in," Mrs. McCullacutty said, gesturing Persephone farther into the spacious room. "I'm afraid I'm a bit too preoccupied for tea today. I simply must get these things packed."

"Do you want some help?" Persephone asked.

"Why, that would be lovely. Thank you!" She motioned to another trunk. "Would you mind helping me with that one? I need to put all these clothes in storage. The house likes to move things around sometimes, and I don't want to lose anything." Persephone nodded, amazed that she wasn't surprised by this. The little white shed did the same thing, after all. She ran a finger over a yellow silk evening gown that looked like it had been at the height of fashion in the 1940s. The fringe detail was exquisite.

"Where did all of these come from?" Persephone asked,

taking the yellow dress from the wardrobe and carefully folding it before placing it into the trunk.

"They came from—well—from everywhere, I suppose," said Mrs. McCullacutty. "Everett found some of them for me, in his many travels. I discovered some of them in various closets in this old house—perhaps from my mother's and grandmother's times here. Some of them I collected myself."

Blue jumped up on top of the trunk's open lid and watched Persephone.

"So," Mrs. McCullacutty began. "It's been some time since we've had a chance to visit! Tell me everything."

Persephone smiled, pulling another beautiful dress from the wardrobe. She told her about Joseph and the apology she'd written him, about Owen's fall and his new scar, about how Malachi had helped fill all the garden beds with dirt. Mrs. McCullacutty listened and nodded and smiled and clapped at all the right places. And when Persephone finished, Mrs. McCullacutty sighed deeply as though she'd just enjoyed a delicious meal. Then the old woman crossed the room and took Persephone's hands in both of hers, squeezing them gently.

"And now," she said, "tell me about the things you've *not* been telling me." Her voice had gone soft but strong as iron, and Persephone carefully pulled her hands from Mrs. McCullacutty's and stuffed them into her pockets.

"What do you mean?" Inside, though, her mind snagged on the gossip buzzing around Coulter. Someone had stood under one of Dad's ladders yesterday while he was out on a job and pestered him for several minutes for more information about "the famous TV show coming to town."

"I finally had to tell them I didn't have any information, and that I was just trying to fix this roof!" her dad had said, exasperated.

"People like to talk, you know," continued Mrs. McCullacutty lightly. "They have been talking for as long as I've been here, and that's a long time." She smiled. "But I heard rumors the other day about you and a certain television show." Mrs. McCullacutty paused. "I didn't think too much about it—I never put much stock in rumors, you know—until my neighbor Mr. Wilson mentioned the improvements being made to my garden. He too, he said, was making improvements on his own home—for the arrival of *Small Town Revival*. He seemed quite certain about everything. Said your family was keeping rather quiet about the matter, presumably out of concern for your brother Levi's privacy, but that an official notification had arrived a couple of weeks ago." Mrs. McCullacutty folded her hands in her lap. "Now, your business is your business, my dear," she said carefully. "But I too am a rather private person, and this"—she swept her arm around the room, encompassing the old white house, the garden, Blue, all of it—"this is rather precious to me. I've entrusted a measure of its care to you. But not for the purpose of exploitation."

Persephone gasped. It felt like the room had suddenly tilted, and she grabbed hold of a chair to keep from falling over. "I would *never do that* . . ." But she trailed off, the taste of the lie bitter in her mouth. Because she *had* been willing to use Mrs. McCullacutty's garden, and anything or anyone else that might make Coulter more appealing to the show's developers. But that had been *before*! She had emailed Rebecca Mathews and told her the truth! She had declined their offer and told them all no—as Levi had wanted. But the town didn't know that. And Mrs. McCullacutty didn't know that.

The old woman waited in silence.

And so, Persephone found a chair, sat down, and did what she should have done weeks ago: she began unraveling and unwinding her lies. She told Mrs. McCullacutty everything, starting with the moment she signed Levi's name to the application instead of her own. Blue climbed up into her lap and listened.

Mrs. McCullacutty listened too.

And the house listened.

And the garden listened as, finally, Persephone spoke the whole truth.

38

THE STORM

That night, the biggest storm of the summer rolled over Coulter with the force of a freight train. Persephone had felt it coming—building in the weight of late-July humidity, the stillness of Galion Lake in the mornings, and the buzz of cicadas in the tops of the Queens. The wind whipped trees in every direction, toppling them and throwing them against the ground, against rooftops, and into yards. Hail fell in sheets, skittering against windows in the dark. The sirens howled storm warnings from the top of the fire station, as they did when a tornado threatened.

People crept into their basements in the darkness as the power flickered in and out, in and out, and then out. Persephone's parents couldn't wheel Levi's bed into the basement, but they wheeled it out of his bedroom and into the hall, away from windows. They all huddled together there, listening to the wind and clutching flashlights like life preservers.

Around four a.m., the storm finally blew over and they all went to bed.

Owen was still scared, so Persephone crawled into the top bunk in his room where she could keep him company. But after her little brother fell asleep, she sat peering out his window into the night, trying to see if there were any trees lying down in their yard. It was still too dark to tell. All the streetlights were out and wouldn't come back on until the emergency crews and linemen got the power back on all over town.

Persephone watched the numbers on Owen's battery-powered clock change, one after the other, until they finally read 4:54 a.m. She couldn't sleep. She could hear the garden. It pulled at her from somewhere out there in the dark. She could picture the rock wall with its new layer of moss, the fruit trees, the vines and flowers, and the Queens, every-thing so alive and so much *more* than a garden should be. But somewhere inside of her, the garden was crying. She didn't know why, but she couldn't bear it.

The morning light was heavy and gray when Persephone finally got up and tiptoed back into her own room to find shorts and a T-shirt. She couldn't wait any longer. She left a note on the kitchen table so her parents would know where she was, and she slipped outside.

Proof of the wild night lay across people's yards like a rowdy party thrown by the weather. One house three blocks down had a tree across the roof. A few people were up and awake, like Persephone, out surveying the damage.

"Kind of a mess for a TV crew, eh, Persephone," called her neighbor Mr. Tellington.

"Yah," Persephone called. "It . . . it really is!" Persephone ducked her head and kept walking.

As she rounded the last block and the old white house came into view, she knew the feeling that had been growing in the pit of her stomach hadn't been for nothing. Because not one, but *two*, trees lay across Mrs. McCullacutty's yard. One had narrowly missed the house, catching the edge of the roof on its way down and pulling a few shingles with it. Persephone started running.

Not the Queens—Not the Queens—Not the Queens.

When she came to a stop in front of the garden, her heart rose into her throat. Not only had the Queens fallen, with their massive, spreading branches twisting and tearing in the wind and getting tangled on their way to the ground, but they had fallen on the garden as well. It was hard to tell how much damage had been done beneath them, but she could see at least two of the freshly filled garden beds had been destroyed.

The garden was weeping. She could hear it. It wailed the way she had cried *that day*, Last Year's June. Persephone fell to her knees and ran her hands through the grass, shaking, tears rolling down her face. She knew. *She knew* how it felt to lose someone irreplaceable. And there was no use trying to pretend something beautiful wasn't lost—that it didn't hurt. The Queens had stood guard here for a hundred years. Perhaps longer. They would be *grieved*.

"Mrs. McCullacutty!" Persephone breathed shakily.

She jumped to her feet and ran, racing through the yard, avoiding the tangle of far-reaching fallen branches, and up the porch steps. She knocked twice, loud and insistent. The door swung wide on quiet hinges, granting her permission to enter. But she just stood there and stared.

Mrs. McCullacutty was putting things away, or perhaps the house itself was—one oddity and piece of art at a time. Dust sheets covered the three carousel horses and many of the pieces of art that adorned the foyer wall. Only a few faces of the people dressed in blue stared down at her now. A giant sheet hung over the mirror as well, and her voice was full of echoes as she called down the hall.

"Hello? Mrs. McCullacutty?" *Silence.* "Hello?" She called again, fear rising. But after a moment the familiar figure of a small gray cat emerged. Persephone knelt in relief as Blue padded toward her on silent feet, and then a moment later, Mrs. McCullacutty herself appeared. She was dressed in a beautiful purple silk skirt paired with a silk lavender blouse, several strings of pearls draped around her neck, and some of her age seemed to have fallen away—as if age were a thing that came and went depending on the day. Perhaps whatever filled the walls and rafters—the bones of this strange old house, whatever had leaked out into the garden—had crept into Mrs. McCullacutty too. And perhaps they had settled things— Mrs. McCullacutty and her old white house. Because, despite the storm that had raged outside, inside it felt peaceful.

"Good morning, Persephone!" Mrs. McCullacutty said.

"Are you all right? It's rather early. Did you come through the storm okay?" Persephone stood up, Blue in her arms, and stared wordlessly at Mrs. McCullacutty.

"You look—" Persephone searched for the words. *"Beautiful,"* she breathed at last. Mrs. McCullacutty laughed.

"Thank you, dear," she said. "The house does what it likes with those who live and belong here." She reached out and patted a wall affectionately. "Blue and I just try to keep up."

"The Queens—" Persephone said abruptly. "The garden—" Her voice caught on tears that were rising again.

Mrs. McCullacutty nodded slowly, her face falling. Those exquisite ancient trees.

"I am so sorry, my dear," she said, squeezing Persephone's hand gently. "I was afraid something like this might happen. Come," she said. "Will you have some tea? We should talk."

The study was cool and quiet as Persephone and Mrs. McCullacutty settled into the old wingback chairs, teacups in hand. The green cupboard had offered Persephone a set of matching cups covered in white-and-yellow narcissus blooms. *Her* flowers—the token blooms of the Greek goddess she was named after. Perhaps the house was offering a little comfort in its own way.

Persephone tried to hold her teacup steady, but all she could see was the broken frames of the garden beds, and the twisted trunks of the mighty silver maples—the crush of branches everywhere.

"It appears the house is getting rather loud," Mrs.

McCullacutty said, studying the delicate narcissus blooms painted on her teacup.

Persephone listened, but compared to the sound of the garden crying, the house seemed quiet to her.

"After all of your truths yesterday, I think it has decided to help."

"What do you mean?" Persephone set her teacup down and clasped her hands in her lap. Mrs. McCullacutty was doing that thing she did sometimes—saying illogical things in a logical voice. It always made Persephone feel like she needed to unravel hidden meanings, but she could never quite do it. This morning it made her feel like screaming.

"Sometimes people need a nudge before they can begin really moving in the right direction. Towns too." Mrs. McCullacutty sipped her tea. That reminded Persephone of what Malachi's grandfather had said the first time she met him.

"In the end," he had said, "bodies, plants, everything, really, have to grow in the right direction on their own."

"But you planted those beautiful old trees," Persephone said, still wondering how that was even possible. "Aren't you *sad*? The *garden* is sad, I can hear it!"

"Sad?" Mrs. McCullacutty thought for a moment and then nodded. "Yes, of course. But I'm also curious. The house likes you. And the garden has become something else entirely since you arrived. It's not strange to think the house wouldn't offer up a little help when it comes to your garden."

"*My* garden?" Persephone leaned back in her chair.

"I think at this point, the house and the garden would both agree that it belongs to you more than it does to me," Mrs. McCullacutty said gently. "Perhaps even more than it belonged to my mother or my grandmother." Persephone felt the weight of the woman's words like a warm hand on her back.

"But how is it helpful for the Queens to have been blown down?" Persephone didn't understand.

"I'm not quite sure yet," Mrs. McCullacutty said. "We never really see how the ruination of something could possibly result in growth." She smiled. "At least, not until we can look back and see what changed because of the mess."

Persephone left Mrs. McCullacutty's house a while later, feeling a little better. Her words had helped, but nothing could entirely ease the ache Persephone felt in her chest. Explanations and reasons never seemed to ease heartache, no matter how much she wanted them to.

But the garden had quieted too, and as she stood on the front step, she could hear the town abuzz with the sound of voices and chain saws as neighbors and friends began helping one another clean up the damage the storm had left behind.

The Queens would have to be removed as well; they couldn't lay as they were—stretched and sprawling and broken across the garden. The thought made Persephone want to start crying again.

And that was when she heard a chain saw buzzing

from somewhere behind the house. Someone was *already* helping. She broke into a jog and rounded the side of the house before stumbling to a halt.

He stood over one of the trees, his foot against the trunk to steady himself. One of the Queens had already been neatly trimmed of limbs and branches while Persephone was inside talking with Mrs. McCullacutty. He had made clean cuts and tidy piles of branches and debris. Such small changes had already begun to restore order to the chaos.

The noise of the chain saw completely drowned out the sound of Persephone's approach, and she stood there for a minute watching as he efficiently began cutting the big old maple trees into slices.

Finally, Persephone stepped into his line of sight, and he paused, smiling a little ruefully. He turned off the chain saw. The silence was unbearable.

Persephone's heart pounded so loud her ears rang.

He wiped his face on his shirtsleeve.

"Hello, Joseph," she said.

39

JOSEPH

"I got your letter." Joseph sat beside Persephone on one of the tree trunks. He'd put his chain saw away and pulled out a water bottle.

Persephone fidgeted with a small branch, slowly stripping the bark away with her thumbnail.

"I meant every word." She hadn't seen him since the Fourth of July, and she honestly wasn't sure he'd ever want to see her again. "I really am sorry."

"I know," he said. "This whole thing sucks."

"Yes." Persephone nodded. "But it doesn't mean I should keep running away. From the truth. Just like you said."

"You aren't running now." Joseph nudged her with his shoulder, and she smiled half-heartedly. There was still so much he didn't know. Still so much neither of them knew. It wasn't the first time she wished the truth would just come out and spread as fast as her lies had.

"So, are you sure you want me to tell you?" Joseph took

a long drink of water, not looking at her. Almost like he was afraid. She had told him, in her letter, that she wanted to hear what had happened. The truth, from him. And the truth about their fight the night before the accident—because she hadn't wanted the truth before, she'd just wanted to feel better. Even if that meant blaming someone who was innocent. But Joseph's words mattered. She understood that now. She was ready to hear his truth.

"If it's not too hard for you to tell me," she said quietly.

"I think it'll probably always be hard, Persephone." He glanced at her and then down at his feet. "But I'm ready to talk about it if you are."

And so, he told her. About their plan to go fishing. About the warmth of the day and how the fish weren't biting. About how they'd decided to go swimming instead. It wasn't unusual or different from any other afternoon. They had done all the same things dozens of times before, a dozen summers before.

"We did fight that night—like you saw," Joseph began hesitantly. Persephone nodded, remembering the way Joseph's shoulders had slumped before he got into his car that night and slammed the door. She also remembered knocking on her brother's door and the sound of his voice, muffled and broken on the other side. *"Leave me alone, Persephone."*

"But everything that happened after had nothing to do with our conversation that night." Joseph scrubbed his hands over his face. "I'll never regret being honest with him that night, but I hate that things didn't go the way I'd hoped. I hate that we argued." He stared at his feet. "Anyway, I'm not going to tell you exactly what we fought about, Pip. That's between Levi and me. But you have to trust me. I loved Levi. I still do. And I'd never do anything to hurt him."

Persephone chewed on her lip.

"So, you weren't still mad at each other?"

Joseph sighed and shook his head. "I mean, things were a little awkward, maybe. But mad? No."

"Then what—what happened?" *How did my brother—my excellent-swimmer-lifeguard brother—end up in the lake that morning?* The accusation disguised as a question was loud inside of her. But she had told Joseph she would listen to his truth. And so she did.

"The water was perfect," Joseph said, remembering. "Still as glass, and the sun was so hot. We put away our fishing poles—nothing was biting anyway, and Levi balanced on the edge of the boat before doing that one flip he always did. That *stupid* flip." Joseph closed his eyes and Persephone sat up a little straighter, feeling her heart squeeze. She could see it in her mind. A perfect arc, hands tucked behind his knees, water spraying out of his hair as his body spun in midair before he hit the water. It was beautiful. Joseph opened his eyes and took another long drink of water before continuing, his voice a little shaky, and Persephone clenched her hands in her lap.

"We didn't know the boat would rebound after he jumped. But his jump rocked it just enough so that it rocked back and hit him in the back of the head as he went into the water." Joseph rubbed his head as if feeling the impact himself. "I knew it was bad right away. I just didn't know *how* bad. But then he didn't kick up for air like he should have. He just slowly bobbed to the surface. So I went in after him."

Persephone didn't realize she'd been holding her breath, but she released it now in a kind of gasp that sounded more like a sob.

"He was so heavy," Joseph said, his voice low. "I couldn't get him back in the boat. I couldn't do CPR in the water. I couldn't do anything except try to keep his face out of the water and scream for help."

Joseph's voice cracked and he swallowed.

Persephone wiped away tears.

"I'm not even sure how long we were out there before that other boat arrived and called for help. When we got up onto that little fishing boat, I started CPR right away." Joseph scrubbed his face over his hands. "But we'd been out there for a long time. I—I tried. But his injury was bad and he'd been without oxygen for a while. Then the paramedics showed up and they tried. But it was too late."

Persephone couldn't stop crying. Joseph stared at his feet, wiping away his own tears with the back of his hand.

They were both silent for a while, and then Persephone took a deep breath.

"I believe you," she said finally. She knew he had tried. Maybe she had always known, deep down. But it had been easier to be angry. "And I—I'm sorry, Joseph. I wish I could go back and fix it. Everything. This whole last year."

Joseph nodded. "Me too," he said. "What would you tell yourself if you could go back?"

It was an interesting question. She'd expected him to ask what she'd *do*, but this was different. She thought about it for a minute.

"I guess I would tell myself to love better. To tell the truth. To *believe* the truth. To be a good friend . . ."

"Sounds like you'd give yourself some good advice." Joseph nodded. "Maybe you should write a letter to your past self."

"My past self?" Persephone frowned. It seemed like such a strange idea.

"No, for real!" Joseph was earnest. "One of the therapists I saw after Levi's accident gave me that assignment. She told me it was better to imagine offering myself some kind words that might help me let go of the things I couldn't change, rather than imagining what I would do differently."

She stared at Joseph, and he shrugged. He had struggled this past year. Just as much as she had. Even if their pain was different.

"I get to decide how this changes me," Joseph said. "It's my choice. Yours too, if you want. It doesn't seem to matter who we are, you know? One way or another, life is going to hurt. But we get to decide what to do with it. At least, that's what my therapist says." His words reminded her of what Mrs. McCullacutty had said about Levi, the night of her birthday party. *We never get to choose when we say goodbye, do we? Only how.*

"Thank you, Joseph," Persephone said finally.

"You're welcome," he said.

"No—I *mean* . . ." She searched for words. *Thank you*

didn't seem like enough. "Thanks for not giving up on me. For not *hating* me." A lump rose in the back of her throat, and Persephone swallowed hard.

"I did hate you for a little while," Joseph said.

"Do you still hate me now?" She needed to know.

"No." Joseph shook his head.

"Why not?" She looked up, waiting for the truth.

"Because hating you didn't help me, or Levi, or anyone. It just made a bigger mess out of what was already broken, and I don't want that. Besides, you're my best friend's little sister. What kind of person does that make me, if I walk around hating the people he loved?"

Joseph wrapped an arm around Persephone's shoulders and glanced up at the big white house. "We get to be angry at each other for hard stuff. You know? We get to make mistakes. But we can't stay that way. Or nothing will ever change."

Persephone knew he was right. And she was certainly ready for change.

Persephone thought about Joseph's words all the way home. He'd told her the truth. And the truth had a way of changing things. Maybe she could be brave enough to let it change her too.

Mya had known the truth all along—Joseph was innocent. She'd believed it. She'd refused to leave, even when Persephone had given her every reason to quit showing up. She had chosen to be her friend, over and over.

Persephone stopped on the sidewalk two blocks from home.

There was somewhere else she needed to go first.

Mya was mowing the lawn—one even row after another across her front yard—but she took one look at Persephone walking down the sidewalk and brought the mower to a halt.

"Hi," Persephone said, her voice a little shaky in the sudden quiet.

"Hi." Mya wiped her forehead on her shirtsleeve, her face full of questions. "What—what's up?" It was the first time Persephone had shown up in over a year. Mya had every right to be a little confused.

"I needed to talk to you." Persephone shifted nervously. "About . . . everything."

"Oh." Mya's eyebrows rose. "Wow. Um, okay. That sounds like a long conversation." She offered a hesitant smile. "Maybe we need some lemonade?" Persephone blinked back tears and tried to smile too.

"Yeah." She nodded. "We probably do."

The girls sat in the shade, sipping tall glasses of lemonade under the birch trees in the front yard, and they talked. Persephone told her about the letter she'd sent to Joseph and all the truths he had shared. The truth she was finally ready to believe.

"I'm sorry," she finally breathed through tears. "I'm so sorry, Mya. I've been mean and unfair and a terrible friend and you didn't give up on me even when you totally should have." She wiped tears off her face with the back of her hand. "This whole year has been awful. And it's still awful. But I made it worse for both of us. And I know I don't deserve to have a friend like you, but . . ." Persephone took a deep breath and her words came out as little more than a whisper. "Do you think you can forgive me?" She cleared her throat and spoke louder. "Maybe let me try again?" She sniffed and looked up into Mya's tear-filled eyes. She had also started crying at some point while Persephone was talking, but now she beamed through her tears.

"You have no idea how long I've waited to hear you say that," Mya said, brushing away tears. "*Of course* I forgive you. And of course we can be friends." She laughed, and sniffed, and threw her arms around Persephone. "I've missed you like crazy."

And Persephone hugged her back, laughing and crying all at the same time.

"Thank you," she whispered. "I've missed you too."

40

PRESERVED

Malachi and Mya showed up in Mrs. McCullacutty's garden the next evening and helped Persephone and Joseph clean up as much of the damage the storm had left as they could. By the time they finished, all that remained was a pile of logs, and the stumps of the Queens where their trunks used to stand. Persephone, Malachi, Joseph, and Mya crouched around the stumps and tried to count the rings, but they kept losing track around one hundred and thirty.

As the four friends returned the shovels and wheelbarrow to the little white shed, the can of lifeguard-chair-red paint seemed to issue an invitation. Persephone had left it on a shelf out of the way, meaning to take it home. But she had forgotten. The shed had not, of course, and the paint had moved to a more prominent place beside the door, as if it were eager to leave. Eager to be used. And instead of just one paintbrush, now there were four.

Persephone emerged from the shed with the can of

paint in one hand, and the four paintbrushes in the other. She held them up, and her friends looked at her, curious.

"Do you want to help me do one more thing?" she asked.

Persephone hadn't gone near the lifeguard chair since Last Year's June—since Levi last sat in it. It stood like a sentinel on the beach; keeping watch over the empty swimming area as the sun began to descend toward the western edge of Galion Lake.

How many afternoons had Levi spent in that chair? How many lives had he guarded? How many had he saved? She had no idea. Sometimes he had let her climb up and sit beside him for a little while if the beach wasn't too busy. She had loved the way even a few extra feet of height had offered a better view.

Persephone rested a hand on the first rung of the ladder. A lump formed in her throat.

She began to climb.

Past lifeguards had carved their names into the edge of the wood seat. It was a privilege and tradition, Levi had explained.

Persephone sat down and traced her brother's name with a trembling finger. He'd carved it there Last Year's June. He'd carved it knowing it would be his last summer guarding because he was going to school. None of them ever could have guessed it would be Levi's last summer guarding for other reasons. Persephone wiped tears off her cheeks and made her way back down the ladder to where her friends waited.

Are you okay? Mya didn't voice the question, but she didn't have to. Persephone could see it all over her face. She nodded, and Malachi handed out the paintbrushes.

The chair had been painted and repainted many times. But no matter how many coats of paint had been added to help preserve the chair, every lifeguard who sat there made sure the names remained, re-carving the painted-over marks, lending them a kind of permeance that couldn't be worn away by weather or time, or covered up by paint. Whoever guarded here next would get to go back over all the names. Including Levi's.

Nothing is being erased, Persephone told herself as she climbed the ladder again and began painting. The bright red paint would preserve the chair and the names etched deep in the wood. Despite knowing that, it wasn't easy to smooth the fresh coat of paint over her brother's name. Mal and Mya and Joseph solemnly dipped their own paintbrushes into the red paint, and together the four of them worked to revive something beautiful.

Not a whole town, Persephone thought to herself. *But the memory of a whole life.* And maybe that was better. Levi would have loved it.

When they finished, Persephone wrapped her arms around Joseph and Mya and Malachi. And the four of them stood in silence, speckled with red paint, watching the sun set over Galion Lake.

41

SURPRISES

"Hello, Persephone," Mrs. Howard said, emphasizing her words and offering a small smile as Persephone walked through the post office door the following morning. The woman seemed almost nervous, fidgeting as she stood behind the counter. "Is there *anything* I can help you with?" Persephone shook her head and held up her mail key.

"Just here to get the mail," she said.

"Right. Very well." Mrs. Howard nodded and then disappeared into the back room. Almost as if she was avoiding Persephone.

And she should, Persephone thought a little bitterly. *She's caused me a whole lot of trouble with her gossip.* Someone had stopped her mother at the grocery store yesterday and asked her for details about the film crew's arrival. Her mother had told her there weren't any film crews coming to Coulter, and that Persephone had simply sent some information to the show *Small Town Revival*.

"I had to ask the woman to please stop spreading rumors, and she got a little upset with me!" her mother had said, unpacking groceries in the kitchen. "It was almost like she had already made up her mind about what was true, and nothing I said mattered!" Her mother had turned to Persephone. "This is not okay. We need to come up with a way to make people understand." Persephone had nodded, guilt swirling in the pit of her stomach. Her mother didn't even know the whole truth about *Small Town Revival*. She didn't see why she needed to tell her now, since she had already fixed things and sent that email to Rebecca Mathews. But rumors had twisted into ideas people had chosen to believe—true or not—and Persephone didn't know how to make people believe something they didn't want to believe. There were two envelopes waiting inside the post office box, but none of them were stamped with any condemning red letters today. Persephone shoved them in her backpack and her mother opened them later with her usual resignation when Persephone got home.

She stood at the kitchen counter and pulled the first bill from the envelope, and then uttered a sudden little cry. Persephone whirled from where she was standing at the sink and watched as her mom dropped the open bill onto the kitchen counter and tore open the next envelope. She made another strangled little sound, and clapped a hand over her mouth.

"*What?* What is it?" Persephone ran to her mother as tears began to slide down Mom's face. With shaking fingers, Persephone snatched the bill off the counter. The number listed at the bottom was impossibly large. But even more impossible were the letters stamped in red at the bottom.

PAID IN FULL

Persephone felt her mouth fall open and she stared at her mom, who was just standing there, tears streaming, her shoulders shaking with quiet sobs.

"What does this mean?" Persephone asked, taking the other bill from her mom's hands and finding another PAID IN FULL stamped in red across another impossibly large amount. "Is it paid? Did *we* pay it?" Persephone searched her mother's face as she slowly shook her head.

"No," she said tearfully. "We didn't pay it. But someone did." She flipped the bill over, searching for clues as to where this miracle had come from, and then she pulled her phone out of her pocket. "I have to tell your dad. Maybe he knows something more."

But Persephone didn't wait to hear what her dad had to say. She was pretty sure she already knew who was behind this. She could think of only one person who might have the kind of money required to pay off such large bills, and she tore out of the house, down the sidewalk through town, and up the three cement stairs through Mrs. McCullacutty's front yard.

The air was heavy with the smell of freshly cut wood and new earth. The stumps and roots of the Queens had been pulled up by a little yellow skid loader from Dupree Excavating and Landscaping. The tear in the garden had been covered over and smoothed down, black dirt spread evenly over the bare patch. And now the vacant space they left behind was the only proof that the beautiful old trees ever stood there.

The front door swung open almost the same moment Persephone knocked, and Mrs. McCullacutty stood in the quiet foyer dressed in a forest-green pantsuit and soft brown sweater. Persephone threw her arms around her in a tight hug.

"Thank you, thank you, *thank you*," she whispered.

"Why, whatever for, dear?" Mrs. McCullacutty squeezed her back.

"For paying those bills!" Persephone said, pulling away, waiting for the look of understanding on Mrs. McCullacutty's face. "Medical bills," she continued. "A couple of the really big ones. We got notices in the mail today that said they'd been paid in full." Mrs. McCullacutty just shook her head.

"I'm so honored that you would think of me, but I am not the one paying those outstanding debts on behalf of your family, Persephone."

"Really?" Persephone blinked. "Well, then who is?"

Mrs. McCullacutty just smiled. "Perhaps whoever it is wishes to remain anonymous for the time being? I am certain everything will be made clear in due time." She squeezed Persephone's shoulder. "Everything blooms when it's ready, dear—even answers to perplexing questions." She paused and then held open the door and extended an arm. "And that reminds me . . . there is something I need to show you." Persephone searched her face at the note of sadness that filled Mrs. McCullacutty's voice. She followed her inside the big old white house that seemed to be quieter and quieter every time Persephone visited.

All the pictures on the walls, all the furniture, all of the oddities that filled the house had been draped in dust sheets. A hush had fallen over everything. The air was cool and quiet, and Persephone stared into each room they passed as they walked down the hall, something in her chest grow-ing heavier and heavier. *Mrs. McCullacutty was really leaving.* Even the house knew it. Maybe the house had told her to go. And even though Persephone had helped her pack up all those beautiful clothes, part of her hadn't truly believed it.

Until now.

She reached out and took hold of Mrs. McCullacutty's wrinkled hand. The old woman squeezed it gently, her face sad.

And then, Persephone saw it.

The orchid sat in its usual place on the window seat, evening light throwing long shadows where leaves *used* to hang. Because every leaf had dropped. A few of them lay shriveled and dry on the window seat beside the terrarium. Even the stems had shriveled.

It was dead.

Unmistakably.

Unchangeably.

Despite her best efforts.

"No!" She clenched and unclenched her fists. "No—" Her voice cracked on the word. She picked up one of the orchid's dried and shriveled leaves and it practically fell apart in her hands. Mrs. McCullacutty sat down on the window seat and wrapped an arm around Persephone.

It seemed silly to cry over the plant. It was just a plant, after all. But Persephone had *hoped*—she had tried so hard.

"There, there—shh," Mrs. McCullacutty said. "It's all right, dear."

"But I did everything right," Persephone sobbed. "I can make things grow! It's the one thing I haven't messed up, or lied about, or ruined!" But the lifeless plant sitting in the sleeping house felt like proof—even that had not been enough.

"*Meow.*"

Blue appeared, the way she did, without warning and without fanfare, wrapping herself around Persephone's ankles before leaping up onto her lap.

"*Meow,*" she said again. Persephone ran her hands through her soft fur as the cat purred. And gradually Persephone's tears stopped.

Blue suddenly hopped down from Persephone's lap.

"Where are you going?" Persephone asked.

"She has something to show you too," Mrs. McCullacutty said, her eyes sparkling now. "And her surprise is far more delightful than mine."

Blue stopped in the hallway and looked back.

"*Come see,*" she said with those bright green eyes.

And so Persephone did.

Blue led them into the study. The house was still awake in this room. The evening light was warm and alive, igniting the red geraniums on the windowsill. Red-gold light threw itself across the wingback chair and the rug. Across the bookshelf and the desk. Across a black-and-white photograph of a girl and a boy—smiles wide and bright. Jane and Terrance, *friends.*

"*Meow.*" Blue jumped up on the window ledge, a dainty acrobat among the geraniums, and almost disappeared into the flowers.

Persephone stepped closer and peered into the shelter of red flowers and pink buds and green leaves. And there— *the most wondrous thing*—three kittens, smaller than her fist. Two tabbies, and a gray, just like Blue.

"Ohhhh!" Persephone crooned, getting down on her knees and peering at them between the flower stems. Mrs. McCullacutty came to stand beside her, her face alight.

"Look what you made, Blue!" Persephone whispered. "They're wonderful!" Blue purred and then settled in among her babies, curling her body around them and tucking them between her paws.

Persephone knelt for several long moments, watching in amazement as Blue fed them and licked their tiny ears— still folded over and curled like the edges of a flower petal. Then she stroked the top of Blue's head one last time and stood up.

"I have to go home," she said to Mrs. McCullacutty. "But is it all right if I come back tomorrow?"

"Yes, of course, dear," Mrs. McCullacutty said. "Blue will expect it."

"*See you later, darling girl,*" Blue said with her bright green eyes.

Mrs. McCullacutty walked back down the hall with Persephone, opening the door to see her out, and then she gasped, her hand flying to her heart as she beheld none other than Dr. Terrance Rathmason standing on the porch. The porch seemed larger somehow, as if the house wanted him there and had made extra room for him while he waited.

Both Persephone and Mrs. McCullacutty stared at him.

There was something about the way he carried himself. Like he had lived his life with twice as much intensity as regular people. Perhaps because he had never been allowed to live in any other way. But as he stood there on the porch, his face softened.

He smiled at Persephone and nodded. And then he smiled at Mrs. McCullacutty, and his eyes went soft.

"Hello, old friend," he said.

"You came back," she whispered.

"And you asked me to." He reached out and squeezed her hand.

Mrs. McCullacutty's words rang in Persephone's head as loudly as if the house itself had shouted them down the hall and out into the garden.

Everything blooms when it's ready.

42

FRIEND

Persephone closed the front door behind her, smiling to herself as she left Mrs. McCullacutty and Dr. Rathmason in the quiet house. Part of her wanted to stand there on the porch, pressing her ear against the door—listening to what they might be saying. What sort of words did you give someone you once loved after so much had happened—after so much hurt, time, heartache, and hope? She wished she knew. Especially when she found Malachi waiting for her in the garden, a strange look on his face, his hands shoved deep in his pockets.

"Hello," she said. But it felt like a question. "Is everything okay?" Her heart began to pound.

"I just learned some really interesting information about a *friend* of mine," Mal said, his voice tight. And the way he said *friend* made Persephone's stomach flip-flop, but not in a nice way. "I walked over here with Gramps tonight, because I figured you'd be here, and I wanted to say hello."

He marched down the sidewalk. Persephone could feel it coming. Like a storm she had made herself. She held up her hands, stumbling down the stairs to meet him, wanting to speak, to explain, but Malachi wouldn't let her.

"Gramps told me about your little *bargain*." He choked on the word. "He was teasing me about liking you." His face went red, and Persephone felt sick. "Gramps said it was *fortuitous* you agreed to hang out with me—to befriend me—in exchange for his help with that orchid. *That* was interesting—suddenly realizing that this friend of mine, this girl I've been hanging out with all summer, was a *liar*."

He almost spat the word, his breath hot against Persephone's face. Something in her heart cracked.

"I mean, I knew you lied about stuff," Mal said, his voice hitching, "but I thought you trusted *me*, because you told me about your lies, your secrets, your big plans. Or at least I thought you did. Turned out you lied about that too! I don't know why I ever thought you'd tell me the whole truth when you weren't willing to tell anyone else!" He laughed, the sound bitter and broken.

Persephone had never seen Malachi angry before. She'd seen him happy and silly, tired, nervous, worried, and scared, but never angry. *Sometimes, anger is just sadness wearing a suit of armor.* The words flickered in the back of her mind. *Hurt.* Mal was hurt. She'd known he would be. But it hadn't kept her from lying to him.

"Your grandfather asked me to hang out with you," Persephone hurried, frantic to explain. "But, Mal, we were *already* becoming friends! I would have spent all summer with you anyway because I *wanted* to hang out with you! Not because your grandfather asked me to!"

Truth.

"I wanted to be your friend! I was just afraid, at first— that if I was friends with anyone again, something bad might happen."

Truth.

"I'm so sorry I didn't tell you—"

Big *truth.*

"I really, really—"

"Just stop." Mal shook his head and ran his hands over his hair. "I don't believe a word you say." The words felt like a gut punch.

Her mountain of lies was crumbling under her. And she was crumbling with it.

How do you make someone believe something when they've already decided not to? Persephone heaved a sob as Mal turned and walked away, his shoulders slumped, and his hands anchored in his pockets like he might never take them out again.

43

EXPLAINING HERSELF

There was a strange car parked in the driveway when Persephone finally stumbled home, her eyes red from crying. She didn't think things could get any worse, but she was wrong. So very wrong.

Both of her parents and the mayor of Coulter were waiting in the living room as she came inside. The printed copy of an email lay open across Mayor Hattie's lap, Epiphany TV's logo printed at the bottom. Persephone stood in the living room, and the weight of every lie she'd told, and told again, all summer long, felt impossibly heavy. She couldn't breathe.

"Persephone—" Dad cleared his throat, like he was trying to keep his emotions in check. "Mayor Hattie stopped by tonight with the most *interesting* email."

"Come and sit down, Persephone," her mother said. Her face was tired.

Persephone's legs shook. It took everything she had not

to turn around and run right back out the front door and as far away as she could get.

But she was too tired to run anymore. And all the running away she'd already done hadn't fixed a single thing. Joseph was right. So, she squared her shoulders. And walked slowly into the room and sat down across from her parents. The mayor said nothing. She simply handed Persephone the printed email to read.

Dear Mayor Carter,

Your information was provided to me by Levi Clark, who recently submitted your town, Coulter, Wisconsin, as a possible candidate to our show, Small Town Revival. *We were delighted to accept, and a formal letter was sent via post notifying Mr. Clark. I then followed up with an email, but I recently received the most peculiar response from his alleged little sister informing me of Mr. Clark's unfortunate accident.*

Miss Clark explained that she had submitted the application on her brother's behalf and forged his name. She then acknowledged the error of her decision and declined our offer.

I have copied her email below.

I am a little confused by this turn of events, and

I'm concerned that there has been a lapse in communication. If what Persephone said is true, then I am deeply sorry for Mr. Clark's unfortunate circumstances, and we will pursue other options for the show.

But I felt it necessary to reach out to you for confirmation before we proceeded, being that the circumstances are so unusual, Miss Clark is a minor, and we are already this far along in the process. Please advise.

> *Best regards,*
> *Rebecca Mathews*
> *Production Lead*
> *Small Town Revival*
> *Epiphany Television Inc.*

The room was silent as Persephone read and then reread the email. She could hear the clock on the wall *tick-tick-tick*ing away the seconds. Finally, she looked up.

"Persephone," Dad said, "do you understand what that email is saying?" He was keeping very careful control over his voice.

Persephone gathered her thoughts together like a handful of tiny seeds. Truth seeds. She chose the best one and spoke it into life.

"Yes," she whispered.

"So this is true?!"

She nodded, but barely. "I'm so sorry." As the words left her mouth, they grew, filling the room, expanding and expanding and expanding until she felt them press against her. Against the walls. Against her parents and the mayor.

"So you lied," said Mom, acknowledging the truth. Her hands were clasped tightly in her lap, but now she unfolded them. And like a balloon deflating, Persephone's own words shrank and shrank and shrank, until they were just words again, no longer holding her prisoner. She was free. Free to tell the truth.

"I only wanted to help." Persephone took a deep, shuddering breath and started at the beginning. "I wanted to help Levi. And you guys." She looked at her parents. "And Coulter." She looked at Mayor Hattie. "*Small Town Revival* seemed like a really good way to do that. One hundred thousand dollars is a lot of money. I know about those treatments for people who have brain trauma. I've heard you talking. And there are so many hospital bills—I know because I bring them home from the post office almost every single day." And even now, though someone was mysteriously helping her family pay for them, that didn't stop new bills from coming.

Persephone's dad slumped in his chair, staring at his soot-stained hands.

"But we *believed* you, Persephone!" Mom said. "I believed you when you said you had sent in that application *but hadn't heard back*. We talked about this! And you lied right to my face! What did you think—that this would all just disappear if you changed your mind?

"Persephone, you let everyone believe something that wasn't true! Our friends and neighbors—people are convinced that a national television show is coming to Coulter because you lied! I don't—" Her mother sat back against the couch, her words suddenly failing. "I don't even know what to say anymore!"

Persephone began to cry. Again. Her mother was right, of course. She had hoped to fix things by writing her brother's name in her own handwriting at the bottom of that application letter. But instead, she had let things go way too far and ruined everything, and she had used Levi's name to do it. She felt like she might throw up.

Her mother stood up, pacing back and forth across the room. Then she stopped and looked at Persephone for a moment before shaking her head.

"I can't," she said, to Persephone, to Dad, to the living room ceiling. "I need some air."

And then she walked out of the room. Persephone heard the front door close behind her as her mother stepped outside. She stared at the empty place on the couch where her mother had been sitting a minute ago.

Persephone couldn't breathe.

Her mother had never done that before.

She had never just *left*. She always stayed. Always fixed things.

But not this time. This time it was too much.

Silence filled the room for several long moments.

"Will you send a response to Rebecca Mathews?" Dad asked finally, turning to Mayor Hattie. "Regardless of the money involved, we do not wish to subject our family or our community to the media or the entertainment industry. Levi made that decision before the accident, and we will honor it now."

"You're certain?" Mayor Hattie asked.

Dad nodded.

Persephone nodded.

"Very well," the mayor agreed, but she seemed reluctant, and Persephone realized that even Mayor Hattie had wanted something more for Coulter. *Small Town Revival* had felt like the perfect kind of more.

Persephone studied her hands, clutched in her lap. She had a bit of garden dirt under her fingernails, and callouses across her palms that had never been there before. Proof that her work in the garden was changing things—changing her. But were they good changes? She didn't know anymore.

44

LETTERS AND MIRACLES

Persephone's lies tumbled around and around in her mind all night, the faces of her family and friends fading in and out of focus, each of them angry, betrayed, hurt. She dreamed she climbed the water tower again to rescue Blue, but when she finally got to the top, Levi was at the top instead of Mrs. McCullacutty's small gray cat. And her brother refused to climb back down with her.

When she finally woke, her blankets and sheets were tangled around her like she'd been trying to swim laps all night; the sky was just turning gray outside her bedroom window. She lay there for a few moments as an idea began to tug at the corners of her heart. A simple, honest, rumor-shattering idea.

She sat up, rolling it around and around in her mind, and then she got up and pulled a sheet of paper from her desk drawer. She had no idea how to fix the mess she'd made, but she knew how to say sorry.

Maybe, like Malachi, no one would believe her. Maybe they would be mad—too hurt to listen. But maybe, she could keep trying. She could keep showing up anyway.

She began to write.

When the sun began to throw light across her bedroom floor, Persephone signed her very own name to the bottom of the page, set down her pencil, and read what she had written.

It wasn't perfect. It might even be a little dangerous, and foolish, and brave. But it was the best she could do. And while she couldn't read it out loud—*personally*—to every one of Coulter's 523 residents—for now, she could do this.

But she couldn't do it alone.

Mrs. Howard was standing behind the postal counter sorting through mail when Persephone opened the door and stepped into the cool post office. Even the bell seemed to jingle a little more sleepily with her early arrival.

"Why, good *morning*, Persephone," Mrs. Howard said. "You're here early. You're my *first* visitor this morning."

"Good morning," Persephone said, shifting nervously from foot to foot.

"What I can help you with, dear?" she asked. Persephone hadn't wanted to ask Mrs. Howard for her help. She wasn't sure she could trust her. But Persephone knew she hadn't been trustworthy either. And she needed Mrs. Howard. There was no one who understood how to send a letter better than she did. And Persephone needed to send *a lot* of them.

"Actually, yes. There is," Persephone said. "I need some

help sending a letter." She fished the letter she had written from her pocket, smoothed out the creases, and handed it to Mrs. Howard.

"For me?" Mrs. Howard adjusted her glasses.

"Well, yes." Persephone nodded. "For you, and for all of Coulter, actually." Mrs. Howard raised her eyebrows, situated herself on a stool behind the postal counter, and for the next several minutes, she carefully read the words Persephone had painstakingly poured out. Her apology. Her explanation. Her truth.

She watched Mrs. Howard's face. Watched her expression change from curiosity, to sadness, to understanding. She nodded several times, and then she sniffed once or twice, dabbing at her eyes with the corner of her sleeve before setting the letter down on the counter and laying her hands over it.

"This is lovely, Persephone," she said. "Tremendously brave." She fidgeted with her glasses. "And it explains a great deal." She cleared her throat. "You didn't say as much, but I believe I have contributed to some of the—*ahem*—rumors this letter untangles." *Truth.* Mrs. Howard stopped fidgeting with her glasses and looked at Persephone. "I am *sorry*, dear. I truly am."

"I forgive you," Persephone said quietly. "And I'm sorry too. For not telling you the whole story when I had the chance."

Mrs. Howard nodded in understanding. "How can I help with that letter, dear?"

"I want to send this to every mailbox in Coulter,"

Persephone said. "But I don't know how many copies to make, or how many envelopes and stamps I'll need to buy."

A slow smile spread over Mrs. Howard's face.

"Well, dear," she said. "You've come to the right place. I know *exactly* how many mailboxes are in Coulter. As for the photocopies and envelopes and stamps, what would you say to allowing me to help with those? It's the least I can do."

Persephone nodded. And so, for the rest of the afternoon, at the kitchen table and with her parents' help, Persephone folded 184 photocopies of her letter. She addressed 184 envelopes. And stuck a stamp to each one.

The letter contained the truest truth she knew how to tell. She explained, 184 times, that while she, Persephone Pearl Cark, had indeed submitted their town to the television show *Small Town Revival*, there would be no fame, or riches, or film crews, because their town and every person in it deserved more than whatever story a television show would tell about their lives. She had wanted things to be better—for her family, the town—but at what cost? They were more than opening credits and catchy jingles, more than the number of views their successes or tragedies might earn, and she was sorry she had been willing to put the town on display.

Change doesn't happen overnight, she wrote, just like the host of *Small Town Revival* liked to say. And he was right. Real change was a slow-growing thing—a forgotten garden full of weeds and potential.

Persephone wanted to deliver a copy of her letter to Mrs. McCullacutty in person, but no one came to answer the door that evening as she stood on the porch of the big old white house and knocked.

She knocked again.

Three times.

Four.

Five.

Persephone's palms were sweaty when she finally turned the knob. The door swung open, and the house seemed to sigh—dust sheets fluttering on furniture and across the faces of covered paintings. Everything was quiet. Empty. As if it had been that way for a long time, even though Persephone knew that wasn't the case. It was as if some of the magic was gone.

"Hello?" Her voice sounded small in the foyer. "Hello?" Persephone stepped inside. "Mrs. McCullacutty? Blue?"

A small table had been moved to the center of the entry-way, like it had been placed there specifically to hold the tall antique vase filled to overflowing with bright orange and yellow chrysanthemums. And leaning against the vase was an envelope with her name scrawled across the front of it.

She took it, slipping the letter she had brought for Mrs. McCullacutty back into her pocket. With shaking hands, Persephone broke the seal and unfolded the letter. Mrs. McCullacutty's delicate script filled the page.

My Dear Persephone,

*I had so hoped to see you one last time before
I left, but it appears that is not to be. I hope you
will forgive me for leaving before I had a chance to
say goodbye properly. Alas. We never get to decide
when, only how. And because of you, my heart
feels as bright as these chrysanthemums. They are
sometimes referred to the flower of goodbyes. The
garden gave them to me this morning before I left
so that I could share them with you.*

*My old friend Dr. Rathmason and I spoke at
length yesterday. (Thank you for prompting me
to write to him; he came because of that letter, you
know.) He will be supervising some finer points of
caretaking this big old house while I am away. I trust
he will fill you in when the time is right. But the
garden and its future belong to you—it always has.*

*I believe some of the magic in this old house
crept outside because it simply no longer fit within
the walls. I had been intent on keeping everything
changeless and safe for so many years that the
house grew restless. You see, everything needs
room to change and grow—even if the process
is hard and painful because you are reminded
of what could have been, if only you had made
different choices . . .*

*The garden didn't begin to breathe until you
appeared in front of my house, Blue in your arms,*

all those weeks ago. I didn't realize you were the
miracle we were waiting for all these seasons, but
the house and the garden and Blue knew, right
from the start. Don't let them get too bossy.

I will miss our visits tremendously and
will think of you often. Please look after Blue
and her children and Piccadilly in my absence,
as we discussed. Blue felt inclined to stay until
her children have grown. She will join me later. I
think she was reluctant to leave you too.

Don't forget to plant those seeds I gave you
for your birthday—you just never know what will
grow with a little time, and a little hope.

Until we meet again,
Your friend,
Jane McCullacutty

Persephone took a shuddering breath and looked around.

Mrs. McCullacutty was gone.

"Meow." Blue padded down the hall, her tail high, eyes bright, and Persephone knelt, scooping her into her arms. The small gray cat purred and purred against her chest—a comforting, assuring sound that settled deep within Persephone.

Piccadilly was quiet in his cage in the kitchen. His little black eyes flashed at Persephone, the way they always did. But he didn't sing. Or tweet. He didn't say anything at all.

Even the little yellow bird knew Mrs. McCullacutty was gone.

"Don't worry, I'll look after you until she comes back," Persephone whispered.

She knew Mrs. McCullacutty had to go look after her grandnephew. The world was probably full of people who could use someone like Mrs. McCullacutty. *But I need her too,* Persephone thought miserably. *I wasn't ready for her to leave.*

Persephone still saw Mrs. McCullacutty everywhere she looked as she made her way down the hall and through the empty house. Even draped in dust sheets—oddity and peculiarity and beauty lived in everything. In the art and furniture, in items of natural history and wonder, things gathered and collected, found and saved and loved. What would happen to it all? Would it just sit here and gather dust until she came back?

If she comes back, a small voice whispered in Persephone's heart. She shut it out.

Persephone crept into the study, returning Blue to her kittens, and sat on the floor in the dim evening light. Mrs. McCullacutty seemed present in this room more than any other place in the house. They had shared pots and pots of tea here; they had talked and dreamed about the garden together. It was here, over plates of scones, that Mrs. McCullacutty had shown Persephone how to be a good friend.

Once she finished feeding her babies, Blue climbed into Persephone's lap again, standing up and rubbing her head under Persephone's chin. She purred as Persephone stroked her from head to tail.

"You're not alone," Blue reassured her with unblinking green eyes.

Persephone left Blue curled up with her kittens among the geraniums, promising to come back and check on them tomorrow after she finished swimming her laps. But as she walked out of the study and down the hall, she caught a glimpse of something—a brush of white in the late-evening sunlight that poured through the beautiful bay window in the hall.

She froze.

"What—?" Her voice was a ragged whisper. She took a deep breath and looked closer. *"Impossible . . ."*

But perhaps not. Because there in the window seat sat Mrs. McCullacutty's orchid. The one that had most certainly been dead.

Only it wasn't.

Not anymore.

Dark green leaves fanned up from among living, twisting roots that vined around rocks and moss in the terrarium. And from every stem, giant white blooms dripped and hung on delicate filaments, splaying bright faces into the light. Persephone's whole body shook. How was this possible? She certainly hadn't been able to keep this plant alive. She'd tried all summer to fix it, and nothing had worked!

She took a few steps closer.

Not only was it alive and blooming but it had *grown.* It had been shriveled and shrunken the last time she saw it. But now it stood tall. Unwavering.

It didn't make any sense.

Tears ran down Persephone's face and she let them. She stopped trying to hold it all in and make sense of it. Instead, she simply sat down on the window seat and admired the miraculous beauty of that flower. She breathed in its delicate perfume. Maybe it could just be enough that it was *here*. And that it was very much alive.

45

THE ORCHID

"*Jane said you wouldn't mind terribly if I helped look after things* while she's gone," said a voice from behind her. Persephone stood on Mrs. McCullacutty's porch step, and she whirled around to find Dr. Rathmason on the curb.

Persephone smiled. "Oh, I'm glad!" she said. "I don't mind at all." *Truth.*

Knowing he and Mrs. McCullacutty had sorted things out between them, at least a bit, and had started to remember what it meant to be friends again, changed things.

But as glad as she was to have his help, and to be able to keep pieces of Mrs. McCullacutty close until she returned, suddenly, the events of the day and the old woman's absence felt like a physical pain Persephone couldn't quite manage.

Dr. Rathmason wrapped an arm around Persephone as she started to cry.

"There, there," he said, patting Persephone's back. "I believe I owe you an apology."

Persephone took a step back, sniffing, her stomach a little twisty.

"I made an error in thinking I should help Malachi navigate his friendships this summer," said Dr. Rathmason. "What I thought was a harmless nudge—a bit of encouragement—ended up hurting both of you. I'm truly sorry."

Persephone nodded, and took his wrinkled hand in both of hers, squeezing tight.

"Thank you," Persephone said. But she was still sad. It had only been two days since their argument, but it felt longer. She missed Mal. More than she'd let herself think about.

"Mal said he didn't trust me anymore," she said. "I need to think of a way to show him that I really am his friend. That I always was."

Mal's grandfather smiled. "Don't give up, Persephone. He's very fond of you. Unfortunately, a streak of stubbornness runs in his family." Dr. Rathmason sighed ruefully. "I can only hope he won't wait too long to remember how precious friendships truly are, even when terrible mistakes have been made."

"I'm learning that too," she said. "Oh!" She suddenly remembered the orchid. "Will you come inside?" She opened the door to Mrs. McCullacutty's house. "There's something I want to show you."

Blue was there to greet them when Persephone opened the door, evening sunlight spilling across the entry and casting a long cat-shaped shadow over the floor.

"Hello, Blue," Persephone said, and then gestured to the small gray cat. "Have you two met?" she asked Dr. Rathmason as the man stared at the cat. He seemed surprised. Or confused. He ran a hand over Blue's head and down her back, just the way Blue liked.

"Yes," he said. "Yes, we've met. Years ago." He mumbled something about nine lives, but Persephone knew better than to ask questions as far as Blue was concerned. She led Dr. Rathmason down the hall toward the study until they came to where the orchid sat on the window seat, in full regalia, dripping and spilling over with white blooms.

"*Impossible*—" he breathed. And he crouched down, studying the magnificent plant. "I thought it was dead!" He looked at Persephone, his eyes full of questions. He had seen it for himself when he came to visit Mrs. McCullacutty last night.

"I know. It was." Persephone knelt beside him and opened one of the deep drawers that nested in the base of the window seat. She pulled out handfuls of leaves. Shriveled. Dried up. Dead orchid leaves. "These were scattered all under the plant. I saved them as proof. It really happened." Persephone shoved the leaves into Dr. Rathmason's hands. "I thought maybe you did something to help it?"

"Just the food I gave you," Dr. Rathmason said, studying the leaves in his hands for a moment. "But after what I saw last night, that didn't do much. This—this is something more—" He stared at the plant before getting to his feet and looking around like he was searching for answers in the quiet rooms of Mrs. McCullacutty's big old house.

"I gave this orchid to Jane years and years ago," he said quietly. "Before our lives fell apart and anger and bitterness and resentment got the better of us. I'd forgotten all about it until last night when I saw it here. Somehow, Jane kept it alive all those years. I realized then it meant something to her still. Perhaps our relationship still meant more to her than I'd let myself believe. Even after all this time. Even after all that brokenness. Hope is peculiar like that . . ." His breath hitched, and he stared at the leaves in his hands. Dr. Rathmason shook his head. "Listen to me!" he scoffed. "I'm not making any sense."

"No!" Persephone insisted. "You're right! Plants know things! Plants grow better when you talk to them and love them. Maybe plants grow better when they have hope. Just like people!"

"I imagine you're right." Dr. Rathmason nodded. "Hope is a seed. It's got to be planted deep. And truth-telling makes for some awfully rich soil. Right here." He patted the palm of his hand against his chest. "You've done some remarkably good truth-telling lately. Jane told me."

Persephone smiled slowly.

"Maybe enough for that orchid?" she suggested.

Dr. Rathmason shrugged. "Stranger things have happened in this house." Persephone nodded. He was definitely right about that.

46

A MILE

On Tuesday, the last week of August, Persephone stood on the dock, adjusting her goggles. Her mother sat beside her, coffee steaming in the early-morning air. Loons wailed their tremolo calls over the water—haunting and familiar.

"How far today?" her mother asked. Her face was peaceful in the morning light. It had been a week and a half since Persephone had come home and found Mayor Hattie sitting in the living room, and things had settled between them, at least a little. Mom had helped Persephone address envelopes to all their friends and neighbors as Persephone signed letter after letter. She had even left a note for her parents on her mom's nightstand—*I'm sorry* written at the bottom. But Persephone had spun a web of lies the past few months, and she knew forgiveness was only possible when her mom could believe her again. That kind of change didn't happen overnight. It might be a while before Mom could really truly believe her. But

Persephone was determined to earn back her trust.

"I . . . I'm not exactly sure." She scrubbed the lenses of her goggles with her thumbs. Listening to Joseph's truth about what had happened on the lake that day had loosened something inside her. She curled her toes around the edge of the dock. "Maybe I'll just start, and see how far I get?" Persephone glanced at the lifeguard chair.

Her mother nodded and followed her gaze.

"It looks beautiful," she said quietly. "Levi would love it." She smiled at Persephone and reached out, squeezing her hand. "Do you still want me to count?" It was the same question her mother always asked, and Persephone nodded as she eased into the water.

"Good luck," her mother said softly.

Persephone smiled and slipped under.

Reach—Pull—Breathe.

She had to pace herself or she'd be tired and breathless before she even got started, so she found a slow rhythm and focused on the beat of it, moving her body to the three-count rhythm inside her head.

Reach—Pull—Breathe. Reach—Pull—Breathe.

Her fingers touched the edge of the dock.

"One." Mom's voice was muffled by the sound of the water. Persephone did a flip turn against the dock and crawled her way back across the water toward the rope on the far side.

Time moves differently underwater than on land.

Slower. But also faster somehow.

Persephone's body seemed to slow down, but her

mind sped up. She focused on counting. And breathing. She watched the weeds sway in long green swaths beneath her. Fish eyed her warily from below, curious. Bubbles followed her hands through the water in a mirrored trail as she reached and pulled. Reached and pulled. She kept her body straight, her legs strong, her rhythm steady.

And her mother counted.

And Persephone swam.

Propelling herself across the distance.

One lap at a time.

And somewhere around lap twenty-six, Persephone decided to keep going. Just one more lap. And then another.

Twenty-nine . . .

Thirty.

And then two more.

And then

one

last

lap.

And then it was done.

Finished.

Thirty-three laps.

Sixty-six lengths there and back again.

One whole mile.

She hung suspended on the edge of the dock, fingers wrapped around the rough boards, half in, half out of the water. She rested her forehead on her arms and tried to catch her breath. A loon called again somewhere out on the lake. Haunting and wild.

It had taken all summer.

It had taken less than an hour.

A lifetime.

A minute.

Her mother knelt over Persephone.

"You did it!" she whispered in Persephone's ear. "I am so proud of you!"

Persephone tried to smile. But she couldn't quite do it. She had hoped that by swimming all those laps, she'd feel different. Better.

Silence hung heavy over the water for a moment and then that loon wailed again, long and mournful.

"What's the matter, sweetheart?" Mom's voice was soft.

"Everything." Persephone's voice came out as a broken whisper. "I swam a mile. *A whole mile.* And everything is still exactly the same."

Tears mixed with the water dripping out of her hair and down her face. Her mother looked confused for a minute and then, slowly, realization dawned. Persephone watched it settle on her like a stray beam of morning sun. Flickering.

"A mile." Her voice caught. "Because—that's how far out they were that day, on the lake. They were a mile offshore." Persephone rested her head on her arms again and nodded, tears flowing in earnest now.

She was tired.

So tired.

"Oh, Persephone." Tears ran down Mom's face as she helped her climb out of the water. Persephone was shaking with the effort it had taken to go so far, but her mother's arms were steady. She wrapped a towel around her and gathered her into her lap like when she was little. Despite everything. Holding her, letting her cry. And when Persephone finally took a shuddering breath, once the waves inside her had quieted, she rested her head against her mother's shoulder.

"Levi's accident *should* change the way we do things," Mom said. "We understand that life is precious and short and important in a way we didn't before." Mom wrapped the towel around Persephone's shoulders a little more snugly. "But his accident and his absence shouldn't change the *why* we do things. Those have to belong to us. Not to Levi."

Mom reached into the water and scooped up a handful of small stones. "Look." She took a stone and dropped it into the lake. It made a small *ploup* sound and then sank.

Ripples formed around the place where it had vanished under the surface, spreading in ever-widening circles until the sheer size of the lake swallowed them up. Mom dropped another stone, *ploup*. It sank again, leaving ripples behind.

"Do you ever think about what happens to a stone after it stops making ripples?"

Persephone shook her head. She'd thought about the ripples they left, of course. Everyone loved that idea—that a small stone dropped into water leaves bigger marks than anyone could imagine. But she never thought about the stone once it stopped making ripples.

"It's still important," her mother said, firmly. "It still matters, there, in the quiet." *Ploup. Ploup.* She dropped two more stones.

"But how?" Persephone watched those two new stones

settle on the bottom. "How is it important if it's not doing anything?"

"Well, to start, nothing holds value because of what it *does,* but because of what it *is.* And those stones aren't just sitting there, even if it looks like it from up here on the dock." Her mother cradled another rock in her hand. "Those stones are becoming something else. Here—" She handed a stone to Persephone. "Feel how smooth that is." Persephone rubbed it between her fingers and then against her cheek. It was smooth from being rubbed against other stones and sand down there in the water—over and over until all the rough places were worn away. "Just by existing in the water, it's being changed, and it's helping to change everything else around it." Her mother's words rang like solid, comforting truth, and Persephone cradled the rock in her hand.

"Both people and stones hold weight in the world, whether or not you can see the ripples they make. It makes them tremendously valuable, just because they *are.*"

Persephone thought of Levi—a quiet stone.

She thought of herself—splashing around and trying so hard to make ripples.

Mom wiped a tear off Persephone's cheek.

"Levi is changing the world just by being in it, Persephone. Even though he's not here like he was before. Look at how he changed you! You never would have swum a mile without him! But that doesn't mean you should walk around trying to make a difference or change the world only because of your brother. The changes you bring about must be a result of who *you* are. Not because of who anyone else is.

Because no matter how big, or small, or rough our edges, or grand our dreams, or broken our hearts, or quiet our bodies, we are all changing the world all the time. We can't help it. We make mistakes. We make ripples. Sometimes we sink. The only thing we get to decide, is what kind of changes we are going to make—both on the surface, and beneath it."

Persephone took a deep breath. Then she let go of the stone she was holding, watched the ripples it made as it hit the water, and didn't look away, even after it was lost to her sight.

47

GOOD MAIL

There were four bill-shaped envelopes waiting inside the mailbox when Persephone turned the little key in its lock. But instead of delivering them to her mother, this time she tore one open right there in the post office, curious. She scanned the notice until she found the words stamped at the bottom of the page.

PAID IN FULL

Again.

She opened the next one, and the next, and the next. All of them *paid*. A small sound escaped—not a sob and not a laugh, but something like both, and she looked up, searching for someone to thank. Someone to explain this impossible miracle. Mr. Perry from the hardware store was at the counter, talking with Mrs. Howard, and they turned, their faces filled with concern as Persephone waved the notices.

"Someone is paying Levi's medical bills," she said, her

voice breaking. "Someone is making all the difference in the world for my family, but we don't know who!" Mr. Perry's face shifted into a smile, and he looked knowingly at Mrs. Howard. The woman came out from behind the counter and wrapped Persephone in a hug.

"Why, we *all* are, dear," she said, delightedly.

"You *all* are?" Persephone looked tearfully between Mr. Perry and Mrs. Howard. "I don't understand."

"Jane McCullacutty set up a fund," said Mr. Perry, and Persephone felt her mouth fall open. She stepped back, surprise and something like hope making her whole body tingle, all the way from the tips of her toes to the roots of her hair.

"What?" She could hardly breathe. "But she told me she wasn't paying for those bills . . ." Persephone trailed off. Mrs. McCullacutty had said whoever was paying them might wish to stay anonymous. And that everything would most likely become clear in time . . .

"I'm not entirely sure what she was contributing herself," said Mrs. Howard. "She reached out to me, and many others around town, about helping your family out, if we could." She gestured to Mr. Perry, who nodded in agreement. "We all just figured it was time your family experienced a little bit of what you've given to all the rest of us. So, Jane set up one of those fund pages on the internet," said Mrs. Howard, smiling. "She just shared a bit of what most folks around here already know about you and your family, and of course, Levi. He was good to all of us. Saved my nephew from drowning, two summers ago—did you know that?"

Persephone swallowed hard, blinking back tears.

"I'll bet he's saved a whole lot of us, here in Coulter," Mrs. Howard said with a wink. "And I doubt there's a person around who hasn't been helped by your family in some way or another, Persephone," she continued. "That's the truth. Your dad has repaired roofs and chimneys all over town . . . Your mother has helped sort out medical records . . . You've helped us all with plants, and even your little brother, Owen, has a smile for everyone! It only made sense to offer what help we could, when you all needed it. Turns out, people on the internet shared that fund page, and a lot of folks beyond Coulter wanted to pitch in too. Guess there's still some good in this old world yet. And a lot more friends than maybe you realized."

"Yes. A lot more," Persephone whispered happily.

❧ 48 ❧

SOMETHING NEW

The following morning, Mya and Persephone knelt in Mrs. McCullacutty's study, peering through the geraniums at Blue and her kittens.

"What are you going to do with them?" Mya whispered, running the tip of her finger over the back of one of the tabby kittens.

"Find good homes for them, I guess." Persephone stroked Blue from head to tail, and the small gray cat purred. "Except for this one." Persephone rubbed one finger over the gray kitten. "I'm going to keep this one. Mom and Dad said I could." Persephone met Mya's gaze. "I named her Periwinkle."

"I love it," Mya said with a smile.

"Me too." Persephone nodded.

"Actually, it's purrrrrfect," said Mya, rolling her *R*s. And they laughed together.

"Speaking of blue flowers—" Persephone reached into

her backpack and took out a package of forget-me-not seeds.

She'd pulled them from her bedside table drawer that morning, knowing what she needed to do. What she needed to ask. Mya's eyes widened a little and she studied Persephone, her body going quiet, like she was waiting for Persephone to change her mind.

Mya had kept showing up, again and again and again. She had refused to give up on Persephone. She had *chosen* to be her friend. No matter what.

"I never thanked you for these," Persephone said. She smiled a little crookedly and cleared her throat, holding the little package of seeds in her hands. "I never thanked you for a lot of things. So . . ." Persephone struggled, searching for the right words. ". . . Thank you. For being my friend, even when I thought I didn't want you to."

"You're welcome, Persephone," Mya said. Her best friend wore a familiar smile, but there were tears in her eyes.

"Do you want to help me plant these?" Persephone asked, holding up the package of forget-me-nots. "I think I know the perfect place."

And so, in the shadow of a big white house, full of art and oddity, potential, and miracles, Mya and Persephone knelt beneath the memory of two Queens—absent branches giving way to sunlight—and sprinkled seeds into the fresh soil where roots once clung. Planting promises, and hope.

49

AN INVITATION

Persephone stood on Malachi Rathmason's front step two days later, her backpack slung across one shoulder. She had spent the last two days at the garden, getting things ready for this, and Jerry from the lumberyard had helped. She had used her own money on the items that were currently rattling around in her backpack. Now she just hoped Mal would listen to what she had to say.

Persephone pulled her hands out of her pockets and stared at a small vine with heart-shaped leaves that had wound its way up the porch rail. It nodded at her in the breeze, reassuring. So, she knocked on the door. Softly at first, but then louder and louder until she heard footsteps. Then the door was open and Mal was in the doorway, just like the first time she'd seen him here.

"Hello," she said. But before she could get another word out, Mal shut the door.

Persephone stood there for a moment, feeling something

inside her begin to collapse. She glanced at the vine clinging stubbornly to the rail.

And she knocked again.

And again.

And *again*.

She was stubborn too.

Finally, Mal pulled the door open, so forcefully she almost fell inside.

"*What?*" he demanded, his face stormy.

"I just want to talk to you." Her heart was pounding so hard she thought he might be able to hear it. She knew what Mal was thinking. The lies he was remembering. "I have something to show you." She tried to keep her voice steady. "At the garden." She waited, hoping. "Please?" she whispered.

After a minute, he nodded. Just once.

They walked in silence until they got to Mrs. McCullacutty's yard. And then Persephone studied his face as Mal took in the changes she had made over the last two days. His eyebrows rose.

All along one side of the garden, Jerry Gilbert had helped her construct a fence. Six feet tall, and freshly painted white. A blank canvas. Just like he'd always wanted.

"I'm so sorry," Persephone began nervously. "I'm sorry I lied to you, Mal. I'm sorry you ever thought I was only being your friend because your grandfather asked me to. You've *always* been my friend." Persephone unzipped her backpack and held it out to him. "I know I lied about a lot of things this summer," she said quietly. "But I never once lied about that."

Mal stared at the contents of her backpack, and then at the fence, and then at Persephone, understanding dawning. His eyes grew wide.

She had filled her backpack with cans of spray paint. As many colors as she could find, as many colors as Mrs. Perry at the hardware store had on the shelves.

Mrs. McCullacutty had paid both Persephone and Malachi for their work in the garden. And while Persephone had refused to accept the money at first, the old woman had insisted. Now Persephone was glad she had, because she'd been able to use it for paint.

"Maybe you would let me try again?" Persephone asked. "Maybe you could show me how to make something beautiful out of all this?" She nodded at the fence, but she was referring to them too. It was an apology, and an invitation.

Mal looked at her for a long moment, his face kind of scrunched against whatever emotion he was fighting.

"Okay," he said at last, breathing a little shakily. His face slowly fell into a familiar smile. A smile Persephone hadn't been sure she'd ever see again, and he handed her a can of paint—a friendship seed. It could be a start. Change didn't happen overnight, and broken friendships couldn't be fixed in a single moment. Persephone knew that better than anyone.

But she would try.

She would keep showing up.

"Let's vandalize this fence," Mal said, and Persephone grinned.

"It's not vandalism," she said emphatically. "It's *street art.*"

50

SEEDS

One morning, the last week of summer, a truck pulled up to the curb in front of Mrs. McCullacutty's house, and in the back was the most magnificent arched trellis Persephone had ever seen.

She had been working in the garden, and she wiped her sweaty face on her shirtsleeve as Joseph and Mya climbed out of the truck.

"That's beautiful!" Persephone skipped down the three cement stairs to where they stood. "Where did you get it?"

"I made it," Joseph said, grinning.

"You *made* this?" Persephone felt her mouth drop open and she climbed into the truck bed to get a better look. The trellis was made entirely of woven branches, twisted and twined together into a perfect arch. She ran her hands along the silver branches and felt a vague sense of familiarity.

"It seemed a shame to just throw them away," Joseph said quietly.

"These are from the Queens." Persephone gasped as she realized what Joseph had done. He nodded.

She hopped down and wrapped her arms around him.

"Thank you, Joseph," she whispered.

"You're welcome, Pip," he said, hugging her back. He took a shaky breath.

"I helped too, ya know," Mya said jokingly.

Persephone smiled. "Thank you, Mya." And she squeezed her best friend's hand.

"All right," said Joseph. "Now let's get this thing unloaded."

A little while later, Malachi showed up too, and together, the four of them situated the trellis where the beautiful Queens used to stand. Already a few seedling forget-me-nots that Mya and Persephone had planted were emerging from the rich soil, and in no time at all, they would form a carpet of blue flowers over the bare patch of ground.

In every corner of the garden, things had burst into bloom. The garden seemed eager to help, and whatever they planted, whether seed or vegetable, it all seemed to mature almost overnight, despite the lateness of the season. No sooner did Persephone set rows of lettuce and radish, carrots, kale, and swiss chard, than seeds sprouted. Tomato plants and peppers went into one bed, along with zucchini and pumpkins, cauliflower, broccoli, and eggplant. Zinnias and cosmos went into another bed beside cornflowers, nasturtiums, and marigolds.

And while Persephone never sent out an official request for help, every day, as she and Malachi and Mya, and sometimes Joseph, pulled on their gloves, others showed up too. Mike Dupree from the excavating company, Mr. and Mrs. Tellington, and Mr. and Mrs. Perry from the hardware store. Rosalyn Howard, Mr. Grove the postmaster, Sam and Mrs. Lin, and her parents and Owen came sometimes too, when they could.

The grown-ups brought kids and the kids brought grown-ups, and everyone brought friends. They carried seeds, and plants in pots, fruit trees, and berry canes, herb starts, and fruit tree cuttings. Some of them even brought their copy of the letter Persephone had sent, tucked into their pockets, because they wanted to be part of something beautiful. Something worth reviving.

Dr. Rathmason helped Persephone in the garden now and then too, and it was nice, having a master gardener for a friend, especially because while Persephone happened to be remarkably good at making things grow, she still had a lot to learn.

Persephone returned *The Maiden* to Mrs. McCullacutty's house, but situated her in the garden where she seemed to belong best. And though she never caught the bronze statue moving, Persephone was certain she was *more* somehow— the way the house was *more*, and the garden was *more*—as if it was all proof that friendship brought things to life.

And while it was all wonderful and good and full of hope, change didn't happen overnight, regardless of what miracles were wrought in the garden. There were still things that did not come with guarantees, like Levi's health, despite the new treatments he would start in the middle of October. His seizures would lessen with the addition of new medicines and therapy, but they would not bring him back. And Persephone knew there was a real chance that one day soon, Levi would leave them forever. So she held on to what she could, and did her best to let go of the things she could not.

She and Levi continued to watch *Small Town Revival* together every Thursday night, and sometimes Owen joined them. Persephone continued to imagine the sound of Levi's voice in her memory, and they talked. She even showed him the list of requirements she was checking off, one by one, as she worked toward earning her lifeguard certification. She had already checked off "swim a mile." He had helped her with that. Next summer, when she turned fourteen, she planned to sit in that bright red lifeguard chair herself, as a junior lifeguard. She would have to wait a few more years to guard on the beach all by herself, but until then, she could help. She would etch Levi's name deeper into the wood of that freshly painted chair. And then she would write her own beside it.

On Friday afternoon, the last day of summer, Persephone found a small hand trowel waiting for her in the little white shed, almost as if it knew exactly what she needed. And digging a hole, Persephone finally sprinkled the packet of mysterious birthday seeds Mrs. McCullacutty had given to her into the ground beside the Queens' trellis.

She knelt in the dirt for a few minutes, and as she watched, tiny green shoots began to emerge from the dark soil, reaching for the sky, impossibly quickly.

At first it was difficult to tell what they might become. But as the minutes passed, the shoots became tiny vines, uncurling familiar leaves, and twining tendrils around every available branch and twig as the shoots climbed.

Persephone had no idea how long she sat there, watching breathlessly as the shoots unfurled one heart-shaped leaf after another, but she suddenly began to remember them—those same heart-shaped leaves on her own front porch, at the post office, and rambling over the chain-link fence around the water tower. She remembered them twisting around the handles of a broken wheelbarrow in an alley, and on a mailbox post in front of Dr. Rathmason's yard when there was blood running down her leg. They rambled over a broken fence slat in her memory as Blue led Mya down the sidewalk, and they nodded at her, first through Levi's bedroom window as she wrote an email to Miss Rebecca Mathews, and again when she stood on Mal's front step, knocking and knocking and knocking. This plant had been following her. Or perhaps she had been following it. Around each decision, through every choice, up one rung of truth after another, this curious vine had somehow been there too. Evidence of—what? *What was it?*

Dashing into the little white shed, Persephone searched shelf after shelf, digging through bins and overturned baskets until she found it. A plant identification guide. But as she carefully turned the pages, looking for the identity of the plant growing from the seeds Mrs. McCullacutty had given to her, a folded slip of paper fell out and landed in her lap. Persephone glanced around the little white shed, mysterious and so full of potential, and then unfolded the note Mrs. McCullacutty had meant for her to find.

Dear Persephone,

I could not seem to find the right time to tell you about the fund I set up to help your family with all those medical bills—forgive me for not explaining earlier. But I never wanted you to imagine that I alone was responsible for the kindnesses so many others extended to your family.

I am so proud of you, dear, for the weeds you pulled when you finally saw them for what they were. And for the seeds you planted, even before you imagined what might grow from them.

It is my deepest hope that this garden will grow wonderous, miraculous things for you, just as you have grown miracles for others—as you have been a miracle to me.

—JM

Persephone pressed the letter to her heart and smiled through her tears before studying the page in the plant guide that Mrs. McCullacutty had bookmarked with her note.

Common Ivy. An evergreen plant that grows well in cold cli-mates. Requires well-drained soil. Identified by its three-lobed leaf, sometimes heart-shaped. Often considered a plant that symbolizes friendship. White globe shaped flowers. Blooms when conditions are favorable.

Persephone read the last bit over and over.

A plant that symbolizes friendship.

Blooms when conditions are favorable.

She glanced up from the page and gasped.

The ivy had climbed, twisting and winding its way over the Queens' trellis, and it had begun to flower. Frothy white globes made up of dozens and dozens of tiny flowers erupted into life, one after the other, saturating the air with sweet perfume.

The garden inhaled. And Persephone inhaled. And then she began to laugh—hope tangling up inside of her with each change that had crept over every wall she'd built around her heart. Hope bloomed and bloomed and bloomed as if the garden, and the girl in it, were celebrating a season of miracles.

ACKNOWLEDGMENTS

This story first came into being about a year before pandemic season arrived, but the work of revising, crafting, and honing Persephone's story happened in some of the darkest days that followed. And yet, this is not a pandemic story. It's a gardening story. Because despite the grief, loss, heartache, and isolation so many of us have experienced, telling a story about a girl who refused to give up on the possibility of making a difference in her world became exactly the balm I needed. It is my dearest wish that Persephone's story serves as a tiny reminder that sometimes hope blooms out of the darkest places.

Thank you first and foremost to my family for being so patient as I raved and ranted about old houses and gardens, broken friendships, swimming laps, magical cupboards, and the oddity of cats.

To my husband, Aaron: thank you for believing in me—for seeing value in the things I dream of doing, even before I bring those dreams to life.

To my children—Caleb, Ella, Lucy, and June: You four are always providing insight and inspiration! You make magic happen every day, and I am so grateful for each of you. You bring light and joy and courage and goodness to the world and this book belongs to you four as much as anyone. Thank you for showing me how to hold on to hope.

And I suppose a word of thanks must go out to our sassy old cat, Henri, who gave me Blue, and to our massive white floof of a Pyrenees, Pearl, who loaned Persephone her name.

Thank you to my parents, who have always been good gardeners, planting seeds and believing in flowers (metaphorically) long before I was able to believe in them myself. I hope this book serves as a note of deepest gratitude.

Thank you to my friends who cheered for me in the midst of drafting and revisions; who checked in and reminded me to breathe—those I have left anonymous and those I've named here—Katie Maine, Sarah Katzenberger, Abby Stevens, Christy Slaughter, Sharri Westin, Laura Huisinga, and Jamie Erickson. A special thanks to Lyric and Jeff Hassler, and their daughters, Aurelia, Eliana, Renata, and Annora, who read and offered their kind insights and lovely artistic interpretations to early drafts. Thanks also to Monica Goodwin, MD, who vetted Levi's role in this story for me. And to both Paige Westin and Olivia Huisinga, who shared their summers with my children so that I could get this book written. Thanks to both Courtney and Lara, who have listened to, affirmed, and validated me through the ups and downs of the last couple years—I wish everyone had access to therapists like you!

To my agent, Danielle Chiotti: Three books! I can't imagine being here with anyone else. You have been my friend, advocate, and writing coach through this whole process all these years, and there's no one I'd rather do this storytelling stuff with. Thank you also to the immensely talented and supportive team at Upstart Crow Literary, especially Michael Stearns. It is an honor to be a part of the flock, and I look forward to many more stories to come!

To my editor, Liza Kaplan: Thank you for loving, supporting, and believing in my books! Because of you and your fantastic team at Viking—Ken Wright, Tamar Brazis, Gaby Corzo, Maddy Newquist, Sola Akinlana, Anna Booth, Theresa Evangelista, Gaby Corzo, Marinda Valenti, Ellice Lee, Kaitlin Severini—the stories that might live only in my head and heart exist in the real world, and I am so privileged and grateful to share them. Thank you for helping me make each one the best version of itself. It is an honor to tell stories with you.

A huge thank-you to my readers, who have been kind and generous with their reviews, their notes and emails, and with their hearts. Because of you all, I get to do work that I love deeply.

And as always, for all my stories (written and unwritten), my thanks to God—for every seed planted, watered, and raised. *Soli Deo gloria.*

AUTHOR'S NOTE

While I am always drawing inspiration from real life, none of the people or places (or houses) in this story exist—each one is fictional and entirely imagined. Too much growth and too many mistakes are required of characters in good storytelling, for me to ever borrow from real life and risk wounding someone.

However, the inspiration for Mrs. McCullacutty's big old white house was drawn from an old mansion in my hometown, built by one of the town's visionary entrepreneurs for his wife, Jessie. No mysterious stories or magical happenings were ever rumored about the place, but it always drew my imagination. Sadly, it finally succumbed to time and age and the push of progress. It lives on now only in memory and photographs, and perhaps, in some small way, in this story—because even old houses should be remembered and celebrated for the life they bring to small towns, and the magic that bloomed because of them.